THE CRIMS #2:
DOWN WITH THE CRIMS!

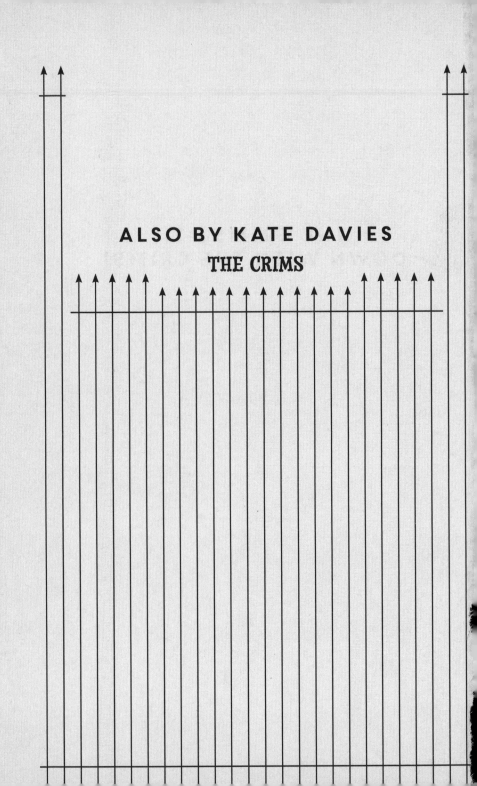

ALSO BY KATE DAVIES

THE CRIMS

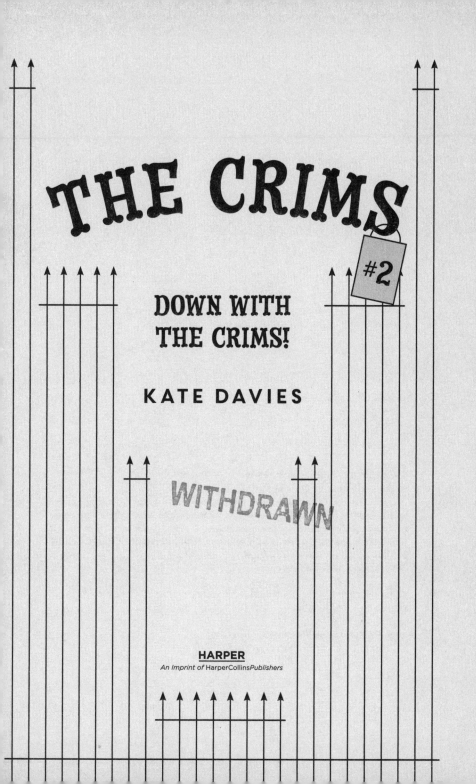

THE CRIMS

#2

DOWN WITH THE CRIMS!

KATE DAVIES

WITHDRAWN

HARPER
An Imprint of HarperCollinsPublishers

In memory of my amazing grandmothers,
Peggy Davies and Brenda Collier,
who were just as funny and wise as Big Nana,
but not nearly as good at crime

FROM THE DESK OF

Big Nana!

PAY ATTENTION, FOOLS

My darling family,

Since you are such exquisite screw-ups, we find ourselves in a unique and challenging position. If we want to retain our reputation as the most terrifying criminals in Blandington, it's time to step up our game. Starting this Monday, I will be collecting your crime journals each week, and I expect to see plans for <u>at least five</u> crimes <u>with a point</u> that can <u>actually be carried out</u>.

Each week, I will select a winner, who will be allowed to choose one item from the loot cellar as his or her prize. I will also select a loser, who will be responsible for feeding Isabella that week. I recommend a suit of armor. (In the unlikely event that the loser is Isabella, she will be responsible for feeding Aunt Bets.)

XO, Big Nana

CHAPTER ONE

IMOGEN WALKED HOME from the library through the beige streets of Blandington carrying a ridiculous amount of books in a duffel bag, until she reached the decidedly un-beige Crim House. She couldn't help smiling when she looked at it. She sometimes fantasized about being back at Lilyworth Ladies' College or living in an ordinary house, with central heating and a doorbell that didn't feature her grandmother singing "Willkommen" from *Cabaret* in a very unwelcoming minor key. Imogen had to admit that she loved her home—the east wing, which Big Nana had recently painted red, because the sun rises in the east; the west wing, which Big Nana had painted white, because there's a West Wing in the White House; and the two airplane wings from a Boeing 747 that Big Nana had stuck on top of the house to celebrate the birth of Isabella, Imogen's youngest cousin. There literally was no place like home.

But as soon as Imogen opened the front door, she wished she hadn't. All the Crims were home, and they all seemed . . . happy. The sound of happy Crims, Imogen realized, was possibly even worse than the sound of sad Crims—like a cross between a distressed eagle and a nineties rap song.

She followed the sound into the kitchen. There they all were, being themselves. Her mother, Josephine, was reapplying her makeup, using a switchblade as a mirror; Al, Imogen's father, was in the corner, feeding minisausages to Barney, their dog; Aunt Bets was crocheting a tea cozy in the shape of a nuclear warhead while Uncle Knuckles looked on fondly, untangling her yarn with his massive hands; the Horrible Children were throwing sandwiches at one another; and Freddie, Imogen's eldest cousin, was helping Big Nana pour champagne into a ragtag assortment of wineglasses (all stolen, of course).

Freddie wasn't Imogen's *most* annoying cousin—that was probably Henry, who liked to try to tattoo his name on Imogen's face when she was asleep; or Sam, who prank-called her every night, even though she always knew it was him because his cracking voice sounded like a fire-truck siren; or Nick and Nate, identical twins who no one could tell apart and who said things like "BOOM!" unironically; or Delia, who periodically set fire to all of Imogen's nice twinsets, "just to keep you on your toes."

Imogen, in other words, had too many cousins. All of whom were horrible. Which is why everyone called them the Horrible Children . . . except their teachers, who were too scared to call them that.

Before Imogen could ask what was going on, Uncle Clyde jumped out in front of her, like a jack-in-the-box that no one should ever have made.

"Imogen!" he cried, looking crazier than ever. He had dyed his shock of black hair red to celebrate his recent release from jail, but unfortunately, it just looked like his head was on fire. Four people had poured buckets of water over him in the month since he'd been released. "Guess what?"

This all felt very familiar. "You won a tadpole at the Blandington County Fair in 1996."

"Yes! But guess what else."

"You've given up on ridiculously overcomplicated heists, and you're going to stick to something nice and simple like internet fraud."

"Ha! Good one. Of course not. No—I've actually just pulled off my best heist yet: the Great Bakery Robbery. I'm a wanted man again!"

Imogen's stomach went cold. The last time Uncle Clyde had come up with a heist, Imogen had been kicked out of school and ended up almost getting murdered by a butler. And a billionaire's dog. And a fully grown man dressed as a terrifying cartoon baby. If this heist was anything like his lunch box heist—and if Uncle Clyde was actually the one to pull it off this time—things were about to go very wrong indeed. Particularly if he insisted on announcing his guilt to everyone around him. When would the Crims realize that getting credit for their crimes wasn't glamorous and just led to spending months in jail, drinking second-rate tea and wearing unflattering orange outfits?

"What . . . kind of robbery?" asked Imogen.

"I didn't steal money exactly. Or dough. Ha! Ha! This was more of a boutique crime. By which I mean, I'm starting small and working my way up."

Imogen relaxed. She clearly didn't need to worry—this crime was obviously more on the scale of Uncle Clyde's less ambitious, preheist efforts, when he had specialized in stealing things no one wanted. "You just walked up to the counter and took a loaf of sourdough while no one was looking, didn't you?" said Imogen.

"No, actually. I walked up to the counter and took a *cake* while no one was looking. And what a cake!" He stood aside, proudly, so that Imogen could see it. "Ta-da!"

Imogen had to admit the cake did look delicious. It was huge—six tiers tall—with what looked like cream-cheese frosting and little marzipan flowers. "Happy Birthday, Daisy!" was iced across the top.

"Who's Daisy?" asked Imogen.

"Whoever she is, she *isn't* going to have a very happy birthday," said Uncle Clyde. "I've got her cake! Ha! Ha!"

Big Nana began to pass the champagne-filled wineglasses out to the adult Crims. "I have to say it's very good timing for a cake theft," she said. "We've something to celebrate." She picked up a newspaper from the kitchen table and passed it to Imogen.

There, spread across pages four and five, was a photograph of the Crims at Big Nana's sixty-fifth birthday party. The headline above the photograph read: "Big Nana— Sixty-Five and Alive!" The rest of the article went on to say:

Spirits were high at Blandington Village Hall last week when Blandington's famous crime family came together to celebrate Gerda "Big Nana" Crim's sixty-fifth birthday. And that's not all they were celebrating. Big Nana has just rejoined the family after faking her death two years ago in the Underground Submarine Heist, which has gone down in legend as the Most Stupid Crime Ever Attempted by an Otherwise Successful Criminal.

"Yeah, we've forgiven her," her grandson Nick Crim told our reporter. "She forgives us whenever we do things wrong, so it's only fair. I mean, Henry set her bedroom on fire a couple of days ago, and Big Nana just called us all in there to roast marshmallows and have a good old sing-along until the flames died down."

Henry Crim—an expert with a box of matches—also lit the candles on Big Nana's cake. The whole family (and a few special guests) joined in singing "For She's a Jolly Good Felon."

Our reporter was surprised to see the officers of the Blandington Police Department out in force for the occasion, but when questioned, PC Donovan Donnelly said showing up was the least they could do. "We accused the whole family of a crime they didn't commit," he said through a mouthful of cake. "We held them in custody for weeks because all evidence pointed to the fact that they'd stolen an extremely valuable lunch box from James Wooster. But it turns out it had just fallen down the back of an umbrella stand. To all the people out there: Before reporting a crime, check behind your umbrella stand. You'll be surprised the sort of things you'll find back there—diamonds, long-lost relatives, missing pets . . ."

The Crim family was eventually exonerated, thanks to the actions of Big Nana's twelve-year-old granddaughter, Imogen Crim, who stopped at nothing—not even stop signs—to prove her family was innocent. "I mean, they're not actually innocent," she explained. "They're all criminals—they're just not very good ones, so I knew they wouldn't have been able to pull off a crime of that magnitude."

When the other Crims overheard Imogen using the word "magnitude," they launched into a round of "For She's a Jolly Good Felon"—long words are highly prized in the Crim clan—and our reporter took his leave. The party bag, for anyone inter-ested, contained a piece of cake, a party popper, a lock-picking kit, and a small gerbil wearing a name tag that said "Nigel." Thanks, Crims, and happy birthday, Big Nana!

Imogen smiled. That had been a good day. It had taken some time to forgive Big Nana for the whole death-faking incident, but now Imogen couldn't be happier to have her back. Big Nana was the only Crim who she aspired to be like when she grew up. Although she'd probably choose a different haircut and not call people "my miniature grapefruit" in public quite so often.

"Cut up the cake, Clyde," Big Nana now said. "We're celebrating the dawn of a new age of the Crims! I'm back, and we're better than ever. Except for 1976—that was a golden year. That's the year I stole Pentonville Prison and gave it to Bets as a playhouse—do you remember that, my unripe pumpkin?"

"I learned to file through iron bars there, so I could escape!" said Aunt Bets, smiling fondly at the memory.

But Uncle Clyde wasn't smiling. He had just cut into the cake, and he was staring down at the slice with a look of confusion on his face. "Mother," he said to Big Nana grimly, "there's something wrong with this cake."

He picked up the cake to take a closer look—and realized that it wasn't a cake after all. "It's made of cardboard!" he wailed like a disappointed ambulance. "There's no cake at all! Even the icing's fake! I've been had!"

"Wait," said Big Nana, leaning down to examine the "cake." "There's a note in here."

She pulled out a crumpled piece of paper and held it up for the other Crims to read. The note, which was made from letters cut out of magazines, read: **We're Coming For You!**

The Crims were stunned into silence, which was quite

unusual for them. Imogen felt the hairs on her arms stand up on end.

"The cake was supposed to be filled with buttercream and raspberry jam, not hate mail," muttered Uncle Clyde.

"What does the note *mean*?" asked Josephine, wringing her expensively moisturized hands. "Who is it from? Are we in trouble? What are we going to do? Why isn't anyone saying anything?"

"Because you won't let the rest of us get a word in edgeways," said Aunt Bets, pointing a fork at Josephine in quite a threatening manner.

"SORRY TO INTERRUPT!" shouted Uncle Knuckles, in his terrifying voice. "BUT I DON'T THINK THE NOTE IS MEANT FOR US. CLYDE *STOLE* THE CAKE, REMEMBER?"

"Exactly," said Aunt Bets. "It's Daisy who they're coming for. Not us!"

"You're right!" said Uncle Clyde, his face relaxing as the Crims smiled at one another, laughing with relief.

Poor old Daisy, though, Imogen thought. *Her birthday is getting worse by the second.*

But Uncle Clyde's smile was fading. "The thing is," he said, ruffling his bright red hair, "that note looks a lot like the one that someone slipped under our front door this morning, tipping me off about the bakery."

Big Nana folded her arms and looked at Uncle Clyde

with narrowed eyes. "What do you mean, 'the note that tipped me off about the bakery'? You said you just took a cake from the counter when no one was looking."

"Yes," said Uncle Clyde, "but how do you think I *knew* that no one would be looking?" He pulled a crumpled paper from his pocket. When he uncrumpled it, Imogen could see that this one too was made from cutout letters. Whoever was making the notes was obviously getting their money's worth from their subscription to *Oh Yes* magazine.

Big Nana took the note from Uncle Clyde and held it up to the light, the way you would to check for counterfeit money. And then she read it out loud:

Hello!!!
If I were you (which I'm not)
I'd go down to Blandington
Bakery at about 5 p.m. today.
There's a really tasty-looking
cake on the counter—frosted
and everything—and no one's
watching it. The fools! I'd grab
it if I were you!!!!
A Well-Wisher

"Well," said Big Nana, "we know one thing about the person who sent this note: They have too much time on their hands. They took the trouble to find eight exclamation marks in eight different fonts."

"They're very good with a pair of scissors, too," said Nate. "Very neat cutting-out-letters skills."

(You're probably thinking: *But how did Imogen know it was Nate? I thought it was impossible to tell the twins apart.* Thankfully, Nick had taken to wearing a ridiculous baseball cap with "Could I Have Fries with That?" on the front. It was part of a clothing line Sam had designed, each featuring one of his favorite phrases, so that he'd have to talk as little as possible until his voice had properly matured.)

"Clyde," said Big Nana, turning to him with a glare. "I can't *believe* you didn't think it was suspicious that someone would tip you off about a cake in a bakery. Have I taught you *nothing*?"

"Of course you have," mumbled Uncle Clyde, looking at his feet. "You taught me how to make perfectly boiled eggs, so that the center is still a bit runny—"

"About *crime*, you overfed giraffe!" roared Big Nana. "We're *Crims*. We think up our own crimes. We're not plagiarists. We don't get tip-offs. We're not"—she spat—"the police!"

"I wasn't really thinking," said Uncle Clyde, looking a little worried now. "I just fancied a cake, and someone was offering me one, so—"

"So you walked right into the trap," said Big Nana,

11

shaking her head. "Clyde, you've been set up. Again." She started pacing the room, the way she always did when she was thinking.

Imogen couldn't help but feel a little exhilarated to watch Big Nana in action again after all these years.

"The note was slipped under our front door this morning," Big Nana said. "Just after the article about my return to Blandington appeared in the paper. Coincidence? I don't think so. Someone is worried that I'm back in charge of the family. And whoever that someone is, they want to send us a message."

"SORRY TO INTERRUPT," shouted Uncle Knuckles, "BUT WHO WOULD DO THAT? IF YOU DON'T MIND ME ASKING."

"Who do you think?" asked Big Nana.

"The Kruks," Imogen said as a small thrill of fear rippled through her. Her grandmother was convinced that, some day soon, the family would have to face their greatest rivals, the Kruks, in a crime family showdown. The Kruk family were extremely good at thinking up interesting ways to kill people, and according to Big Nana, they were keen to try out some of their latest murder techniques on the Crims.

"Right, as usual, my darling kumquat," said Big Nana, smiling at her. "Elsa is in charge of the Kruks now. And what is Elsa?"

"Crazy," chorused the Crims.

Just a few weeks previously, Big Nana had discovered that "crazy" Elsa Kruk was taking over the Kruk crime empire. And Imogen knew Big Nana didn't mean "crazy" as in "That crazy Elsa Kruk is a bit of a liability at parties," or "That crazy Elsa Kruk wears mismatched socks to work." It was more like "That crazy Elsa Kruk fed her next-door neighbor to a tiger," and "That crazy Elsa Kruk sharpens her teeth on diamonds every morning just in case the tigers aren't hungry."

"Exactly. And she's obviously decided to throw everything she's got at us . . . so watch out when you're walking underneath windows, in case she chucks some bricks at you."

But something about this wasn't sitting right with Imogen. It felt . . . too *small-time* for the Kruks. "Are you *sure* it was the Kruks?" she asked. "Wouldn't they be a bit more . . . well, blunt than a cake switcheroo?"

Big Nana blinked at her. "What do you mean, my overcurious tangerine?"

Imogen sighed. "It's just . . . We've been to the Kruk headquarters. It is an exact replica of Buckingham Palace, except it's underground, and with tighter security. You know how all the ice from the Arctic sea is melting? It's not! They've got it all in their basement, keeping their Diet Coke supply cool. Right, Freddie?"

Freddie nodded. "They have some pretty impressive loot, too. There's a dodo down there, running around with a pterodactyl. If there were some sort of criminal Olympics, they'd win gold. And silver and bronze."

Imogen nodded. "I just think, if the Kruks wanted to send us a message, they'd clone a velociraptor and set it loose in our yard. Or build a bomb out of steak knives and throw it into the living room. I don't think they'd try to get to us with a *cake*."

"It's not a cake, darling," Josephine pointed out, patiently overemphasizing each word. "We *can't eat it*. See, they've fooled us with cardboard."

Imogen pushed down her annoyance with her mother. "Yes, well, even so. Isn't it more likely that we've made an enemy here in Blandington? Again?" said Imogen. "Freddie, could it be someone in your . . . secret club?"

"What," said Freddie, "my gambling ring? I gave that up. Pummeling people all the time is very hard on the biceps. Plus, it was much less fun after you found out what I was doing."

"Or, Mom, what about that woman you hit with your car?" said Imogen.

"Oh, no," said Josephine. "We don't need to worry about her. She's dead, thank goodness."

Big Nana smiled grimly at Imogen. "I promise you, my little matzo ball, the threat from the Kruks is real.

And Elsa is really, really nuts. More nuts than those honey roasted cashews Uncle Knuckles likes."

"THOSE ARE VERY NUTTY. AND DELICIOUS," said Uncle Knuckles.

"But—" started Imogen.

"No buts," said Big Nana, shaking her head. "What have I always taught you?"

"Big Nana is always right, except when she's turning left."

"Exactly. Everyone, I want you to be on your guard. The Kruks could strike anytime, any place. If you see any slightly overweight lampposts, pick up your pace—it's probably a Kruk in disguise. If you hear a particularly tuneful bird, take a second look at it—those Kruk children are small, deadly, and they know how to whistle."

The Crims all looked at one another. They didn't feel like celebrating anymore. One by one, they trooped out of the kitchen. But as Imogen was about to follow them, Big Nana touched her on the shoulder.

"Come with me," she said. She tapped on an old photograph of Great-Uncle Umbrage, and part of the wall suddenly swung open. "I'd hoped to tell you on my deathbed where these tunnels are—but, well, desperate times call for desperate measures."

She followed Big Nana through a narrow, dusty tunnel until they reached a windowless room. All the furniture was covered in sheets, so the room looked as though it was home to a lot of lumpy ghosts.

"This is where I come to think," said Big Nana, locking the door behind them. "I covered up the furniture so it can't see what I'm up to. You can never be too careful!"

She whisked a sheet from an old velvet chair and indicated that Imogen should sit down.

"Now," she said. "Remember, Imogen: I need you to be ready to lead the family in case anything happens to me."

"Nothing's going happen to you," Imogen said quickly. Losing Big Nana once had been hard enough—so hard that Imogen had turned her back on her family and started to believe that crime didn't pay. She had only just gotten her grandmother back. She couldn't bear to think about losing her again.

Big Nana shook her head. "We have to be prepared," she said. "I'd feared that the Kruks would make a move once they realized I was back in power, and now we've received a credible-looking threat."

Imogen didn't want to believe what she was hearing. "It can't have been from the Kruks. They would never leave a note in a cardboard cake. It's so *basic*."

"Never say never," said Big Nana. "Unless it's in answer to the question 'Would you like pineapple on your pizza?'"

Imogen still wasn't convinced. "But are you *sure* they're

after us? Really? Remember the last time we thought the Kruks were behind something?"

She was thinking of Derek Hornbutton. The awful, vain CEO of Charm, Inc. children's entertainment conglomerate and owner of Charmtopia—the world's least charming theme park—had gone missing around the time Big Nana had come back to Blandington. Imogen and Big Nana had been convinced the Kruks were responsible, and they'd considered sneaking back into Krukingham Palace to see if they could find him in one of the dungeons. But just before they caught the train to London, Derek Hornbutton had appeared on the news. It turned out he'd just been on a very long scuba diving vacation and had forgotten to turn on his out of office.

Big Nana rolled her eyes. "If that ridiculous man *had* been kidnapped, the Kruks *would* have been behind it. The fact that he wasn't doesn't mean anything. Except that you should never believe what you read in the papers. Apart from the horoscopes. I promise you, Imogen, my defrosted hamburger: The Kruks are planning to attack us. And I think they've already put their plan into action."

"But how do you *know*?"

"I just do," said Big Nana. She reached up and pulled down another sheet, revealing a massive whiteboard. "Enough questions," she said. "It's time to get to work."

Scribbled across the whiteboard was a detailed grid—a

little like a school timetable, only with the words "larceny practice" where "lacrosse practice" might have been.

"What's this?" asked Imogen.

"This is your crime timetable," said Big Nana. "We need to ramp up your criminal training so you can take over the family if the time comes."

"Which it won't," said Imogen. "Not soon."

"Even if it doesn't, my little extractor fan, I still need you in top shape."

Imogen studied the crime timetable with a feeling of rising panic.

5 a.m.: Get up. Cold shower.

6 a.m.: Pickpocket enough money to buy breakfast.

7 a.m.: Tiger wrestling (if no tigers available, tie one arm behind back and practice with five stray cats).

7:30 a.m.: Rehearse evil monologue in mirror.

8 a.m.: Vandalism. Destroy one Blandington landmark per week, starting with the bakery, because their doughnuts aren't as good as they used to be.

9 a.m.: Disguise making. Dress up as a piece of fried chicken and lie on the street corner until a dog tries to eat you.

10 a.m.: Forgery. Make a credit card and use it to book a holiday for two to the Bahamas. Thank you for asking—I would love to come with you.

11 a.m.: Bikini shopping for the Bahamas.

12 p.m.: Go to primary school and steal lunch from weakest-looking child.

1 p.m.: Steal a motorbike and teach yourself to ride it.

2 p.m.: Possible trip to the ER, depending on how the motorbike training goes.

3 p.m.: Help four wild animals escape from the zoo. Suggest lemurs, as they're cheerful and also portable.

4 p.m.: Collect Crim children from school, disguised as a stay-at-home dad. Extra points for convincing facial hair.

5 p.m.: Scout out new criminal headquarters in case Crim House is invaded and occupied by the enemy.

6 p.m.: Call prime minister, convince her that you are the head of her security team, get her to reveal classified information to you, leak it on the internet.

7 p.m.: Dinner—pasta with tuna sauce (very good for the brain).

8 p.m: Bed. Practice sleeping with one eye open.

"But when am I supposed to go to school?" asked Imogen.

"It says . . . You'll collect the other children at four p.m.," said Big Nana.

"No, I mean, to class," said Imogen. "It starts tomorrow, you know. It will take up a lot of my day. And it's illegal for me to drop out of school unless I'm sixteen."

"Exactly! Crimes that involve *not* doing something are

the easiest of all to commit!"

"But I *want* to go to school! I *have* to!" said Imogen, starting to feel a bit desperate. Truth be told, she'd been constantly fantasizing about going back to school since moving back to Blandington—even if she'd be attending her old public school and not the posh boarding school she'd left, Lilyworth Ladies' College. At Lilyworth, Imogen had learned that her intelligence—when not used for criminal pursuits—could actually be *useful*. That it made other students look up to her. And *that* meant she wielded quite a lot of power.

Power she'd been missing these last few weeks back with her family. "Please?"

Big Nana looked at her. "Fine," she said. "In that case, you're going to have to get up earlier and stay up later to fit in all your crime homework. The future of the Crims is in your hands!"

Imogen looked down at her fingers.

"Not literally," said Big Nana. "That was a metaphor."

"I know," said Imogen. "I was just checking my cuticles."

"Good," said Big Nana. "Now. Put on a boilersuit and some insect repellent. It's time to get started."

Imogen already felt defeated by the sheer amount of work ahead of her, and the prospect of having to take over as head of the family so soon. Yes, she wanted to rule the

Crims, Big Nana–style, when she was older, but she was only twelve. She'd thought that before she took over the family, she'd have time to be a teenager and do all the stupid things that teenagers do, like dye her hair an extremely neutral color and lie to her parents about who she was on the phone with (it would be the UN) and date boys who her parents disapproved of, like valedictorians and junior chess champions. But no. This was going to be her life now.

For the first time in a long while, two words wriggled their way to the front of her brain. She said them out loud: "I can't."

Big Nana blinked. "*What* did you say?"

"I can't start my crime homework now," said Imogen, in a smaller voice.

"There's nothing a Crim can't do," said Big Nana, "except pay their taxes on time."

Imogen needed an excuse, and she needed it now. "I have schoolwork," she said. "My class had a summer assignment. I have to write a report on global warming by tomorrow morning."

"You know that's caused by the Kruks blow-drying all the polar bears, don't you? Elsa hates looking at photographs of polar bears with messy fur."

Imogen nodded. "I'll be sure to mention that."

Big Nana studied Imogen as though she were an

interesting painting. She sighed. "Fine," she said. "But I want to see you back here tomorrow morning to start work in earnest."

Imogen rushed out of the room before Big Nana could change her mind. After several wrong turns—who knew there was an aviary in the basement of Crim House?—she made it out of the secret passageway and back to her apartment. She locked her bedroom door, collapsed onto her bed, and closed her eyes. It had been a long day. And tomorrow was going to be even longer.

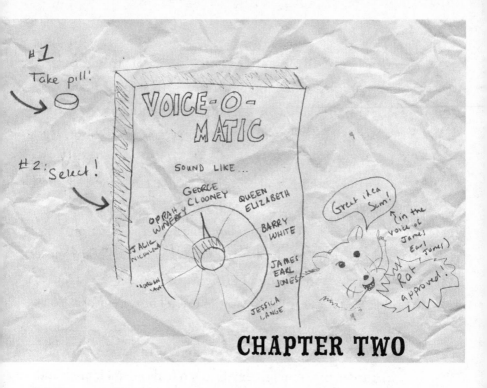

CHAPTER TWO

THE NEXT MORNING at seven thirty a.m., as scheduled, Imogen Crim was staring at herself in the mirror, delivering an evil monologue.

"As soon as I walked into Blandington Secondary School, I knew I was going to kill it," Imogen said to her reflection. "And I did. I slayed it. I assassinated it, maimed it, made it beg for mercy." Imogen nodded to herself. She didn't really know what 'it' was, but that was beside the point. Today was her first day at a new school, and though Imogen would never admit it to anyone—particularly to her own reflection—she was a little bit nervous. She'd been queen bee at Lilyworth. And as a child, she'd been a baby queen bee at Blandington Primary School, ruling over a slightly ramshackle clique of three girls named Penelope, Hannah, and Willa. It seemed reasonable to expect that she be queen bee of Blandington Secondary School. But what if another queen was already in control? She'd been out of the Blandington school game for a few years—long enough for someone new to buzz in.

Not possible, Imogen assured herself. Blandington Secondary School was in Blandington, after all, one of the most boring towns in the most boring part of England—so dull it didn't even have hills. It was the town equivalent of a YouTube ad for car insurance that you're not allowed to skip. And while Penelope, Hannah, and Willa were perfectly nice girls—nice enough that Imogen had called Hannah and asked her and the other girls to meet her in the schoolyard to flank her for her Big Entrance—Imogen felt confident that none of them had the charisma, talent, intelligence, or powers of manipulation necessary to rule the school.

Still, she was nervous, so she was practicing one of Big Nana's favorite confidence-building techniques: criminal visualization. "If you can do it in your imagination, you can do it in reality," Big Nana liked to say, although Uncle Knuckles had proved this statement false when he convinced himself he could fly and jumped off the roof of the house. Still, in her desperation, Imogen was willing to give it a try.

She closed her eyes and pictured herself as the undisputed ruler of Blandington Secondary School. She even gave herself a crown—a boring one, obviously. "You," she said, stretching an arm toward her imaginary classmates, "I feel almost sorry for you. None of you stood a chance against someone as strong, confident, and criminally gifted as me. The moment I walked in that classroom, I knew I'd have everyone at Blandington Secondary School under my thumb in no time. Luckily, I have surprisingly big thumbs." She opened her eyes and smiled at her reflection—a smile so evil, she actually felt a bit intimidated. *Still got it,* she thought, and tipped back her head in preparation for her maniacal laugh. "Ahahahahaha! AHAHAHAHAHA!" She was working her way up to her big, terrifying ending—quoting a few Latin poets, maybe throwing in a bit of ancient Greek—but before she could really get into the flow of things, her door burst open.

There, framed in the doorway like a cat-eyed version of Munch's famous painting *The Scream,* was her cousin Delia.

"Hurry up," Delia said.

"How did you get in here?" Imogen asked, smoothing down her hair—all that maniacal laughing had messed up her ponytail.

"How do you think?" asked Delia, holding up a screwdriver.

Imogen nodded. "Stupid question." All the Crim children had learned to pick locks before they could walk. "Can you give me a minute? I need to do the sinister cliffhanger ending and twirl my imaginary mustache."

"But it's *my* turn," said Delia, pouting. "I have the seven thirty evil monologue rehearsal slot. The twins did theirs at seven, Sam does his at eight, and Freddie's helping Isabella with hers at nine."

Isabella couldn't really speak in sentences yet, but she certainly could cackle maniacally. "There's no time like the present," Big Nana always said. "Except the past, but that's full of dead people and slow internet connections."

Imogen sighed. Now that Big Nana had ordered the Crim children to practice evil monologues every morning before school, the bathroom line was going to be a nightmare. Imogen usually liked to do her monologue in her own bathroom—the one in the apartment that she shared with her parents at the top of Crim House—but her mother had been in there for the last hour and showed no sign of getting out; she had stolen some caviar-infused shower gel from the Russian mafia and insisted on "getting her money's worth," even though she hadn't spent any money on it, and it left her smelling vaguely of fish.

Imogen stepped aside, allowing Delia to take up her place in front of the mirror. "Are you nervous?" she asked.

Delia turned to look at Imogen, frowning. "Why would I be?"

"You know," said Imogen, fiddling with her watch. "First day of a new school year . . ."

Delia laughed. "NO!" she said. "The only people who get nervous about school are goody-goody teacher's pet types, like—"

"Me?"

"Exactly!" said Delia. "So I bet *you're* terrified. Which is pathetic, by the way."

"I'm not terrified," said Imogen, her cheeks reddening. "And it's not pathetic to want to do well—"

"This school is in Blandington. In case you hadn't noticed, you're not going to Lilyworth anymore." Delia gave Imogen a nasty smile, pushed her out of the bathroom, and slammed the door.

Imogen stomped back up the stairs to her family's apartment. Yes, she *had* noticed she wasn't at Lilyworth anymore. And the more time she spent with the Horrible Children, the more she had to keep reminding herself why she'd left her posh boarding school, where she'd ruled over the other students and had been top in every class except needlework, which didn't count—unless you were planning on being a housewife in an eighteenth-century novel when you grew up.

Imogen wasn't planning on being a character in an eighteenth-century novel—not even a really good one with bonnets and horses and multiple uses of the word "hitherto."

She was planning to be the head of a crime empire.

And if there's any chance Big Nana's right about the Kruks, she thought, *I need to get the Crims in top criminal shape. . . .* The only trouble was, Imogen still couldn't work out why the Kruks, who were actually *good* at committing crimes, would bother fighting the Crims at all. The Kruks had once stolen an Alp and installed it in their backyard so that the young Kruks could learn to ski. The Crims had once stolen a single, broken ski from a trash can. Uncle Clyde, whose "heist" it had been, had spun round and round in circles for a few minutes before falling over, getting a concussion and calling everyone "Your Majesty" for a few weeks until he recovered. The ski now sat in the Loot Cellar, along with the spoils of all the Crims' other pointless crimes.

So yes, maybe Imogen did have a bit of work to do to help transform her hopeless relatives into a world-class crime organization. But she wasn't convinced that a showdown with the Kruks was imminent, so what was the rush? Besides, there was a while yet before she'd have to take over the Crim empire—and there was nothing wrong with wanting to do well academically in the meantime.

Or wanting to rule the school like a dictator with really smooth hair. . . .

Just as Imogen opened the door to her apartment, something small and red whistled past her head. She turned around to see who had thrown it and was immediately knocked to the ground by a massive poodle.

"Barney!" she yelled, except her face was squashed into the carpet, so it came out as "Bmmmnmmmfh!" She tried to push Barney off her, but he was surprisingly heavy. He was also unbelievably stupid and ridiculously loyal—in other words, he fit right in at Crim House.

Barney was the first pet the Crims had ever had, unless you counted the piranhas in the piranha pond; or the deformed snakes that patrolled the front garden; or the live, rabid fox that Josephine sometimes wore as a scarf. Barney had followed Al Crim home from work a few weeks' previously (though what an oversize poodle had been doing in an accounting firm was anyone's guess), and he'd refused to leave, no matter how politely he was asked. He'd refused to leave no matter how impolitely he was asked, too, so Nick and Nate decided to adopt him and train him as an attack dog. Which wasn't going very well. Barney, unfortunately, was a lover, not a fighter. He loved many things: Henry, Aunt Bets, lit matches, Delia, eating other people's food, Imogen, Uncle Knuckles, Uncle Clyde, chasing squirrels, chocolate, the color orange, and, above all, Imogen's father, Al. Which was weird, because most other people forgot Al Crim existed, unless they needed help with a particularly tricky math problem. He was the quietest and nicest of all the Crims, and he only ever committed minor bookkeeping offenses.

The only thing Barney seemed interested in attacking was his toy bone—which, Imogen, realized, was the small, red thing that had whistled past her head and which was now lying on the floor next to her. She managed to grab it and hurl it down the hall. Barney bounced off her and chased after it. At last.

Imogen sat up and brushed the curly white dog hairs from her gray school uniform. "Nick!" she called. "Nate! Stop throwing Barney's bone at people!"

"It's the only way we can get him to attack anyone!" said Nick.

"Barney didn't attack me. It was more like a very heavy hug," Imogen said.

"Well, that's a start!" said Nate, ruffling Barney's fur. "He's definitely getting scarier. He growled at me the other day, and he bared his teeth. It was adorable."

"Adorable isn't going to save us from the Kruks," Imogen pointed out. But before she could meditate further on how totally incapable Barney was of protecting her family, her father ran down from the upstairs of the apartment and started cooing at him.

"Who's a lovely boy, then?" said Al, taking Barney's toy bone and throwing it down the stairs. Barney bounded off to fetch it while Al beamed at him.

Imogen actually felt quite jealous; her father had never shown her the attention he showed Barney. He wasn't usually one for public displays of affection—he preferred public displays of equations (he had a gallery of framed math problems in his office that he liked to show off to visitors). But Al was different with Barney. He seemed to glow whenever the dog was near, like a lightbulb in a suit.

Of course, Imogen thought, *once I'm back in school, outshining the other students on a daily basis, I'm sure he'll take notice. . . .* Al had always been the proudest of Imogen when she'd been flying high (academically speaking) at Lilyworth Ladies' College. *Speaking of which . . .* Imogen looked down at her watch and was stunned to realize it was almost eight o'clock. She was five minutes behind schedule. Her heart began to race the way it always did when she wasn't exactly on time. School didn't start till nine, but she wanted to get there early, to get the lay of the land, scout out the best locker—and figure out how soon she could take control. She rushed into the apartment and grabbed her schoolbag from her bedroom floor. "Delia!" she called down the stairs from the apartment. "Let's go! Now!"

The sun was shining as Imogen and Delia walked toward Blandington Secondary School. The birds were tweeting, and the clouds looked fluffy and delicious, like vanilla meringues, even though Imogen knew they were just collections of frozen water droplets because science was one of her favorite subjects. But the moment the cousins walked past the school gates, the sky above them turned gray, the birds stopped singing, and it looked as though it might rain at any minute.

Delia pulled up the hood of her coat. "Summer vacation really wasn't long enough," she muttered.

Imogen hugged herself. *I want to go home,* she caught herself thinking. And then she shook her head and put her hands on her hips like confident people do. *No I don't,* she thought. *I love school.* But was she going to love *this* school?

Lilyworth's red bricks had seemed to glow from within, the way places do when they're filled with rich people and politeness and children who thought "Gosh!" was a rude word. Blandington Secondary School didn't glow at all. In fact, it seemed to snuff out light. The school was a solid lump of gray concrete, with unwelcoming gray doors and tiny windows. It looked like a really depressing LEGO building made by a really depressed giant. The whole place seemed bleak and empty; there were a few other students clustered in small groups in front of the school, but it was hard to see them because their gray uniforms (and gray faces) blended in perfectly with the building behind them. Imogen could tell it was going to be quite an adjustment from Lilyworth.

"I can't believe we're actually at school *early*," said Delia, looking around suspiciously. "I never even get here on time. Who *are* these people who turn up to school before they have to?"

Delia's question was answered when three mousy-looking girls rushed up to them. "Imogen!" said the one in glasses—and then she noticed Delia and backed away a little. It took a moment for Imogen to recognize her.

"Hannah?" she asked. Hannah had been Imogen's best friend before she'd left Blandington—partly because she seemed to have absolutely no interest in becoming queen bee herself. Hannah looked incredibly innocent, but she'd been responsible for more than one of their primary school teachers running screaming from the building, singing the lyrics to obscure Sondheim musicals, never to return. Imogen had never quite worked out what Hannah had done to them . . . but it couldn't have been pretty.

Beside Hannah stood Willa, who was much more intelligent than Imogen but also much more socially awkward (she couldn't bear to look people in the eye unless she had one of her own eyes shut, which is why everyone called her "Winky"), and Penelope, who looked exactly the same as she had two years previously, except she now had braces on her teeth. *My old clique!* thought Imogen. But then she realized that Penelope was wearing her frizzy hair in a ponytail. *Interesting,* Imogen mused. Everyone knew that only the queen bee was allowed to wear her hair in a ponytail. Without Imogen there, Penelope had obviously become ruler of the school. Imogen was surprised—Penelope had always been a bit of a sheep (she was always cast as one in the school Nativity), so eager to please, and Imogen had never had any trouble getting her to do exactly what she wanted. She'd once convinced Penelope that "wonderbits" was the new word for "cool," and Penelope had gone around saying it for an entire week before Imogen revealed that it been a hilarious joke. But now that she thought about it, "wonderbits" had actually caught on in a big way. . . .

"So here you are," said Penelope, staring at Imogen.

"I am," said Imogen, staring at Penelope.

The other girls looked from Imogen to Penelope and back again, seemingly trying to work out who would crack first. Imogen hadn't lost a staring contest since she'd been beaten by Great-Uncle Umbrage when she was eight—and that didn't really count because it turned out that Great-Uncle Umbrage had two glass eyes. So it wasn't very surprising that after a couple of minutes Penelope blinked.

Yesssss, thought Imogen.

Penelope pulled out her ponytail and combed her

fingers through her hair, smiling at Imogen with a "you win" sort of expression, which was Imogen's favorite type of facial expression on other people.

Good, thought Imogen. *This isn't going to be hard at all. I'm queen bee again already.*

Penelope actually looked a little relieved not to have to be in charge anymore. She linked arms with Imogen as they walked toward the school building. "Everyone is going to die when they see you," she said. "Like, *literally* die."

"I hope not," Imogen said. "I don't fancy doing time for manslaughter."

"You're still a total legend here," Hannah said. "Everyone remembers that time at primary school with the worms and the caretaker—" But then she stopped speaking. She was looking at someone off to the side.

Delia. She was standing where Imogen had left her, arms crossed, foot tapping as though she were feeling very angry—and a little bit left out. Imogen had completely forgotten that she was there.

"Sorry!" said Imogen.

"Whatever," Delia said, looking away, her lips pursed.

Imogen felt a stab of guilt. She and Delia had only just properly become friends again, and now here she was, abandoning her for her old clique. "See you after school?"

Delia rolled her eyes. "If I don't find someone older

and cooler to hang out with." And she stalked off to the other side of the school.

Hannah hadn't been exaggerating, Imogen realized, when she walked into her classroom. She really *was* a legend in Blandington. Maybe not a good one, like *The Legend of Zelda*—more like an old Greek myth that seems sort of familiar, even though you haven't actually read it. Her classmates fell silent when they saw her . . . and then they started whispering to one another, making her feel like she had something embarrassing written on her forehead (which she definitely didn't—she'd checked just before she left the house). But she just smiled at her new subjects. *I don't blame them for whispering,* she thought. *Things must have been pretty boring around here without me and my caretaker-defeating worms.*

Imogen marched straight to the back of the classroom and took the seat next to Penelope. At Lilyworth she'd always sat front and center, and generally behaved like an insufferable goody-goody. But Imogen Collins, her Lilyworth alter ego, was dead and gone like an out-of-date dodo bird. Everyone here knew who she was: Imogen Crim, math genius, criminal mastermind, junior tiddly-winks champion. And they liked her already. Or feared her, which was pretty much the same thing.

The boy in the seat in front of her swiveled around and

stared at Imogen. "Is it true?" he asked.

"Probably," she said.

The boy looked impressed. "So when do you turn into Catwoman? Where do you get your powers from? Were you bitten by a cat or something?"

Which wasn't the response Imogen had been expecting. "What?" she said. "I'm not Catwoman. Catwoman isn't real."

"Right," said the boy, giving her a wink.

"Anyway," said Imogen, who had read a lot of Sam's comics, "Catwoman doesn't have powers. She's just a very good burglar."

"Like some other people around here, eh?" said the boy, winking again. "Everyone knows you managed to get your family off on the whole Lunch Box Heist and that you can leap across buildings like a cat—"

This was ridiculous. "Seriously, not even Catwoman can do that."

"I thought you said Catwoman wasn't real."

Imogen sighed. It probably wasn't a good sign that she was exhausted after just five minutes inside. *Fine,* she thought. *Let him think I'm Catwoman.* There were worse reputations to have.

"Sorry I'm late!" said a small man with a very large bow tie who rushed into the classroom carrying a huge stack of books. Imogen recognized him at once—it was

Mr. Stanton, her old primary school teacher. He looked a little less gray than he had back then . . . possibly because he hadn't had Imogen in his class for two years. *Such happy, innocent days,* Imogen thought, remembering her tenth birthday, when she had set off explosives during silent reading so she would be able to go home early for birthday cake with her cousins. . . . Hm. She'd forgotten just how badly behaved she had been before she left for Lilyworth.

Mr. Stanton dumped his books on the desk, and then realized he couldn't see the students because the pile of books was so tall, so he walked around to the front of the desk. And then he took one look at Imogen and screamed.

Imogen looked behind her, thinking for a moment that he might have seen a rat, or a ghost, or someone with an even bigger bow tie than him, but no: Mr. Stanton was screaming because of *her.*

"Hello, boys and girls and Imogen Crim," said Mr. Stanton, edging as far away from Imogen as possible. "I'm Patrick Fry, and I'll be your teacher this year."

Hang on a minute, thought Imogen. *His name isn't Patrick Fry. . . .*

"Yes it is," said Mr. Stanton/Mr. Fry, as though he could read her mind. "I had to have my name . . . legally changed. . . ."

Oh yes. Imogen remembered now. Mr. Stanton had testified against the Horrible Children regarding the Milk

Carton Heist they'd pulled off just after she'd left Blandington. He must have changed his name through a witness protection program. He had obviously left his job at the primary school and come to teach at Blandington Secondary School. Which had been pretty pointless, seeing as the Crim children had followed him there.

Mr. Fry straightened his bow tie, his hands shaking slightly. "Let's get started, shall we? Sooner we start, sooner we can get out of here and back to the safety of our own homes!" He gave Imogen another terrified glance. "Open your history books to chapter four, 'The Russian Revolution.' Will the czars survive? Spoiler alert: No, they will not!"

Everyone clattered around, trying to find their textbooks, and just as they were settling down again, there was a sharp knock at the classroom door.

"Come in!" said Mr. Fry.

A tall girl with an unnecessarily wide smile walked into the room. She was beautiful. Not only was she beautiful, but she was stylish. And not only was she stylish, but she was wearing her hair in a massive, glossy ponytail that put Imogen's to shame. Honestly, a horse would have been proud of it.

"So sorry I'm late," she said, smiling her wide smile. "My mother's Rolls-Royce broke down. They're so much less reliable than BMWs, am I right?" She tossed her glossy ponytail and walked confidently up to the teacher, her hand outstretched. "Hello . . . Mr. Fry, is it? What a fantastic name. Is it German? My last school was in Germany. *Es war fantastisch!*"

"Why, yes!" said Mr. Fry. "'Fry' does derive from the German word '*frei*,' meaning 'free.' What a clever thing to know."

"Oh, well," the girl said with a shrug, smiling. "I *am* clever, so I can't help knowing things."

"And what's your name?" asked Mr. Fry.

"Gud," said the girl, turning her unnerving smile on the classroom like a toothy searchlight. "Ava Gud."

"Welcome, Ava!" said Mr. Fry, showing Ava to a seat right at the front of the classroom. The seat that at Lilyworth would have been Imogen's.

Ava put down her expensive designer bag and pulled out an expensive designer pencil case, and unzipped it to reveal some expensive designer stationery. The classroom oohed appreciatively. Who knew Gucci made pencil sharpeners?

Imogen looked over at Penelope, who was staring, openmouthed, with undisguised admiration at Ava.

Uh-oh, thought Imogen. *Reclaiming my queen bee status is going to be tougher than I imagined.*

CHAPTER THREE

"WHY, YES," AVA was saying to a circle of admirers who'd materialized around her desk. "I did live in Paris for a while before I moved to Germany. Can you tell because of my amazing skin? I'll let you in on a secret—the French smear Brie on their faces at night. I've lived all over the world, actually, which is why I have so many friends and can speak seven languages, plus Welsh."

Penelope had already pushed her seat back and rushed over to introduce herself to Ava. She wasn't the only one—all the girls in the room (and most of the boys) were now buzzing around the new girl like flies around an annoyingly attractive trash can.

Imogen crossed her arms and studied Ava. Listening in on Ava's conversation, she'd learned that she was glamorous, well-traveled, and extremely rich . . . and Imogen was pretty sure that the sparkly specks on her tie were diamonds. ("If you can't identify precious stones from a distance, you might as well become a wig salesperson" was one of Big Nana's favorite sayings.) Ava would have fit right in at Lilyworth, where pupils were dropped off at the start of the term by private helicopter, and the badly behaved girls spoke to one another in ancient Greek just for fun (the good girls preferred Latin).

Then there was the ponytail. If Ava had been another girl—smaller, less sure of herself, someone who didn't use soft cheese as a moisturizer—Imogen would have marched up to her and demanded that she wear her hair in plaits. But something about Ava made Imogen feel strangely insecure—and Imogen had never felt insecure, not even during Uncle Clyde's failed circus heist, when he had forced her to do very dangerous tricks on a very rickety trapeze.

What was a girl like Ava doing in a place like Blandington?

Mr. Fry clapped his hands in a futile attempt to get the class's attention. "Settle down now!" he said. "That's enough excitement for one day!"

Everyone kept on talking and whispering and generally admiring Ava.

"Please?" said Mr. Fry, getting red in the face. Even his bow tie looked a bit upset. "Please be quiet? Just for a teensy-weensy second?"

"Yeah, come on, guys," said Ava, turning around to look at the rest of the class. "Let's show Mr. Fry some respect."

Of course, as soon as Ava asked them to, the class fell silent. You could have heard a pin drop. And then everyone *did* hear a pin drop—one of Imogen's bobby pins slithered out of her ponytail and dropped to the floor, sending her cowlick sproinging back across her forehead. *Great,* thought Imogen. *Even my hair thinks Ava should be queen bee.*

"*Thank you,* Ava!" said Mr. Fry. "Right, class. Now that I have your attention, I'd like you all to give a great big Blandington welcome to our newest student."

"Newest students," corrected Imogen. "This is my first day too, remember?"

"Oh dear, I suppose it is," said Mr. Fry. "It feels like you've been here a lifetime already." His bow tie was beginning to droop. It really was very expressive. "Right, then. Let's give a great big Blandington welcome to our newest students: Ava Gud! (And Imogen Crim.)"

You could hear the parentheses.

A great big Blandington welcome, unsurprisingly, turned out to be a lukewarm round of applause.

"Lovely!" said Mr. Fry. "Now, why don't we ask our

new students to tell us a bit about themselves. Ava, would you like to go first?"

Ava turned to Imogen and smiled her toothy smile. "I don't mind if you go first, Imogen," she said.

"That's okay," said Imogen. "You go first. I insist."

"You're just being modest," said Ava, still smiling.

"I'm not. I'm being polite," said Imogen, whose smile was beginning to crack like a nasty egg.

"But I'm too *shy* to go first," said Ava, batting her suspiciously long eyelashes.

"That settles it, then!" said Mr. Fry. "Miss Crim will speak first. Just remember: no swearing, no violence, no incitement to violence, no threats, no describing murders in disturbing detail, no references to *Fiddler on the Roof*, no tap-dancing, and absolutely no distracting the class so that your cousins can come and pickpocket everyone before your speech is over." He patted his pocket to make sure his wallet was still there.

Imogen walked with purpose to the front of the room and cleared her throat. She opened her mouth to speak—and suddenly realized she had absolutely no idea what to say. She thought she'd left speech giving behind at Lilyworth, along with her hopes of being a future world leader and a secret supply of pretzels (which were probably past their sell-by date now anyway). Since when was public speaking a thing at state schools?

Just say something. Anything, she told herself. *Come on.* "Kill it. Garrote it. Slay it, murder it, make it beg for mercy . . ."

Mr. Fry's bow tie looked like it was trying to escape from his neck. Which is how Imogen realized she'd been speaking out loud.

Think fast. ". . . which, where I come from, means 'I'm so happy to be here at Blandington Secondary School, and whatever you've heard, I've never harmed anyone intentionally with a pencil sharpener.'"

The other kids looked at one another, confused and a little nervous. Hannah frowned at Imogen and mouthed, "You okay?"

This was not going well.

Don't panic, Imogen thought. *You can still pull this back.* She took a deep breath. Maybe it was time to tell the truth. . . .

"Some of you may have heard that until a few weeks ago, I was at the top of my class at Lilyworth Ladies' College. I left because my family was wrongly accused of stealing a very valuable lunch box from a toilet entrepreneur, and I had to prove that they were innocent. Which I did. I successfully investigated the theft of the lunch box, secured my family's freedom, and now here I am, starting a new school, seizing the day, as Horace would put it—"

"Is Horace your boyfriend?" asked a boy in the front row.

"He's a famous Latin poet, actually," said Ava.

"Thank you, Ava," said Imogen, forcing herself to smile. She took a deep breath, gearing up for her big finish. "And as that other great Latin poet Catullus once said—"

BRRRRIIIIIIIIIIIIIIIIIIIING!

"Ooh!" said Mr. Fry, jumping up, a little too happy that Imogen's speech had been interrupted. "That's the fire alarm! Quiet now, everyone. . . . Leave the room in single file . . ."

What's a girl got to do to finish a monologue in this town? Imogen thought as she followed the rest of the class into the courtyard.

The good thing about having a clique is that it doesn't matter how badly your speech has gone, or how terrified your teachers are of you, or how much your school uniform makes you look like large human trout—they'll always make you feel better.

"You killed it," said Hannah.

"You slayed," agreed Willa.

"You made it beg for mercy," said Penelope.

"I didn't," said Imogen, scuffing her shoe on the pavement. "I just sort of slightly injured it."

"Imogen!" Delia was walking toward her across the courtyard.

"Let's get out of here," Hannah muttered.

"You're not scared of Delia, are you?" Imogen asked.

"She *is* quite violent," said Willa. "Particularly in the mornings."

"She threw me across the science lab because I wouldn't let her borrow my fountain pen," said Penelope.

"She does have a surprising amount of upper body strength," Imogen said thoughtfully, remembering the time Delia had picked up Uncle Clyde and tossed him across the living room for calling her "sweetheart." "But once you get to know her, she's really not that bad. . . ."

"She's bad enough," said Hannah. "See you later, Imogen." She linked arms with Penelope and Willa and made for the benches on the other side of the schoolyard.

Imogen went to follow them, but Delia grabbed her with her surprisingly strong arms and yanked her backward.

"Wait," said Delia. "What are you doing for the rest of the day?"

Imogen frowned, confused. "Going back to class, as soon as they figure out how to turn off the fire alarm."

"No you're not," said Delia, still holding on to her arm.

"Yes I am," said Imogen, pulling herself free.

"You're not. Because that would be a waste," said

47

Delia, giving her an evil grin.

"A waste of what?"

"Of the fire alarm, stupid. Who do you think set it off?" Delia pointed to herself, in case Imogen hadn't gotten the message.

"Delia," Imogen said wearily. "You're too old to pull stupid stunts like that. You disrupted everyone's morning and wasted valuable learning time. Plus, you ruined the end of my speech. You *always* ruin the ends of my speeches."

"It wasn't a stupid stunt," said Delia, pouting. "It was a very *effective* stunt. Now no one's going to notice when we sneak out of school." She started marching Imogen toward the gates.

"I'm not sneaking anywhere," said Imogen, disentangling herself again. "I have a school to control and a new nemesis to destroy."

"You have the *Kruks* to destroy. Isn't that more important? I was thinking we could make a plan—"

"I *have* a plan," said Imogen, crossing her arms. "I plan to graduate first in my class. I'll deal with the Kruks in the evenings, when everyone else is eating Cheetos and watching *Gilmore Girls* for the hundredth time on Netflix."

Delia shook her head, disgusted. "Whatever. You're just a teacher's pet, like you always have been."

The other students were beginning to filter back into

their classes. Imogen didn't have time for this ridiculous argument. "You can call me whatever you want—"

"Idiot! Loser! Law-abiding citizen!"

"Hey," Imogen protested, stung. "That last one was below the belt. It's totally possible to do well at school and be a brilliant criminal at the same time. Geometry comes in very handy during jewel heists. And chemistry is basically Poison 101."

"You tell yourself that," Delia said. "You always have to be better than everyone else, don't you?" Her eyes were beginning to shine suspiciously. She was actually upset, Imogen realized. She was genuinely hurt that Imogen wouldn't skip school with her.

"Wait," said Imogen. "Delia—"

But Delia had marched out of school and was already disappearing down the road, getting harder and harder to see, like the little numbers at the bottom of an eye test.

Imogen felt a twinge of guilt, but she shook it off. She and Delia had been spending way too much time together over the past few weeks, and it always seemed to be on Delia's terms. Imogen had lost count of the horrible pink outfits they'd shoplifted, and the terrible romantic comedies they'd sneaked into at the movies to watch without paying, and the number of times they had listened to Kitty Penguin's album on repeat. The words to every awful song were now taking up valuable space in Imogen's valuable brain—space that could have been used to remember pi to forty decimal places, or the reigns of all of the kings and queens of England, or the names and fatal flaws of all of the Kruks. . . . It would probably be for the best if she and Delia spent some time apart. Imogen was obviously getting on Delia's nerves as much as Delia was getting on hers, and it would be good for them to hang out with new people for a while. *Besides,* said a mean little voice inside Imogen, *Delia will get in the way of my quest to be queen bee.*

Imogen was now standing on her own in the empty courtyard. She was late for class, and she was *never* late for class, not even on the day she had been arrested for aiding and abetting Big Nana in the Bookstore Break-In, three years ago. In fact, Imogen had persuaded PC Donnelly to grant her bail, turned up ten minutes early for class, and answered the question about oxbow lakes before anyone else.

Imogen ran back to class and burst through the classroom door, out of breath.

"You're late!" said Mr. Fry. And then he remembered who he was speaking to. "Which doesn't matter at all! Be as late as you'd like!" He laughed nervously, and then he started choking, and Ava had to jump up from her seat and slap his back until he got himself under control.

"Thank you, Ava," said Mr. Fry, with a sickening smile—the sort of smile *Imogen* had prompted from teachers at Lilyworth. "Now, my dear, are you ready for your speech?"

"Sure," said Ava, taking her place at the front of the room.

Ava actually looked a little nervous. Maybe she would be a terrible public speaker! Maybe everyone would realize that Ava was actually pretty average and come flocking to Imogen's delightful hive for some queen bee honey (or something that sounded less disgusting).

But then Ava planted her feet in the traditional speech-giving position and pulled out a stack of note cards—pale gray ones that matched the school color, yet looked chic at the same time, which should have been impossible. She had actually written her speech out. She was PREPAREDD. That's "prepared" with capitals P-R-E-P-A-R-E-D and an extra D on the end for good measure.

Ava gave a modest smile—just the right amount of modest, just the right amount of smile—and started to speak. "I come from a little place called London—not sure if you've heard of it?" she said. "My family moves around a lot, because of . . . reasons." Creating an air of mystery. A classic move. Why hadn't Imogen thought of that? "But nowhere has ever really felt like home. Until now."

"Aaaaaaw," said everyone in the classroom.

"It's true," said Ava, beaming. "There's something

about Blandington that makes me feel like I've lived here all my life."

Imogen's stomach gave a twist. She looked around the room. The boys were staring at Ava like they wanted to date her. Damn it, the girls were staring at Ava like they wanted to date her.

No doubt about it—Ava was killing it way harder than she had. *I hate her,* thought Imogen.

"And—maybe it's because I don't know how long I'm going to be here—but I'm not really that worried about being popular. What I *really* want is to be a part of the Blandington community and to make everyone's lives better in any way I can." With that, Ava stepped back, and she actually took a little bow.

Mr. Fry jumped to his feet and started to applaud. One by one, the students followed suit. Ava was getting a standing ovation.

Imogen felt as though she was about to be sick.

"Well," said Mr. Fry, when the applause had died down several very long minutes later. "Wasn't that just *fantastic?*"

The class agreed that Ava's speech was fantastic.

"So, Ava, you want to help the community?" said Mr. Fry.

"More than anything," chirped Ava, eyes twinkling.

"That's marvelous. Because we have a charity drive coming up!"

"Wonderful!" said Ava, clapping her perfectly manicured hands. "Do you need someone to head it up?"

"Actually, yes we do!" said Mr. Fry.

Imogen stood up. "I volunteer to lead the charity drive too!" she cried.

Mr. Fry looked nervously at Imogen. "Are you sure?" he said. "Are you sure you wouldn't rather be—I don't know—robbing a bank or something? Which would be totally fine, by the way, I'm not judging."

"I'm sure," Imogen said in her steeliest voice.

"All right," said Mr. Fry, adjusting his bow tie, which seemed to be twitching around nervously. "You and Ava can be co-chairs." He turned to the rest of the classroom. "Aren't our new students generous?" he asked. "You could all learn a thing or two from them!"

But Imogen was barely listening. Ava was smiling at her—a smile as cold as a shark's smile would be if the shark had been stuck in a freezer in the Arctic for five years. Imogen forced herself to smile back. Her smile was as cold as a polar bear's smile would be if it went to open the freezer to grab itself an ice cream and found a shark in there smiling back.

What was it that Big Nana had always said? "Keep your friends close. Keep your enemies closer. And keep your nemesis so close that if you get the flu, she'll be sick in bed for a week."

CHAPTER FOUR

IMOGEN LOOKED FOR Delia after school, but it seemed that Delia had already left—if she'd ever come back from skipping class. *She must be really angry,* Imogen thought. Whenever Delia was angry, someone somewhere suffered, and Imogen knew that this time, that someone would be her.

So Imogen went home, consulted the whiteboard, and looked up her crime homework: *build a diorama of the perfect dungeon in which to let your enemies rot. No glitter, please! It gets everywhere.*

Suddenly tired, Imogen decided to lie down on her bed and have a think. *I do all my best thinking horizontally,* she told herself, even though that wasn't entirely true. The next thing she knew, it was dark outside, and someone was knocking on her door and shouting "Imogen! Are you in there?"

Delia.

Maybe she's here to apologize, thought Imogen. *Maybe she's grown up a bit, and she knows she was being unreasonable about the whole you-have-to-skip-school thing.*

But of course she wasn't. She was Delia, after all.

Imogen opened the bedroom door, and Delia pushed her way inside and sat down on the bed. "If I were you, I'd redecorate," she said, bouncing on the mattress, which everyone knows is bad for the springs. "I mean, you still have a poster of the Hatton Garden robbers up in here. They're so 2015."

"Haven't had time yet," said Imogen, sitting down next to Delia.

Delia edged away from Imogen, a disgusted look on her face. "What are you doing? I haven't come up here to *hang out* with you. As *if*! I was sent up to find you. Everyone's wondering where you are. It's the family meeting tonight. Remember?"

Ugh. Imogen did remember. The weekly meetings were part of Big Nana's "family rebuilding plan," now that she was back from the not-really dead. For some reason she thought that getting all the Crims together in one room to talk through their problems would help them bond and reconnect. But it was quite clear to Imogen that getting all the Crims together in one room on a regular basis would be a lot like reenacting the Battle of the Somme over and over again. Some or all of them would end up dead. The others would be traumatized forever. But still, Big Nana knew best. Or so she believed.

"This is going to be awful," said Imogen.

"I know," said Delia. And she gave Imogen a half smile before remembering that she was angry with her, and scowling again.

Good, thought Imogen. *So she doesn't* completely *hate me.* . . .

"Are you worried about the Kruks, then?" Delia asked as they trudged downstairs to the main part of the house.

"I don't know," said Imogen, feeling a bit overwhelmed. "Big Nana says they're after us, so I guess we should believe her. But why *would* they be?"

"No idea. Big Nana isn't usually wrong about things like this, though. There must be something she's not telling us."

"There always is," said Imogen with a grim smile.

They had reached the living room. Imogen was about to open the door, but Delia stopped her. "Hey," she whispered, grinning. "Why don't we investigate? Find out what Big Nana's keeping from us?" She was excited, the way she used to be before she decided excitement wasn't cool. "We can *totally* figure out what's going on. Want to meet up tomorrow before school and make a plan?"

Imogen wanted to say yes—but then she thought about her crime timetable, and about her schoolwork, and about the charity drive she was supposed to be heading up. "I'm sorry," she said, shaking her head. "I don't have time."

Delia scowled. "You mean you don't have time for *me*," she said. "Not since you've got your old clique back, anyway." She pushed open the living room door and took the last remaining seat on the sofa.

"You're here!" said Big Nana, waving to Imogen, who was hovering by the entrance. There was something different about the way her grandmother looked tonight. And then Imogen realized: She was wearing a *caftan*—a kind of floaty tunic favored by the sort of people who like incense and meditation and songs about sharing and rainbows. What madness was this? "Wonderful," said Big Nana in the calm, waft-y voice of a person who wears caftans. "Let's get started. Now, I read a lot of self-help books while I was pretending to be dead—*How to Kill Friends and Intimidate People* was particularly instructive—and I picked up many great tips and techniques for improving family dynamics."

Imogen had a feeling that that would take more than a self-help book; the adult Crims were all shouting at one another and didn't seem to have heard Big Nana, and the Horrible Children were busy ignoring her too. Henry was strumming the electric guitar that Delia had stolen for him in a moment of insanity, singing a song called "I Hate Everything Except Knives and Fire"; Nick and Nate were practicing football throws by tossing Isabella back and forth; and Sam was throwing jail-y babies at everyone. (Jail-y babies are like jelly babies, except they're shaped like famous criminals—the blackcurrant flavor is Jack the Ripper!) But Big Nana carried on regardless.

"Does anyone have any concerns that they'd like to raise at this stage?" she asked.

The Crims raised their concerns very loudly, all at once.

"Clyde keeps eating my porridge," Josephine complained.

"I hate everyone," said Aunt Bets.

"I DON'T UNDERSTAND WHY WORLD PEACE ISN'T A THING!" shouted Uncle Knuckles.

"PEAS! WANT PEAS!" wailed Isabella.

"Not just any old concerns, you bunch of idiotic bananas. Concerns about how we can support and respect one another more as a family," said Big Nana. "Or concerns about the threat from the Kruks."

The Crims were silent.

"No offense," said Delia, "but we're not that concerned about the Kruks."

Big Nana raised her eyebrows in an extremely threatening way. Delia had obviously caused quite a lot of offense.

"You *should* be concerned," said Big Nana in a quiet, sinister voice. "You need to be on guard against any threat. If you see or hear or even *smell* anything suspicious, tell me immediately. Everyone knows that Elsa Kruk has a fondness for lavender-scented perfume. It's extremely overpowering."

"Well, someone cut in front of me at the Blandington Grocery the other day," said Aunt Bets, cracking her small but powerful knuckles. "He didn't smell like lavender, though. He smelled like toilets."

"And the Thompson children have started eating bananas instead of cheese in their sandwiches. Someone must have told them I hate banana sandwiches. I can't steal their lunches anymore," said Nate.

Big Nana shook her head, looking older and more tired than Imogen had seen her in a long time, despite the caftan. She clapped her hands.

"Forget it," she said. "I don't actually care what any of you think. I'm in charge around here, and you idiots are all going to do as I say. When the Kruks attack—"

"*If*," interrupted Imogen.

"WHEN," said Big Nana, "they attack, we will congregate in the Loot Room. That will be our designated emergency meeting place. Understood?"

Everyone nodded.

"Good," said Big Nana, crossing her arms. "Now. Freddie?"

Freddie, who had dozed off for a moment, woke up. "What? Where? Yes! No. I didn't do it!"

"You're in charge of defending Crim House in case of attack."

"Right you are, Big Nana," he said. "There are a lot of poker players who still owe me money, and some of them bite. I can station them around the house and then construct a few booby traps in case anyone actually manages to make it into the house. I have a lot of time on my hands now that I don't have to pretend to go to bookkeeping classes anymore."

"Hey," said Uncle Clyde, looking up angrily from his laptop—he was playing *Solitary Confinement*, which is like *Solitaire* but for ex-cons. "Booby traps are *my* thing."

"But your booby traps never work," reasoned Big Nana. "Freddie, go ahead with your plan."

Uncle Clyde muttered something that sounded like "ungrateful" and "The children were only slightly injured." He went back to his laptop. Imogen saw that he was opening an internet browser and bringing up the Blandington police's "Most Wanted" page. Uncle Clyde looked at the "Most Wanted" page every day, which was a little bit like looking into a mirror and asking "Who is the fairest of them all?" The Crims had always occupied the top spot, even though the police knew exactly where they were, came to their birthday parties, and didn't really want them very much at all. But today, something was different. Uncle Clyde looked pale. "Mother," he said, in a faltering voice. "Something is wrong with Blandington's Most Wanted list."

"What are you talking about?" Big Nana said impatiently.

"There seems to be some sort of fault with it. We're not number one."

The room grew horribly silent.

"What do you mean we're not number one, darling?" asked Josephine, horrified. "We're always number one! It's tradition! It's our birthright!"

"You're not even a Crim," Big Nana pointed out. "You married into this family."

Josephine looked as though she'd been slapped. "After everything I've done for you lot," she muttered. "Before your son met me, he didn't even know what tax evasion *was*!"

But Big Nana wasn't listening. Uncle Clyde had turned his laptop around so that the others could see what he was looking at. There, at the top of the most wanted list, was someone called the Masked Banana Bandit.

The Crims gasped.

"What even *is* a masked banana bandit?" Sam asked squeakily.

"Someone who wears a mask and steals bananas from Tesco?" laughed Henry, as though that was the most ridiculous crime he could think of.

"Yep," said Uncle Clyde. He brought up another web page—the *Blandington Times*'s. Beneath the headline "Banana Drama" was a blurry photo of a thief in a black mask, running out of a supermarket with an armful of bananas.

Imogen was intrigued. The Crims had always been the only criminals in Blandington. Maybe this would make the other Crims up their game. . . .

Big Nana crossed her arms. "Things have come to a pretty pass," she said. "Someone stealing bananas is irritating, sure—but it's *nothing* to the kind of crimes we've committed over the years! This bandit must be pretty pathetic if he's gone to the trouble of putting on a mask and the only crime he can think of to commit is a little fruit-based shoplifting. And yet Blandington Police think he's *more of a threat than we are*." (Big Nana always assumed that successful criminals were women and rubbish ones were men. "If you want a crime done properly, do it yourself. Failing that, ask your aunt or your mother to do it for you.")

Uncle Clyde nodded sadly. "I was dreading something like this happening. Now the police know we're not behind the heist, they must think we're . . . soft."

At this, the room erupted.

"This is outrageous!" shrieked Josephine.

"Unacceptable," muttered Aunt Bets, pulling a sharpened knitting needle from her bag and looking around for someone to attack.

"I can*not* let people at school hear about this," grumbled Delia.

Even Imogen felt offended on behalf of her family. But then she looked around and realized . . . Uncle Clyde was an accidental genius. The idea that the police thought they were soft seemed to have upset and galvanized the Crims more than anything Big Nana had said. Nick and Nate actually got a bit tearful. Isabella banged her head on the wall, apparently trying to prove how hard she was.

Big Nana pounded on the table to call for calm. "That's more like it, my frozen dinners," she said. "We need to get our reputation back. We need to prove that we are a criminal force to be reckoned with. We need to TAKE ACTION."

"Yes!" said Uncle Clyde, jumping to his feet. "We must commit as many crimes as we possibly can until we're at the top of the list again!"

The Crims all cheered—except Imogen, who already had quite enough on her plate, and Big Nana, who, from the looks of it, was starting to regret coming back from the dead.

"I'm very pro committing crimes," said Big Nana, "but stay focused. I'm hereby setting up the Crime Directive: Everyone is to commit at least one crime a day, to sharpen your criminal skills. But choose proper crimes—nothing as small-time as banana theft. Don't forget: We still need to be ready for when the Kruks attack!"

But the Crims had definitely, completely, 100 percent already forgotten about the Kruks.

It was almost ten p.m. by the time the meeting finished and Imogen could head back to her apartment. She felt a little bit panicky as she trudged up the stairs. In no time at all she'd have to get up again and start Big Nana's insane criminal training program.

"Wait for me!" said a cheerful voice behind her.

She turned; her father was bounding up the stairs, two at a time. Al really did seem a lot more energetic and cheerful these days. Maybe he was just really happy that Imogen was back in Blandington. Or relieved not to be serving time for a crime he didn't commit. Being released from jail was enough to put a spring in anyone's step.

"What do you think of the Crime Directive, then, my dear? Are you going to start committing crimes immediately?" he asked Imogen, unlocking the apartment door.

"I have to," Imogen said. "Big Nana's drawn up a whole timetable for me. But I'm going to stick to low-effort crimes for now, because I'm in charge of the school charity drive. I might do a bit of fraud, a spot of hacking on my way to school, poison a few people. . . . We really need to start building up Isabella's tolerance to cyanide. . . ." Even talking about it made her feel exhausted. She smiled at her father and started toward her bedroom, but he called her back.

"Hey," he said, "isn't it thrilling about the Kruks being after us?" There was a strange light in his eyes. Imogen hadn't seen her father this excited since 2011, when he'd won an unusually powerful calculator in the Blandington Chess Tournament. One thing that never excited Al Crim was crime—certainly not dangerous crime. He used to be *terrified* of the Kruks. What had come over him?

"Are you okay, Dad?" Imogen asked.

"Of course! Never been better!" he said chirpily, which is a word that should never be used to describe the way an accountant speaks. "I just think it would be fantastic if there really was a proper rivalry between the Kruks and the Crims. A sort of old-school, mafia-style underground war, with people turning up dead in rivers, and horse heads being left in beds. That sort of thing. Don't you?"

"Not really," said Imogen, more concerned than ever. *Horse heads in beds?* Perhaps her father needed a new hobby—indoor croquet, maybe, or tiddlywinks, or embroidery. . . .

But Barney had come bounding out of her parents' bedroom, and Al turned to ruffle his fur. "Play dead, Barney!" he said, and the big, stupid dog rolled over onto his side with his tongue lolling out of his mouth.

Maybe this is what happens to people after the age of forty, Imogen thought as she watched her father. *They lose their hair, get obsessed with their pets, start to think that attention from murderous psychopaths is better than no attention at all.* . . . Her father was probably just having a strangely upbeat midlife crisis.

LOOT ROOM

Step One: Create disturbance in Loot Room!

Ahh, No!

Step Two: Engage booby trap!

Let us out, we are so annoying!

BUTTON

Step Three: Enjoy peace and quiet!!!

CHAPTER FIVE

IMOGEN'S ALARM WENT off at five the next morning. She hopped out of bed (literally; she'd fallen asleep wearing handcuffs on her feet—she'd been practicing escaping from them), went for a swim with the piranhas, stole Sam's eggs on toast, and still got to school at eight thirty. So it wasn't surprising that by lunchtime, she was tired, grumpy, and more determined than ever to beat Ava any way she could. Starting with the charity drive.

At noon, Imogen set up camp outside the dining hall and started trying to persuade her fellow students to give to charity (by threatening them with extremely violent consequences involving rats if they refused). Big Nana had always told her: "If you want people to do something for you, make them feel special. Make it clear you know their darkest secrets and where they live." So Imogen called over the students she knew by name. There weren't that many of them—she still struggled to remember any of these people—but she found she had a surprisingly high hit rate just by shouting "Noah!" and "Ruby!" at people as they walked past. If someone said, "That's not my name," she'd say, "It is now," and they were usually too scared to argue.

By one p.m., her bucket was filling up. She looked around the dining hall in case there were any weak-looking people she'd missed, and there, at the popular table, was Ava, eating a cheese sandwich (*so* not a queen bee lunch choice), surrounded by admirers. Imogen smiled to herself. Ava clearly didn't have the eye of the tiger needed to beat Imogen in the charity drive. She thought she had time to eat? And *talk*? *Please!*

Imogen had just persuaded one of the Noahs (real name Kevin) to hand over his new sneakers, as well as his lunch money, and was watching him walk away barefoot when she saw Penelope walk into the dining hall, smiling and chatting with her little cousin. Penelope's cousin was really little. It was quite hard to see her without glasses on, even if you didn't need glasses.

"Penelope!" called Imogen.

Penelope walked over with her cousin, who looked

tinier than ever as she registered who Imogen was. "What's up?" Penelope asked brightly. Earlier that day, she and Imogen had had a perfectly *delightful* conversation about isosceles triangles and the little songs they'd invented to remember the angles and what was the point, really, because how relevant were isosceles triangles going to be to their adults lives and . . . *Anyway,* Imogen thought sharply, trying to harden her heart. *That was then, this is now. Being part of my clique means being focused on the end goal!*

"What do you *think*'s up?" Imogen asked harshly, and Penelope's smile collapsed. "Isn't little Emily here—"

"Her name is Veronica."

"That's what I said. Isn't she going to help starving children by donating her lunch money?"

Penelope looked nervously from Imogen to Veronica and then sighed. "Excuse me for a minute, Veronica," she said. Veronica looked all too happy to be excused. "Please, can we leave Veronica out of this?" said Penelope when she and Imogen were alone. "Look at the size of her. The doctor said she might literally disappear if she doesn't eat regularly. And no one likes an invisible eleven-year-old."

Imogen crossed her arms. "Absolutely not. If you want to be in my clique, you need to understand who's in charge. Me. And what really matters: raising more money than Ava and making her look stupid."

Penelope looked disappointed, but only for a second.

Then her face turned cold. "Fine," she said. She called Veronica over. "I'm really sorry," she said. "You have to hand over your lunch money. Don't worry. I'll let you have some of my lasagna."

Veronica fumbled in her tiny wallet and handed her coins to Imogen.

"Thank you, Emily," said Imogen. She felt bad for a moment—but it was a very small moment, even smaller than Emily. She didn't keep a clique to have *friends*. She kept a clique because calling them "minions" was apparently not socially acceptable.

Aside from protecting my family, I have only one goal, Imogen reminded herself. *To rule the school.*

As lunch was winding down and Imogen was counting her take, she heard someone calling her name. She looked up, and there, walking toward her, was Ava, her glossy ponytail swinging and her white teeth shining. Heads turned to watch her as she passed. It was as if she was walking in slow motion.

It was terrible.

"Hi, Imogen!" Ava said sweetly, looking at Imogen's collection bucket. "Wow! Looks like you've raised a little bit of money already!"

"This isn't a little bit," said Imogen.

But Ava didn't seem to hear. "I was thinking: If we

want to raise *real* cash, we should hold an auction. Are you up for it?"

"Sure," said Imogen. She smiled to herself. *I have awakened the sleeping tiger.* "I'll approach local businesses and see if they'll donate stuff. Apparently, the frozen yogurt place is very generous."

"Great!" said Ava, flipping her ponytail. "And I'll see if I can get my friends to donate anything. Effie's family has a spare private jet . . . and Jack's dad has a second home in the Bahamas he was thinking of selling. Plus, François's dad is president of France—maybe we could auction off the chance to be the French prime minister for a day or something. Just to mix it up a bit."

"Great," Imogen said, through gritted teeth. "It's always good to mix it up. . . ."

But she felt disappointed in herself. She had been outplayed, and she was never outplayed, not even at Scrabble.

She was going to have to up her game.

Imogen headed straight to the basement when she got home. It was time to look in the Loot Cellar. The Loot Cellar was where the Crims stored the spoils of their crimes: bad copies of Impressionist paintings, party bags stolen from toddlers' parties, half-used ketchup bottles taken from diners—that sort of thing. She typed in the code, pushed the door open, and walked inside. She was immediately hit by the smell of a thousand pointless stolen goods. If you're wondering what that smells like, it's a bit like that musty smell you get in secondhand clothing shops, mixed with the smell of fried chicken (fast-food restaurants were one of the Crims' favorite targets).

The Loot Cellar was the most ridiculous room in Crim House, and that was saying something. Crim House also contained a room filled entirely with MC Hammer memorabilia and another called "the Success Room," where the Crims went to celebrate particularly brilliant heists (it had been collecting dust for years). Imogen knew it was unlikely, but she thought maybe—just maybe—she'd find something she could donate to the auction. Okay, she thought, noticing a book called *How too Speill* on one of the long, loot-filled shelves that lined the room, that was really unlikely. Still, it was worth a look.

But as soon as she'd stepped into the room, a huge net snagged her up and flew her straight to the ceiling.

"Help!" screamed Imogen. "Let me down!" She started to panic. Had the Kruks attacked them after all? She wriggled, trying and failing to get free. Big Nana had sent her an essay on net-escape techniques just the day before, but she had decided to put off reading it till the weekend. She could have kicked herself, except her legs were twisted underneath her, and she couldn't move them at all. What if, despite Big Nana's Crime Directive, no one scored any loot for weeks and so had no reason to come down to the Loot Room? She was going to die a miserable, lonely death, surrounded by things that nobody wanted—and she'd still be an also-ran at Blandington Secondary School, meaning that nobody impressive would come to her funeral. Imogen shuddered as she thought about what people would say about her: *Sadly, it would appear that her best years were behind her, as the former head girl struggled to manage a charity drive at her third-rate high school. . . .* "HELP!" she screamed again.

At what felt like a very long last, Freddie appeared in the doorway. "Ha! Got you now, you nasty, sneaky, thieving Kruk," he said in the voice he had used to terrorize members of his gambling ring.

Imogen felt an odd mixture of relief and rage. "Freddie," she said. "It's me."

"That's what they all say," said Freddie.

"No, it's Imogen. Your cousin? Let me down." The rope holding the net was starting to creak. Any minute now she was going to plummet to the ground.

"Oh," said Freddie, disappointed. "I really thought I'd gotten one of them. There was an eighty-seven percent chance you were Elsa Kruk, according to my algorithms. What are *you* doing here?"

"Do you think we could continue this conversation at ground level?" Imogen said as terror joined the jumble of emotions she was experiencing.

Freddie reluctantly lowered her to the floor. She landed on her face. It wasn't very dignified.

"At least I know the trap works," he said.

"*Works?* Yes—on your family members," said Imogen, disentangling herself from the net. "Why did you set the trap to deploy after the target correctly enters the code to the Loot Cellar door and gets inside?"

"Because I worked out there was a one in twenty-six chance they'd crack the code, and a two in seven chance they'd be so pleased with themselves for doing it that they'd let their guard down as soon as they entered the cellar."

There was silence for a moment while Imogen tried and failed to figure out what Freddie was talking about.

"Look," she said. "Never mind. Want to help me? I'm trying to find things to donate to a charity auction. This annoying new girl at school is apparently friends with Elton John's nephew, and he got his uncle to donate seven actual tiaras, a songwriting lesson, and a pair of glasses shaped like the sphinx."

"We have a toilet brush shaped like a canoe down here somewhere, if you're interested," said Freddie.

"I'm definitely not," said Imogen.

She and Freddie rooted through all the bizarre junk in the cellar—a box of nappies marked "Used"; a cassette tape labeled "Learn Esperanto!"; the original Broadway cast of *Cats* (they had formed a new breed of musical-theater superhumans at the very back of the cellar and communicated only in high kicks and Andrew Lloyd Webber songs). *This is pointless,* Imogen thought. The only valuable thing in the cellar—Uncle Clyde's Captain Crook lunch box—was too important to the family to give away.

After reaching into a bag marked "Gold" and pulling out a handful of half-chewed chocolate coins, Imogen gave up.

"See you upstairs, Freddie," she called to her cousin, who seemed to have been distracted by a 1980s edition of the board game Who's Who?

"Wait," Freddie said, looking up. "Big Nana said she'd like to talk to you this afternoon."

"About what?" Imogen asked.

Freddie shrugged.

Imogen sighed. Freddie had given up his "I don't know anything" persona and turned out to be a total mathematical genius, but he was still as much use as a chocolate hand grenade. Which is to say, only useful in very specific circumstances—delighting soldiers and terrifying parents, for instance.

Imogen walked back upstairs, disappointed. She still had nothing to donate to the charity drive. She would have to admit defeat, and she didn't like to admit anything, unless it would buy her a plea deal. She pushed open the door to her apartment and found her parents standing on the landing, together—not a very common occurrence. Josephine was usually more interested in looking at herself in the mirror than paying Al any attention. And Al usually preferred chatting to his bank manager than his wife.

But here they were, giggling together—and were Imogen's eyes deceiving her, or was her father fastening an extremely expensive necklace around her mother's neck?

Imogen's eyes were not deceiving her. They were the most honest of all her body parts. Imogen recognized diamonds, sapphires, emeralds, rubies, and amethysts on the necklace. To be honest, the colors looked terrible together, but it must have been worth thousands.

"It's stunning!" Josephine said breathlessly—she didn't really care what things looked like as long as they were worth a lot of money, which is why she could often be seen wearing designer track pants and very heavy solid-gold shoes. "Where did you get this?"

"I stole it!" said Al.

Josephine gasped. "Darling! *Did* you? Really and truly?"

"It was nothing."

But it wasn't nothing, Imogen thought. *Not for Al Crim.*

"Look, darling!" Josephine said, turning to Imogen. "Look what your father just stole for me! Can you believe it?"

Imogen couldn't believe it. "Dad would never steal a necklace," she said.

"What did you say?" said Josephine. "I couldn't hear you, I was too busy polishing my necklace."

Imogen pulled her father aside. "Dad, are you *sure* you're okay? Are you sure there's nothing wrong?"

Her father looked confused. "Of course I'm okay!"

"But this isn't like you."

Al flushed slightly. "Well, Big Nana said we had to up our game and commit as many crimes as possible," he said slowly. "And there was an article in this month's *Accounting Today!* about how crime gets the adrenaline flowing and improves blood pressure over time. . . ."

"Really? *Accounting Today!* is persuading its readers to become felons now?"

"They didn't phrase it like *that*," said Al. "The article was based on a survey of accountants doing time for money laundering. Apparently, they have a better quality of life than other accountants. Did you know they teach stand-up comedy in some prisons?"

"But, Dad," said Imogen, "you've spent time in jail. You hated it."

"It wasn't all bad. . . ."

"And you *hate* stand-up comedy! You don't like being the center of attention! You don't even have a sense of humor!"

"Yes I do!" said Al. "Ha! Ha! See?"

I should just drop this, thought Imogen. She had a horrible feeling that any minute now, her father was going to try to prove how hilarious he was, and it would be so extremely un-hilarious that she might be forced to eat her own arm just to get through it. *He really is having a midlife crisis,* she mused sadly. She remembered Uncle Knuckles's midlife crisis all too clearly; he had tried to steal the principality of Liechtenstein and had ended up stabbing himself on one of the country's many mountains.

Thinning hair could really do a number on a man.

Imogen went to her bedroom. She looked at her crime homework timetable—write an essay on techniques for escaping a net, steal a small plane and land it on the highway, and file fingernails into razor-sharp points—but she just couldn't motivate herself. What she really needed to do was research businesses that looked as though they might be willing to donate expensive goods for the charity auction.

She sent out a few emails, calling herself "the Duchess of Blandingshire"—companies were always more willing to give free things to rich people—and had so far secured promises of a set of electric nose-hair trimmers and a subscription to *Posh Lady* magazine (her fault for posing as a wealthy eighty-three-year-old). She was just about to email a computer store to see whether they'd give her a free laptop when there was a knock at the door.

"Come in," said Imogen, by which she meant, "Please go away and leave me alone."

The door creaked open, and Big Nana's face appeared. "Hello, my wrinkly passion fruit," she said. "Where have you been?"

Imogen felt a sudden rush of guilt. She had completely forgotten to find Big Nana. "Sorry!" she said. "Freddie said you were you looking for me earlier? I've been caught up with this school charity drive. . . ."

Big Nana settled herself onto Imogen's bed. "That's what I wanted to talk to you about," she said. "I'm worried you're already falling behind with your crime homework. You still haven't handed in yesterday's essay—and you were supposed to steal a cherry tree today and replace it with a hatstand to see if anyone noticed. But you didn't, did you?"

"No . . . ," said Imogen.

"Have you committed a single crime today?"

"Yes," said Imogen, reddening. "I'm committing internet fraud right now, I promise."

"Yes, but for a good cause," Big Nana pointed out. "You know how I feel about good causes."

"'Helping others is only worth it if they can get you free tickets to the Emmys,'" chanted Imogen.

"Exactly."

"But look," said Imogen, pulling out her criminal plans journal. "I've been doing proper crime homework too—see? I'm working on a programming code to skim money out of Blandington Police's online bank account."

"How very twenty-first century of you."

"I know. And guess what—it turns out their password is 'password.'"

"So how much have you stolen from them so far?"

Imogen felt her face reddening even further. "I haven't actually put the plan into action. I'm still finalizing the details. I don't want them to be able to trace it to me. . . ."

Big Nana folded her hands in her lap. "You're prioritizing school over your crime homework, in other words," she said.

Imogen was starting to feel a little desperate. "You know that it's important for me to do well in school!" she said. "You don't want me to be like Uncle Clyde, do you? At least when *I* come up with a heist, you know it will work."

"But Clyde has passion," said Big Nana. "And a sense of urgency!"

"But there isn't a deadline on my crime homework, is there?"

Big Nana pushed herself up from the bed. "There is no

time to lose!" she said. "We don't know when the Kruks will launch their next attack—"

"*Next* attack?" Imogen asked skeptically.

"THEY SENT US A THREATENING NOTE IN A CHILD'S BIRTHDAY CAKE!" Big Nana reminded her—the shoutiest reminder Imogen had ever received.

"But that *can't* have been the Kruks," Imogen said. "It wasn't sophisticated enough to be them!"

Big Nana shook her head. "I understand why you're claiming not to think they're a threat," she said. "Denial ain't just a river in Egypt, eh, my trepidatious persimmon?"

Imogen stared at her. "What?"

Big Nana tilted her head, studying Imogen as if she were a work of art. "You're afraid to believe it might be true. After all, it's a pretty terrifying prospect. But ignoring it isn't going to make it go away."

"I'm not ignoring it—"

"You are," said Big Nana. "You're behaving just like you did when you were at Lilyworth. You're behaving like you don't *want* to be head of the Crims one day. Like there's more to life than crime."

Imogen looked away. "Maybe there is," she said quietly.

There was a silence. Imogen's words hung in the air like horrible helium balloons.

"What did you just say?" Big Nana asked in the calm, quiet, dangerous voice that she normally only used to threaten judges.

"Nothing," Imogen said quickly. "Let's just pretend I didn't say anything."

But Big Nana was so angry, her hands were beginning to shake. "Crime is what keeps this family together!" she said.

"I know," said Imogen, edging backward.

"NOTHING IS MORE IMPORTANT THAN FAMILY!" shouted Big Nana, looking more like Uncle Knuckles than Imogen was comfortable with. "EXCEPT CRIME! AND DINOSAURS!!!" And with that, Big Nana stalked out the doorway, slamming the door behind her and stomping downstairs.

Imogen stared after her. That had not gone well. In fact, it had gone badly. In fact, it was the most disturbing conversation she'd had that day, and that morning Aunt Bets had called her "a turnip with a face." She shook herself, trying to get rid of the guilt and shame she felt from disappointing Big Nana. As soon as this charity drive was out of the way, and she was secure in her position as queen bee, she would give all her attention to her family.

Nodding to herself, she turned back to her desk and tried to carry on with her email to the computer store. The screen seemed to swim in front of her eyes, but that would have been weird, because laptops are very bad at the breaststroke.

Then she realized she was crying.

I'm not sad, Imogen told herself fiercely. *I'm just exhausted.*

But she *was* a bit sad. She hated disappointing Big Nana more than she hated anything else—even more than cheese from a can, and toothbrushes with all of the bristles splayed out.

She shut her laptop and opened her crime homework timetable. She really was behind—she was supposed to write yet another essay today: "You and your entire family are in the custody of a master criminal. You're handcuffed, dangling over a pool of acid. The master criminal is delivering an evil monologue. He is using long words like 'heretofore' and 'unrepentant' and 'filibuster.' How do you begin the process of escaping?"

Imogen chewed the end of her pencil. (She preferred to do her crime homework by hand so that the Blandington Police Department would never find it if they searched her laptop.) "First," she wrote, "I would distract the master criminal by flattering his authoritative speaking voice and asking for details of his genius plan. While he explained, I would look around for an exit. . . ."

CHAPTER SIX

IMOGEN STAYED UP till three in the morning finishing her essay and then got up again at five to make herself a bank robbery uniform (dressmaking, according to Big Nana, was an essential part of every criminal's skill set). She arrived to school on time, but she was so tired that her eyes were burning and her brain felt buried in cotton wool, which sounds cozy but is actually quite unpleasant.

By lunchtime, Imogen was ready to collapse. As soon as the bell sounded, she pushed back her chair and walked, zombielike, toward the classroom door—but then Mr. Fry called her back. Or stammered her back, really. He seemed so terrified that he could hardly get the words out.

"I—I don't think you meant to hand this in," he said, passing her the essay she had given in that morning on the symbolism of beards in ancient Egypt. Imogen looked at the essay, confused. Of course she had meant to hand it in. She was particularly pleased with her analysis of the correlation between the pointiness of a pharaoh's beard and the earliness of his death. And then she read the title of the essay and realized why Mr. Fry looked as though he'd rather be anywhere than talking to her—even in a cheap hotel in the dodgiest part of Bucharest, famous for its high murder rate and scratchy complimentary slippers.

She hadn't handed in her schoolwork. She'd handed in her crime homework by mistake. No wonder Fry looked terrified. You'd have been terrified too if you had read such a detailed description of what acid can do to human feet.

"I'm so sorry," she said, trying to look innocent, even though she knew that he knew that she knew how to murder someone with a skipping rope. "I promise you, this is all totally theoretical. My grandmother is quite eccentric—"

"Please stop talking," said Mr. Fry, wide-eyed, his hand covering his bow tie, as if protecting it from her. "The less I know about you, or your grandmother, or your dangerous sporting equipment, the safer for me. How about we never talk about this again?" With that, he ran off down the corridor like a lamb who has just learned what the word "abattoir" means.

Somehow Imogen got through the rest of the day without falling asleep, though it probably wouldn't have mattered if she had—word had clearly gotten around to the other teachers about her crime essay, and they were all behaving as though she might bite them at any minute, which she obviously wouldn't do because everyone knows that teachers taste revolting. Mrs. Mariposa, her physics teacher, actually asked her not to hand in her homework the next day. It was an essay on particle physics, too, and Imogen loved writing about atoms—but she decided not to argue. She was regretting leaving Lilyworth more with each passing day.

All Imogen wanted to do after school was go home, eat a large amount of ice cream, watch videos of cats freaking out about cucumbers, and forget about her teachers and her grandmother and Ava Gud and the fact that she was Imogen Crim. But she couldn't. There was a charity committee meeting that afternoon in the dining hall. The charity committee consisted of Ava and Imogen, Penelope, Hannah and Willa, and five boys who had clearly just joined so they could spend the entire meeting staring at Ava.

"I brought brownies!" said Ava. "Baked them before

school." She arranged them neatly on the plate in front of her. "I've got a thing about symmetry," she explained.

Smart move, Imogen thought. *Way to get the committee on your side.* Even Imogen's friends were grabbing the brownies and cooing "Thank you!" to Ava. Imogen shot glares at them, and they had the decency to look chastened—but not enough decency to put down the brownies, which, Imogen had to admit, looked delicious.

"So," said Ava, taking charge of the meeting.

"So," said Imogen, taking charge of the meeting too.

Ava smiled her toothy smile at Imogen, her head tilted to one side. "Is it okay with you if I chair this meeting? I've brought a notebook. . . ." She reached into her bag and pulled out a notebook with "Ava Gud, Chair of Charity Committee" embossed on the front in gold letters. "My mom had it made for me," she said with a shrug as the others oohed and aahed over it.

"Hang on—" Imogen started.

But Ava blew her a kiss. "Thanks, Imogen!" she said, as if Imogen had agreed, which she definitely hadn't. "Okay. Let's run through the donations we've collected for the auction so far. I'll start! I've been really busy, doing a bit of modeling in the evenings, but I have managed to scrape a few things together. So, we have Elton John's glasses and tiaras and a songwriting lesson—you know about that already. I persuaded Le Cordon Bleu cooking school in Paris to donate a weeklong cooking course, and then there's a disco-dancing lesson with Academy Award–nominated actor Don Vadrolga!"

Everyone on the charity committee burst into a round of applause. Everyone except Imogen, that is. She shot a fierce look at her friends, and they stopped clapping.

"Don Vadrolga, wow— I thought he was dead," Penelope said loudly, winking at Imogen like she'd just delivered a huge *zinger*. Imogen tried not to sigh. *Amateurs*.

"Oh, no, he just played an angel in a movie once. Maybe you got confused?" said Ava, smiling and shaking her head. "Anyway, it's nothing, really. I'm sure you guys have got much cooler donations. Penelope—what about you?"

"Well, my grandmother has promised some knitting lessons," she said, sitting up and looking a little too proud of herself. "Knitting is all the rage among bored hipsters!"

"Cool, how retro!" said Ava. "How about you, Willa?"

Willa glanced at Imogen, turned bright red, and looked at her feet as she said, "Um . . . the frozen yogurt place has donated a two-pound gift card. . . ."

Ava nodded, her head tilted again to one side. "That's about enough for one scoop, isn't it?" she said. "Which is great! We don't want anyone getting diabetes! What else?"

The other girls were silent.

"What about you, Imogen?" Ava said, smiling at her expectantly. "I know you're going to blow the rest of us out of the water!"

"Well, I could," said Imogen, "but I don't think anyone would want to bid for a homemade bomb!"

No one laughed.

Ava shook her head. "Please don't bring a homemade bomb, Imogen," she said.

"Oh, no," said Imogen, "I was joking! That was a silly joke!"

Everyone kept not laughing.

What had she been thinking? Jokes had never been her strong point. *And queen bees,* she reminded herself, *don't have senses of humor.*

"Do you have any *actual* pledges?" Ava asked, a hint of sourness in her sickly sweet voice.

"Yes, actually," Imogen said, thinking quickly. "My family might be willing to donate a secondhand Boeing 747. It's attached to the roof of our house at the moment—my uncle Knuckles and aunt Bets live in it, but we can probably find room for them somewhere else. We just need to find someone to pry it up—"

"Awww," said Ava, pasting on a huge, obviously fake smile. "How sweet! That's *super*nice of them! But 747s are a bit out-of-date—it's all about the 787 Dreamliner now, isn't it? Which means that so far, Imogen has gotten . . . no donations."

Imogen blushed. She hated blushing—pink didn't suit her. She looked down at her phone so no one would see, and noticed a text from Big Nana: **Where are you? You're supposed to be breaking into the post office this evening. We need stamps.** She turned her phone off without replying. Big Nana was much more demanding alive than she had been dead.

When she tuned back into the meeting, Ava was still talking. "So, who wants to volunteer to be auctioneer?"

Imogen and Ava both raised their hands.

"Okay," said Ava. "Let's have a vote. Who wants Imogen to be auctioneer?"

Imogen shot her hand into the air again. She looked over at Hannah, Penelope, and Willa. Penelope and Hannah raised their hands too—but Willa kept hers firmly down.

Hmmm. Imogen cocked an eyebrow in Willa's direction. *Rebellion from the troops?*

"And who wants *me* to be auctioneer?" All five boys and Willa raised theirs.

"I win!" said Ava, giggling in false modesty, which is the worst kind of modesty.

She's beating me at everything, thought Imogen. *I'm going to have to bring her down somehow!*

Imogen was so irritated by Ava that she forgot to steal stamps on the way home. She was even more irritated when, while walking up to the back door, she suddenly fell into a deep trough hidden by pine needles—another of Freddie's booby traps.

"FREDDIE!" she shouted, trying to scramble out of the pit. If she hadn't fallen into it, she might have been impressed—it was very deep and very well hidden. But she *had* fallen into it, and she had mud under her nails and all over her school uniform, so she was mostly just furious.

Freddie lumbered around the corner, a hopeful look in his eyes. Once again, he seemed very disappointed to see Imogen.

"Oh," he said. "It's you."

"Yes," she said. "Help me out of here." She reached out her arm to him, and he heaved her out.

Freddie helped her pick the pine needles out of her hair. "I really thought I'd gotten them this time," he said.

Imogen gave a sigh of frustration. "Don't you think it's time to give up on the booby trap idea? The only person you've caught is me."

"Twice!" said Freddie, who seemed much prouder of this than he should have been. "Plus a couple of cats. And anyway, they work as a deterrent. How many times have the Kruks attacked us since I set the traps? Zero, that's how many."

"And I'm sure that's all thanks to you."

Freddie looked pleased. "Really?" he said.

"You're really good at recognizing sarcasm," said Imogen.

"Thank you!" said Freddie.

Imogen shook her head and pushed past him into the house.

All Imogen wanted to do was take a shower and go to bed and forget about her complete failure of a day. She stomped upstairs, but as she passed Delia's room, she heard the unmistakable screechy tones of Kitty Penguin singing her hit single "Bad Beak." Imogen paused outside the door. She had barely spoken to Delia since the first day of school—and she hadn't had any fun since then, either. Maybe that wasn't a coincidence. She wondered how many crimes Delia had committed since Big Nana had announced the Crime Directive. Delia had so many grand plans. Had she stolen the giant hamburger sign from Blandington Burgers and put it in the kitchen as a subliminal message for whoever was cooking dinner that night? Had she kidnapped Makeup Boy, her favorite YouTube star, and forced him to teach her how to contour? And had she decided to try to find out what Big Nana was supposedly keeping from them, about why the Kruks were coming after them?

She decided to find out.

Delia was lying on her bed, doodling in her criminal plans journal and "singing" along to Kitty Penguin. She sounded like a vacuum cleaner in a lot of pain. She slammed her journal shut when she saw Imogen and asked, "What do you want?"

"Nice to see you, too," said Imogen. "I just thought we could hang out for a bit."

Delia sat up, arms crossed. "Why? I thought you were too good for me, now that you're queen bee."

Imogen sat on the edge of Delia's bed. "Actually, I don't think I *am* queen bee," she said miserably. "There's a new girl in my class. Ava Gud—I mean, what kind of name is that?"

"A bad one."

"Right. And she's good at everything. And everyone likes her. And her voice sounds like angels singing. And she's rich—like, the other day she said, 'Taylor Swift doesn't come to stay anymore, because she got upset that our house was so much nicer than hers.'"

Delia raised an eyebrow. "What does she look like?"

"She's beautiful. Obviously."

Delia shifted closer to Imogen. "There must be *something* wrong with her. What does she smell like?"

Imogen tilted her head, remembering. "It's like . . . roses and butterscotch and freshly cut grass."

Delia shook her head, grimacing. "Man. You're in trouble."

"I know." Imogen sighed, kicking her legs against the bed. "I probably shouldn't be focusing so much on school stuff when Big Nana's so worried about the family. It's just . . . I knew it would be hard to leave Lilyworth, but I thought at least I'd be best at everything in Blandington. No offense." She looked at Delia. "Anyway. Enough about me. How are you? How's the Crime Directive going?"

"Not great," said Delia. "I tried to steal a car earlier. Only it turned out it was a self-driving car, and it took me straight to the police station. I mean, I managed to run away before they caught me—those police officers really need to work on their cardio—but it was a total setup!"

"How was it a setup?" Imogen asked.

"The car just happened to be parked with its window wide open, right in front of the ice cream parlor I go to when I skip school."

"Couldn't it just have been bad luck?"

Delia gave an angry laugh. "OPEN YOUR EYES! Who would leave a self-driving—"

But before she could finish her sentence, Big Nana's

head appeared around the door. "It's time for a family meeting!"

Delia and Imogen looked at each other. The last thing they wanted to do was go to another family meeting. But they knew that if they didn't go, it might *literally* be the last thing they did—Big Nana owned a lot of chainsaws for a sixty-five-year-old. So they stood up and walked sulkily downstairs.

The other Crims were already assembled on cushions on the living room floor, apart from Big Nana, who was standing by the door, holding what looked like a police baton covered in glitter and hearts and pictures of weeping unicorns.

"PLEASE, CAN I SIT ON THE SOFA?" said Uncle Knuckles, shifting uncomfortably, his massive knees knocking together. "THIS IS A LITTLE UNDIGNI-FIED FOR A MAN OF MY AGE. AND MY HERNIA IS ACTING UP AGAIN."

"No," said Big Nana. "This way we're all equal."

"You're standing up," observed Aunt Bets.

"Some of us are more equal than others," said Big Nana. "Now. We have a lot of important issues to cover today, so we're going to treat one another with loving kindness. Everyone's opinions are valid. Particularly mine. So, we're going to use the sharing stick." She held up the strange-looking baton. "Only the person holding this stick can speak. If anyone interrupts, the person holding it can use the stick to hit them until they shut up. With loving kindness, obviously."

No one said anything. The stick was very large, and Big Nana was very strong.

"Right," said Big Nana, satisfied, thwacking her hand with the sharing stick in quite a threatening manner. "Delia told me she had a rather upsetting experience with a self-driving car earlier on. She tried to steal it—as anyone in their right mind would—and it drove her straight to the police station."

"Outrageous," muttered Uncle Clyde.

Big Nana pointed the sharing stick at Uncle Clyde. "Clyde," she said, "are you holding the sharing stick?"

Uncle Clyde looked down at his hands. "I am not."

"So are you allowed to speak?"

Uncle Clyde shook his head.

"That's better," said Big Nana. "So, I wanted to check with the rest of you— How has the Crime Directive been going? Have you had any trouble committing crimes in the last couple of days?"

Sam, who was covered in gold paint, put up his hand. Big Nana handed him the sharing stick.

"Someone left a note on my locker at school, saying that the security guard at the art supply store was legally blind, so obviously, I followed up on that. It went very badly."

"Is that why you look like an Academy Award?" asked Delia.

"I DO NOT WANT TO TALK ABOUT IT!" yelled Sam.

Uncle Knuckles put up his hand, and Sam passed the sharing stick to him.

"I HAD TO BAIL SAM OUT OF JAIL!" shouted Uncle Knuckles. "AND I'D BEEN PLANNING TO USE THAT MONEY TO BUY MYSELF A MUD PACK."

Aunt Bets nodded. "Happened to me too," she said. "I tried to raid the knitting store, but someone had set up a trip wire in front of the really expensive yarn."

"I tried to steal bananas from the supermarket, but the Masked Banana Bandit had already got them all," said Nick.

"What were you doing trying to steal bananas any-way? I specifically told you not to commit such pathetic crimes!" said Big Nana.

Nate smirked at Nick. "That'll teach you for not being original."

"You can talk," said Nick. "Your face isn't even origi-nal. IT'S THE SAME AS MINE."

"Now, now," said Big Nana, grabbing the sharing stick

97

and raising it threateningly. "Loving kindness, remember? And if anyone speaks without the stick again, they'll be sorry. And in a lot of pain."

The Crims fell silent.

"Does this mean that *none* of you have successfully pulled off a crime today?"

The Crims nodded miserably.

Big Nana frowned. "This just goes to show that we need to be on our guard. Particularly since Uncle Clyde was targeted inside Crim House, and Sam was targeted *at school*. Whoever left that note knew exactly which locker was his."

"And whoever parked that self-driving car knows where I go when I'm not at school," said Delia. "Which means someone has been spying on me."

Big Nana nodded, looking serious. "It's time to address the elephant in the room," she said.

"WHERE IS IT?" said Uncle Knuckles, jerking around to look over his shoulders. "I HATE ANIMALS WITH TRUNKS!"

"Not a literal elephant, Knuckles, you oversize balloon," said Big Nana. "A *metaphorical* elephant: There may be a mole in Crim House!"

"A MOLE?" said Uncle Knuckles. "THEY'RE EVEN WORSE! ALL FURRY AND SMOOTH AND BLIND!"

"NOT A LITERAL MOLE!" shouted Big Nana.

"What I mean is, someone in this room is passing information to our enemies!"

"NO!" screamed Uncle Knuckles.

"YES!" Big Nana screamed back.

"NO!" Uncle Knuckles screamed again.

Imogen thought about this. Could there really be a mole in Crim House? She looked around at her family. There was no way any of them would pass information to the Kruks. They were all stupidly loyal to one another, even when they were stealing one another's belongings and attempting to murder one another with tulip bulbs (which is quite difficult). Besides, even if one of them wanted to spy for the Kruks, none of them was actually competent enough to pull it off. Except Big Nana, who clearly wasn't the mole, seeing as she was the one who had brought it up. In any case, Imogen still didn't believe that the Kruks would actually *want* to spy on the Crims. Why would they bother foiling the Crims' petty crimes? Why would they leave a note on a schoolboy's locker?

Imogen took the sharing stick. "Is there actually any *evidence* that there's a mole?" she asked. "Couldn't this all just be bad luck? Or, worst-case scenario, someone's probably trying to prank us. There are loads of people who hate us in this town. Jack Wooster . . . Freddie's whole gambling ring . . . the family of that dead woman Mum ran over . . ."

Big Nana shook her head and took the sharing stick back from Imogen. "Jack Wooster is far too busy sitting on his golden toilet to prank us. Sorry—his golden toilet *empire*. I don't know why you aren't taking this seriously. The threat from the Kruks is real. These people are dangerous. They're stopping us from pulling off crimes, which means we have no food in the house, which means we're going to have to go to the supermarket and *pay for our groceries!*"

"NO!" cried Uncle Knuckles.

"I wouldn't be seen *dead* in a checkout line," muttered Josephine. "So *demeaning!*"

"What do you even *do* in a checkout line?" asked Henry.

"NO CRIM SHOULD EVER KNOW THE ANSWER TO THAT QUESTION!" cried Big Nana. "See what these people have driven us to?"

"Hang on a minute," asked Sam in his squeaky voice. "Have *you* tried pulling off any crimes recently, Big Nana?"

"I shouldn't have to," snapped Big Nana. "I'm supposed to get you lot to commit crimes for me—it's called delegation! It's a management technique! And if I really were your manager, and you were my employees, I'd have fired you all by now!" She took a deep breath and closed her eyes, clearly trying to calm herself down.

Imogen sighed. "Look," she said. "Even if it *is* the Kruks

who were leaving us notes and stopping us from committing crimes—which I really don't think is the case—I'm not convinced that we need to be this worried. Sure, they're psychopaths. But they're not unbeatable. I took them on just a few weeks ago, and I won . . . remember?"

"A very happy memory indeed," said Big Nana.

"And they had no idea I was even *in* Krukingham Palace. So why would they come after us?"

Before anyone could answer, Nick and Nate leaped on Imogen, pinning her to the couch.

"Get off!" she shouted. "What are you doing?"

"Isn't it obvious?" Nick said.

"It really isn't," said Imogen, shoving his arm away from her throat so that she could breathe more easily.

"Why are you so sure the Kruks aren't behind this?" said Nate. "YOU MUST BE THE MOLE!"

"It all makes sense!" said Uncle Clyde.

"No it doesn't!" said Imogen, beginning to panic.

"Yes it does!" screamed Aunt Bets, raising an extremely heavy-looking crossword dictionary over her head. "LET'S KILL HER!"

Imogen's heart was racing. She looked at Al, waiting for him to come to her defense. But for some reason he wouldn't look her in the eye. And if her dad didn't believe in her, no one would.

"One," counted Aunt Bets, taking aim with the

crossword dictionary. "Two . . ."

"WAIT," said Big Nana, banging the sharing stick on the table. "I appreciate everyone's enthusiasm for rooting out the mole . . . really, I do. It's touching. But we have no evidence it's Imogen."

Imogen took a deep breath. Thank badness for Big Nana.

"Since when have we cared about evidence?" said Aunt Bets, still holding the crossword dictionary aloft; she'd obviously been looking forward to a little spot of murder.

"Bets," Big Nana said warningly. "If you kill Imogen, you'll have me to answer to. And the questions I'll ask you will be very hard. Trigonometry related, mostly."

"I hate trigonometry," said Aunt Bets, reluctantly lowering her dictionary but giving Imogen an "I've got my eye on you" look.

Imogen's pulse began to return to normal. The danger was over. For now, at least . . .

Silence fell over the Crims once again, like a strange, itchy blanket.

"I think that's enough for today," said Big Nana. "And remember, all of you: If you see something suspicious, say something. And not just to yourself in the bathroom mirror."

💣 💣 💣

That night, Imogen woke up with a jolt from a vivid dream. Big Nana was on a train full of Kruks, calling for her help, but Imogen was stuck on the platform and couldn't move. She knew it had just been a dream—Big Nana had been dressed as a clown, and Big Nana *hated* clowns—but she couldn't get back to sleep. She felt too hot and couldn't get comfortable on her pillow.

What if Big Nana is right about the Kruks? She'd never doubted Big Nana when she was younger. She thought Big Nana was right about everything—until she had discovered that Big Nana had pretended to be dead for two years. But Big Nana had never been wrong about something as important as this. *She must have some reason to believe that the Kruks are after us,* she thought. *And for some reason, she doesn't want to tell me what it is. . . .*

She looked at her alarm clock. Four a.m. She'd have to get up in an hour to start her crime homework before school. This week's essay: "Your neighbor, James J. Cranky, dies suddenly, under suspicious circumstances. Forge a will, leaving everything to yourself, that can satisfy the authorities." She would get up and do it. She'd take the threat from the Kruks more seriously. She just needed to get a little more sleep first. . . . She closed her eyes again, but then she heard a strange sound coming from the garden. A sound of creaking wheels.

Could it be the Kruks?

Imogen was wide-awake now. She pushed back her duvet, crept downstairs, and opened the back door. There, in the moonlight, someone was pushing a heavy-looking wheelbarrow.

But it wasn't a Kruk. It was—

"Dad?" Imogen called.

Al Crim looked around, startled. "Oh! Imogen! It's you! Just the person I was looking for!"

"What are you doing?"

Al laughed, a little too loud and a little too long. "Well, I've found a few little things to donate to your charity auction!"

Imogen looked through the contents of the wheelbarrow. A genuine first edition of *Harry Potter and the Philosopher's Stone* (Imogen knew what to look for, as Uncle Clyde had stolen at least five fake ones while he was reading the series to Delia), a briefcase with "$100,000 in unmarked bills" written on the front, something massive and metal and green that looked as though it might be the Statue of Liberty's torch.

"That's not real, is it?" she asked.

Al nodded. "Fell off the back of a very large, transatlantic truck," he said.

Imogen stared at him. The father she knew would never have stolen such impressive things. He'd never have been *able* to steal such impressive things.

But what if she didn't know her father that well after all?

"Why were you taking this stuff into the garden?"

"I didn't want the mole to get their hands on it," said Al. "Whoever that is."

Imogen felt a prickle of fear. Could her *father* be the mole? No, Imogen decided. He couldn't be. She had known him her whole life, and there was no way he'd do anything to hurt his family. In fact, he was trying to help her, right now. Just in quite an uncharacteristic way.

Imogen looked at the wheelbarrow. She hadn't seen loot this amazing since she'd visited the Kruks' Loot Cellar. And if she brought this stuff to the charity auction, she'd be in, with a chance of reclaiming her queen bee crown from Ava. . . .

But how had her father managed to pull off these incredible crimes when the rest of the Crims couldn't even steal a banana from the supermarket?

What to do . . . what to do . . .

"Dad?" Imogen said gently. "I know we don't really talk about feelings in our family—"

"'If you don't have anything nice to say, physically injure someone instead,'" said Al, quoting one of Big Nana's favorite sayings.

"Exactly. And you know you can always talk to me."

Al frowned. "We're talking to each other right now."

"About anything you're going through, I mean," Imogen said. "Like . . . do you think you might be having a midlife crisis? You usually avoid committing crimes, and here you are, with a cartload of amazing loot. . . ."

"Oh!" said Al, visibly relaxing. "Yes! That's it! I'm having a HUGE midlife crisis. I've already stolen three sports cars! And a wig, just in case I start to lose my hair. I'm probably going to die soon! Isn't that terrible?"

Imogen had never seen anyone look so cheerful when confronted with their own mortality.

"Anyway," Al continued, "I've been looking deep inside myself, which is difficult to do—I had to borrow some equipment from the doctor—to work out what I really, truly want to do with what's left of my life. And the answer I came up with was—"

"Steal parts of major American monuments?"

"No. I want to live my life in accordance with the values of our family. Which mostly involves committing lots of crime. So I went on a little stealing spree—not too hard once you get the knack." He shrugged. "But that was before someone starting sabotaging all of our crimes . . . obviously . . ." He smiled at Imogen nervously. "So . . . will you take this stuff to school?"

There's something really weird about this, Imogen thought. *Maybe I should push this further. Maybe Dad needs help.*

But the lure of the loot was too strong. *She* needed help too, if she was going to step out of Ava Gud's wealthy, glossy-haired shadow. And with Al's stolen goods, she had the tools to do it.

So she smiled, and said, "Yes, I will. Thank you."

CHAPTER SEVEN

THE NEXT MORNING, after Imogen had done her ten laps around the piranha pond and applied antiseptic to her piranha wounds, she packed up her dad's loot in her old Lilyworth trunk and dragged it to school. She couldn't wait to see Ava's expression when she showed her what she had collected for the auction.

But before she could reach her classroom, Delia tapped her on the shoulder.

"Let's get out of here," she whispered, looking up and down the corridor. "The goose has eaten the contraband."

"What does that mean again?" She still hadn't gotten her head around the code the Horrible Children used to discuss their crimes at school.

"It means that the mole is *somewhere in the school*. I just broke into Giles van Loaded's locker—"

"The really rich guy?"

"Yep. But guess what was in there? Nothing but BOOKS."

"Wow. What a shocker," said Imogen, willing Delia to leave so she could show Ava her loot.

But Delia wasn't going anywhere without Imogen. "Come on, then," she said. "We've got to go and tell Big Nana."

"I need to do something first, actually," Imogen said.

"I'll come with you."

"It might be better if you didn't. . . ."

Delia narrowed her eyes and crossed her arms. "What are you up to? There's something in that trunk, isn't there? Show me."

Imogen couldn't be bothered to argue. She opened her trunk and showed Delia the contents.

Delia gasped. "Holy paroley!" she muttered. "Where did you get all this stuff?"

"From my dad," Imogen said, shutting the trunk quickly.

"Come on," said Delia. "Be serious. Did you steal it all yourself?"

"I *am* serious," Imogen said. "He stole it and gave it to

me for the charity auction." She didn't want to dwell on how massively weird that was; her father's midlife crisis wasn't anyone else's business.

"Hold up," Delia said. "*Your* dad? Al Crim? Stole all that stuff?"

"Apparently."

Delia laughed. "That's obviously a lie."

Imogen shrugged. "My dad doesn't lie."

Delia leaned back against the lockers, frowning. "Wait," she said. "That reminds me of something. Does your dad drink?"

"What? *No!*" said Imogen. Surely Delia knew that by now? "He can't handle alcohol—he gets drunk after a couple of sips. Haven't you heard about what happened when he was in college? He drank one beer and jumped out of a window shouting, 'I am a dragon! A lovely green dragon! Aren't my scales shiny'?"

"I thought so," said Delia, eyebrows furrowed. "But get this: There were a couple of nights I went up to your apartment to see if you wanted to hang out, but you were already asleep. And your dad was in the living room, smoking a cigar and drinking a Hefeweizen."

"A what?"

"You know, that German beer that Isabella orders when we go to the pub. He was *not* pleased to see me. He slammed the door in my face."

"He was smoking a cigar and he slammed a door in your face?" said Imogen, still trying to process this. "He *never* smokes! He's obsessive about carcinogens! He doesn't even eat burned toast!"

Delia and Imogen looked at each other.

"And Big Nana thinks there's a mole in the house . . . ," said Delia.

Imogen felt sick. Her real father would never be the mole, but what if the man currently calling himself Al Crim wasn't her real father? It was hard to deny the mounting evidence.

But if he wasn't her father . . . where *was* her father?

Panic gripped at her gut. She had to find out!

"Come on, Delia," she said, grabbing the trunk and running to the door. "I think it's time to talk to Big Nana."

The house was in chaos, as usual. Aunt Bets and Uncle Knuckles were sitting on the living room sofa while Big Nana bandaged their hands. "Another fake tip-off," she said grimly when she saw Imogen and Delia. "Someone told them you can get a lot of ransom money for porcupines."

"But they didn't mention they shoot their quills when they're angry," said Aunt Bets.

"AND I HAVE SUCH DELICATE, SENSITIVE SKIN!" shouted Uncle Knuckles.

Josephine bustled into the room, carrying a plate of ham and cheese sandwiches.

Big Nana took a sandwich, bit into it, and grimaced. "Revolting," she said. "You *bought* the ingredients for this, didn't you?"

Josephine nodded. "It was so *humiliating*," she said, shaking her head. "I tried to steal them, but the cashier stopped me as I tried to leave the shop! Someone must have told her who I was!"

"See what we've been driven to?" said Big Nana, banging her hand on the table and making Uncle Knuckles jump (he was very sensitive to loud noises).

"Listen, Big Nana," said Imogen, "we need to talk to you. Look what Dad stole this week."

She opened the trunk.

When Big Nana saw the loot, her eyes lit up like cheap, dangerous Christmas tree lights.

"Plus, Al has been drinking beer," said Delia. "And smoking cigars. Not candy ones—I checked."

Big Nana nodded slowly. "Your instincts are right on, my miniature pork chops. Something about this smells fishy. And not in a good way, like someone's about to serve us salmon en croûte. It would take a very sophisticated criminal to pull this off. . . ."

Josephine froze. "Are you saying what I think you're saying?"

"If what you think I'm saying is 'your husband isn't who you think he is,' then yes. I think an imposter is in his place."

Imogen felt sick. Hearing Big Nana say it out loud made it seem horribly real.

"No!" cried Josephine, dropping the sandwiches, which were instantly snaffled by Barney.

So she does *love Dad,* Imogen thought, feeling a sudden rush of affection for her mother.

"The imposter is so much better at stealing jewelry than Al!" wailed Josephine. "Do we really have to find the real Al and switch them back?"

Imogen's affection drained away.

"I'll pretend I didn't hear you say that about my son," Big Nana said dangerously. "I'm going to have a word with this so-called 'Al.' Who wants to come?"

They all did.

Heart racing, Imogen followed Big Nana, Delia, and Josephine to Al's office. He was sitting at his desk, with Barney on his lap, watching what appeared to be an illegally downloaded German show about luxury yachts called *Sehr Gut Boot.* Looking at him now, Imogen was more certain than ever that this man wasn't her father. Al hated yachts—they made him seasick—and German accents gave him unpleasant flashbacks to the Bavarian nanny who had forced him to wear lederhosen to kindergarten.

"Al," said Big Nana, "You're coming with us."

Al swiveled in his chair. "Thanks for the invite," he said, "but I'm busy at the moment."

"That wasn't an invitation," said Big Nana. "It was an order." And she grabbed him by the arm and marched him downstairs to the secret room in the basement. Imogen snatched up Al's latest copy of *Accounting Today!* and followed behind, heart thumping and Barney yapping happily at her heels.

"Sit down," Big Nana said to Al, pointing to the velvet-covered chair in the middle of the room.

She pulled a dust sheet from a large lamp and turned it on, shining the light straight into Al's face. He squinted and held up his hand to cover his eyes.

"Bit bright for you, is it, Al, my sweet?" said Big Nana.

"Yes," Al said falteringly.

All of Imogen's instincts told her to reach out and comfort her father, but she had to stop herself, because he almost certainly wasn't her father at all. She hugged herself for comfort instead.

"LIAR!" shouted Big Nana.

"I'm not lying!" said Al. "It really is extremely bright! I don't think that's an energy-saving lightbulb!"

"You *are* lying," said Big Nana, "because you are not Al. And therefore you are most certainly NOT MY SWEET."

"Of course I'm Al!" said Al. "Look at me! Imogen, darling, you know I'm your daddy, don't you?"

Imogen felt her hairs stand on end. "I've never called my father 'daddy,'" she said.

Al's eyes grew cold, in a way her father's never would have. "Well, it's not too late to start," he said.

"If you are my father," said Imogen, handing him the copy of *Accounting Today!*, "show me that article you were talking about. The one that said that crime was good for your blood pressure."

She willed him to succeed. She willed him to be Al Crim, so that she wouldn't have to worry about where her father was and what was happening to him.

Al, looking slightly panicked, took the magazine and started flipping through it. "I'm sure it's in here some-where. . . . Oh, no. I remember now. It was actually in *Calculator World* magazine—"

And that's when, without warning, Big Nana reached down and grabbed Al's nose, which just *broke off in her hand.*

"ARGH!" screamed Al.

"ARGH!" screamed Imogen and Delia and Josephine.

"RARGH!" barked Barney.

"AHA!" screamed Big Nana.

Because it wasn't Al's nose that had broken off—it was his *fake* nose. Which was part of his entire, thick, fake, rubbery face. Big Nana grabbed a piece and pulled the rest of the mask off, to reveal . . .

"GUNTHER KRUK!" screamed Big Nana. "OF THE BAVARIAN KRUK COUSINS! *YOU* ARE THE MOLE!"

"*Bitte*, don't shout," said Gunther, in his real voice, which was extremely deep and German sounding. "My ears are very sensitive to the words of hopeless criminals."

Imogen felt sick with dread and fear and shame. Big Nana had been right all along. The Kruks really *were* after her family—enough so that they'd kidnapped Al and replaced him with this imposter! How could she have been so blind? How could she not have realized that her father had been replaced by a psychopathic master criminal? Because she hadn't *wanted* to believe it. Because she had been more interested in being popular at school than saving her family. And because she hadn't been able to bring herself to fully trust Big Nana. Well, it was time to start trusting her now.

She felt hot with anger and cold with fear at the same time. "Where's my father?" she managed to say. "What have you done with him?"

"Answer her," said Josephine, her voice shaking with rage. "What have you done with my husband? And do you have any spare rubies lying around?"

Gunther just sat there, an irritating smile on his irritating face.

"If you don't tell us where Al is RIGHT THIS SECOND, we'll set Barney on you," warned Delia.

Barney, at the mention of his name, scrabbled over to Gunther and started licking his (real) face.

"Pathetic," muttered Delia.

"Fine," Big Nana said quietly. "You asked for it, Gunther. KNUCKLES!" she called.

An incredibly loud crashing sound came from above them, which was the sound of Uncle Knuckles walking downstairs as quietly as possible. He appeared in the doorway, blocking out all the light from the passageway.

"YES, MOTHER?" he said.

"This is Gunther Kruk," she said.

"PLEASURE TO MEET YOU, SIR," said Knuckles.

"It is *not* a pleasure," said Big Nana. "This man has been impersonating your brother for the past few weeks. He is the mole we've been looking for. Please take him to the interrogation room."

"RIGHT AWAY," said Uncle Knuckles, and he picked up Gunther between his thumb and forefinger, like a miniature sausage, and carried him out of the room.

"Do whatever it takes to make him talk," Big Nana called after him.

"We have an interrogation room?" said Imogen.

"I want you to forget you ever heard this conversation," said Big Nana, turning toward the door. "What you don't know can't hurt you. Apart from the nuclear codes. Now, why don't we ladies go to the kitchen for a nice cup of tea while the gentlemen are . . . getting acquainted?"

Imogen loved tea—no matter what was going on, the fragrant, warming taste of it usually made her feel as though everything was going to be okay. But today it seemed to curdle in her mouth. Her mother was having no such trouble. She slurped it down, pinky finger raised, as she moaned on and on about all the things Fake Al had promised to steal for her. "A small castle with a real moat, a badger-fur coat, dishwashing liquid made from greyhounds—apparently they have great cleansing properties . . ."

Imogen wasn't really listening. *My father's missing,* she thought. *I've failed him. I've failed my whole family.* She felt disgusted with herself. She prided herself on being the cleverest of the Crims—and yet they had all been right about the Kruks, and she had been very, very wrong. She should never have doubted Big Nana. She should never have allowed herself to be distracted by school.

But then her thoughts were interrupted by an incredibly loud ripping noise from upstairs—followed by a scream.

"Auuuuuuuugh!"

MEANWHILE

THE LOO

CHAPTER EIGHT

IMOGEN CHARGED UPSTAIRS to find—
there *was* no upstairs.

"Wait!" Imogen called to Big Nana and Delia, who
were running up the stairs behind her. She clung to the
banister, which was now . . . *outside*. She stared down at
the rest of Blandington, which was horribly visible considering she should have been indoors.

The incredibly loud ripping noise had been the sound
of a Boeing 747 being torn from the top of a house. By
what looked like a military-grade helicopter. Which was
now whirring away from the house, dragging the plane
behind it, like a cat with an extremely heavy, dead mouse.

A figure was dangling from the tail fin, making rude gestures at them with his free hand—Gunther Kruk.

And then she heard a polite cough coming from somewhere around her ankles. "TERRIBLY SORRY!" shouted Uncle Knuckles. "BUT DO YOU MIND GIVING ME A HAND UP? I THINK I'LL FALL TO A PAINFUL DEATH OTHERWISE, WHICH WOULD BE A SHAME, BECAUSE IT'S A LOVELY, SUNNY DAY, CONSIDERING IT'S SEPTEMBER."

She looked down and saw Uncle Knuckles hanging from the jagged edge of the house by his extremely large fingertips.

Suddenly, Imogen realized she had a fear of heights, which was terrible timing, all things considered. She couldn't seem to let go of the banister. Luckily, Big Nana and Delia reached down and hauled Uncle Knuckles back onto the staircase.

"What happened, Knuckles, you overpriced tin of spam?!" said Big Nana, when he was safely back "inside" the house.

"Could we maybe have this conversation downstairs?" said Imogen, who could no longer feel her legs.

They descended shakily back to the safety of the living room and huddled together on the sofa with cups of tea.

"IT ALL HAPPENED SO QUICKLY," said Uncle Knuckles. "WE JUST TOOK A LITTLE BREAK

FROM THE INTERROGATION, SO THAT GUN-
THER COULD USE THE LOO—"

"Uncle Knuckles!" groaned Delia.

"WHAT?" said Uncle Knuckles. "I'M NOT A
MONSTER, NO MATTER WHAT THE LOCAL
CHILDREN THINK WHEN THEY SEE ME! ANY-
WAY, WE TOOK A BREAK, AND THAT'S WHEN I
HEARD THAT LOUD STRETCHING NOISE, AND
I SCREAMED."

"And didn't you notice that two entire wings were
being ripped off the house?" said Delia.

"THERE WASN'T MUCH I COULD DO ABOUT
IT BY THAT POINT!"

"To lose one wing might be regarded as a misfortune,"
said Big Nana, sipping her tea. "To lose both looks like
carelessness. Anyway, what's done is done." She turned to
Imogen, a grim smile on her face. "Well, my dear. It's
official now. You can't deny it any longer. We are at war
with the Kruks."

Imogen couldn't bring herself to meet Big Nana's eye.
"I'm sorry I didn't believe you," she said. "I feel terrible."

"You're not terrible," said Big Nana, reaching over to
pat her hand. "You're just an idiot. A very intelligent one."

Not that intelligent, Imogen thought. Not intelligent
enough to realize that a cigar-smoking, boat-loving
imposter had taken the place of her father. How could she

not have noticed? Probably because she hadn't wanted to notice.

Well, now she knew the truth. And she was going to find her dad. Somehow. Even if that meant being second best to Ava Gud.

"Imogen! Guess what!" Penelope and Hannah cornered Imogen outside the dining hall the next day, just before the charity committee meeting was about to start.

"I'm not in the mood for guessing," Imogen said.

"This is good, though." Penelope smiled. She didn't smile very often, because it made her look like a vampire bat, so when she did, it was a bit unnerving.

Hannah nodded. "Get this. We're catching up to Ava in the charity drive," she said. "My dad owns a Bentley dealership—I forgot."

Imogen stared at her. "You forgot your father is a luxury car salesman?"

"Yeah, well," said Hannah, shrugging, "he's always changing jobs. He was an insurance salesman for a while, and then he worked at Blandington Zoo, but they fired him for trying to sell life insurance to orangutans. The point is, he's donating a Bentley. Much more useful than a stupid pair of glasses a celebrity doesn't even want anymore. And I told Ava that *you* got the donation, obviously. . . ." She smiled at Imogen expectantly.

"That's great," Imogen said, and she did feel touched by the way Penelope and Hannah were still working to help her—even if she wasn't giving them much in return. But she was too worried about her father to really care, and acting had never been her strong point. It was one of the things Big Nana had asked her to work on for her next crime homework assignment.

Hannah looked at her, concerned. "What's wrong? Do you want me to try to convince him to donate two?"

"Or three?" Penelope suggested, and Hannah glared at her. "Three is a very pleasing number, visually."

Imogen shook her head. "I don't care about this whole queen bee thing anymore," she said. "You managed to get the Bentley, you should take credit for it. And Penelope, I'm sorry I took your cousin's lunch money. You guys keep being really nice to me, and I keep being a brat." She reached into her pocket and pulled out some bills. "Here," she said. "Tell Emily I'm sorry. I mean, if she hasn't disappeared."

Penelope looked down at the money. "But this is way more than you took from her."

"It's compensation for how horrible I was to her." Imogen shook her head again. "I'm sorry I've been so awful."

Penelope looked confused now. Apologizing wasn't something Imogen usually did. "Are you okay?" she asked.

But Imogen had already turned away and pushed open

the door to the dining hall.

Ava was already there, laughing and joking with the rest of the committee. "Imogen!" she said, looking up. "Well done on the Bentley! Such a lovely little car!"

"Hannah donated it, actually," Imogen said, hovering in the doorway.

"Oh!" said Ava. "Well—well done, Hannah! Come and sit down, guys, the meeting has started already."

"I'm not here for the meeting," Imogen said. "I'm not going to be able to help with the charity drive anymore. I quit."

Everyone stared at her in silence for a moment. And then Ava said, "Ha! That's a good one!" and started laughing.

"I'm not kidding," Imogen said. "I'm too busy. I need to focus on my schoolwork." Which was a lie. She was going to focus on finding her father and beating the Kruks, preferably with something large and deadly, like an ax.

"But you're the most important person in the committee!" said Ava. "Apart from me." A look of panic flashed across Ava's face. Why was Ava upset about this? Surely it was what she wanted?

"I'm sorry," said Imogen. She turned to leave, waving at her friends, who looked as though they couldn't believe what was happening.

"Just stay for this one meeting," Ava said. "We need to

catalog all the auction donations before we go home. And everyone knows you've got the neatest handwriting."

"I'm sure you'll manage without me." Imogen turned away.

"Wait! What would you call this?" Ava ran to Imogen, spun her around, and held up an incredibly valuable-looking piece of diamond jewelry. "Should I put 'diamond *choker*'? Or 'diamond *necklace*'?"

"'Choker,'" Imogen said, squinting. "Looks like around eight carats of diamonds. Probably Tiffany, circa 1988. But really, I have to go." She turned and walked out the dining hall without looking back.

Ava chased down the corridor after her, her feet *tap-tap-tap*ping across the parquet flooring until she caught up. "Don't go!" she said. "We have something that looks like a ruby bracelet. Can you tell us if it's real?"

"Scratch it with a knife," Imogen said, still walking. "If the knife makes a mark, it's a fake."

"What about this?" Ava held up an old violin. "It might be a Stradivarius."

Imogen turned and looked at it. "It's not," she said. "Wood's too dark. I'm really leaving now."

But Ava had her phone out. "Wait! Google Maps says your road has been blocked off. Apparently a truck overturned on Unusual Crescent. They're not even letting pedestrians in! So you might as well stay."

"I bet one of my cousins was driving that truck," said Imogen with a fond smile. "The two-year-old, probably. She's still working on her braking. They'll need my help." She walked out into the gray courtyard.

She noticed her shoelaces were undone and bent down to fasten them when something heavy and gold came flying through the air behind her, narrowly missing her head, and landed with a *thunk* on the floor. Imogen bent down to pick it up. It was a solid-gold paperweight.

She turned, confused, to see where it had come from. Ava was standing right behind her, eyes wide with apparent innocence.

"Oops!" Ava said, holding her hands up. "So sorry! Must have just slipped out of my hand!"

But there was something cold in her eyes that Imogen hadn't seen before.

Imogen turned and began walking faster now. She looked over her shoulder to see Ava disappearing into the school.

Imogen walked through Blandington, past the laundromat, the doughnut shop, and the police station, where a big blurry photo of a figure in a robber's mask was displayed beneath the words "Wanted: The Banana Bandit. Reward: Some Bananas." She turned on to Unusual Crescent, where she'd lived all her life (apart from those two blissful years at Lilyworth). The street hadn't always had that name—it had been called Nothing to See Here Crescent until Crim House was built.

Why did she feel so uneasy?

And then she realized: *I've never told Ava where I live.*

So how did Ava know?

Imogen felt sick with dread as she walked along Unusual Crescent to Crim House. There was no overturned truck. Nothing was blocking the road, unless you counted Isabella, who was practicing being a highwayman, crawling out in front of cars and lisping "Your money or your life!"

Imogen had thought that Ava was just an annoyingly perfect, competitive, disgustingly capable rival for queen bee.

But Ava had lied to get Imogen to stay at school. And when Imogen had left, Ava had tried to kill her. With a weapon made of solid gold.

A very Kruk sort of weapon, in other words.

Could she be . . . ? It seemed impossible.

But Gunther Kruk was living in my house. Stranger things have happened. . . .

Imogen whisked her little cousin out of the street and walked toward the house, but before she could open the front door, Big Nana came running out, looking shocked and horrified and scared all at the same time.

"Get inside now, both of you," she said. "Nick and Nate have gone missing. And so has Delia."

Delia and Nick and Nate were at the bowling alley. They'd stolen some coins from a little old lady using the pinball machine—their first successful crime since the Crime Directive had been put in place—and were playing Guitar Zero, *which is like* Guitar Hero, *but the idea is not to get any of the notes right. Delia had just beaten the twins for the second time when a strange boy walked up to them. He had piercing blue eyes and black curly hair, and they knew he was strange right away because his jacket had "strange" written on the pocket. Plus, he kept winking at them for no apparent reason.*

"Hey," he said. He had an accent of some kind . . . French, maybe? Or Austrian? "Do you want to play Skee-Ball? Best of five?"

"What do we get if we win?" asked Nate.

"My soccer shirt," said the strange boy, opening his jacket to reveal the latest home jersey for Blandington Football Club, which looked exactly the same as every other home jersey Blandington FC had ever produced—gray, with the word "Blandin" written on the front because the designer had got so bored making it that he'd fallen asleep halfway through. "And if I win, I get your hat," he said, pointing to Nick's "Can I Get Fries with That?" cap.

Nick held on to his hat protectively. He loved it, and there was only one of them in the whole world—Sam had moved on to making caps with the slogan "A Cup of Tea Would Be Lovely."

"What's the matter?" asked the strange boy. "Scared you're going to lose?"

"No," said Nick. "I'm just feeling sorry for you already because of how badly you're going to get beaten."

And they shook on it.

So they played Skee-Ball. There's no need to describe the game to you—you really had to be there. All you need to know is that the strange boy won, and Nick was very upset.

"Hand over the hat," said the strange boy.

Nick shook his head. "Can't you take something else? I'll give you anything you want."

"Yeah," said Delia. "Don't take the hat, please. It's the only way I can tell these guys apart."

"I've got a couple of rabbits at home that know how to sing 'It's a Long Way to Tipperary,'" said Nick. "They were Irish, originally. Want them instead?"

"No. I want the hat," said the boy, hands on his hips. "Tell you what—come back to my house, and we can play a different game, double or nothing. SimPin3000. Have you heard of it?"

Nick and Nate looked at each other. They prided themselves on being up on the latest games—they planned to be cybercriminals when they were older, kidnapping characters from computer games and holding them ransom in virtual dungeons. But they'd never heard of SimPin3000.

"It's really cool," said the boy. "It's like pinball, but you go *inside it—like you are the pinball. I've got two controllers, if you want to come over."*

Nick and Nate looked at each other again and agreed silently, the way twins do.

"Sounds good," said Nick.

"Sehr gut!" said the boy. "I only live a couple of blocks from here." He started leading them through the arcade to the exit.

"Funny that we haven't seen you around before," said Delia. "Do you go to Blandington Secondary School?" There was something strangely appealing about the boy. She wondered how old he was, and whether he was single, and whether he'd consider dating someone with a sizable criminal record.

"I'm homeschooled—" And then he paused. "To tell you the truth, I've just gotten out of jail. Juvie, I mean."

"Ooh!" said Delia, eyes wide. "What did you do?"

"I killed my kindergarten teacher with one of those little wooden blocks."

"OOH!" said Delia, touching his arm. "You must be, like, really strong. . . ."

"I guess." The boy shrugged. "They reinforced the bars on my cell because I kept bending them with my amazing muscles."

The boy had led them to the fire exit. "I always go out the back door. That way you don't have to give back your bowling shoes." He winked at them again and pushed the door open.

The door opened onto an alley. It was getting dark now, and there was no one else around.

"My house is just around the corner," said the boy, motioning for the others to follow him.

"So," said Delia. "Did you join any prison gangs?"

But she never got to hear the answer. Because that was when she heard the footsteps approaching.

Before she could scream, a bag was shoved over her head, and everything went black.

CHAPTER NINE

IMOGEN DIDN'T FEEL like doing her crime homework that weekend—she was too aware of how quiet the house was without Delia—but she forced herself through it. It wasn't an essay this time; it was a practical test in welding. "You never know when you'll need to forge something out of metal," Big Nana had told her, "like a gun or some money or a statue of Lenin." At least the heat and the smell of molten metal and the flash of the sparks took Imogen's mind off her missing cousins for a few hours.

But once the homework was done, it all came crashing back. Apparently, Nick, Nate, and Delia had gone to the bowling alley and never come home. Imogen and Big Nana had searched all over town for them, with no luck. Imogen was sure Ava had lied to her. She had definitely tried to kill her with that golden paperweight. Or at least knock her out. She had been so desperate for Imogen to stay for the charity committee meeting because she wanted to keep Imogen occupied while her cousins were kidnapped.

Which meant she was either a Kruk, or she was working for them.

As soon as she and Big Nana had realized Delia and the twins had gone missing, Imogen had told her grandmother about Ava.

"No wonder she's been irritating you so much," Big Nana had said thoughtfully. "I thought you were just getting distracted at school, but really, your criminal instincts were honing in on another felon."

Imogen had considered that. She had to admit she liked the theory. It made her feel less guilty for getting so tied up in the charity drive. "It's possible," she'd said. "But what do we do now?"

Big Nana had frowned. "I'm afraid we don't have enough evidence to go after her yet, my rising loaf of pumpernickel. But keep an eye on her," she had said. "Actually, keep several eyes on her."

"I only have two eyes," Imogen had pointed out.

"Then that will have to do."

Imogen walked to school alone on Monday, crunching through the fall leaves as she marched up to the gates, feeling angrier and angrier with every step. The more she thought about it, the more "keeping an eye on" Ava didn't seem like enough. She was going to confront her. Which, considering Ava was probably a Kruk, would be a very dangerous thing to do indeed. So she was going to do it in public.

Ava was in the courtyard, laughing and joking with an eclectic group of people: the school caretaker, the captain of the soccer team, and a girl everyone called "Dribble Face" because she always had dribble on her face. Ava brought people together. Even people who should never be brought together.

Imogen marched up to Ava. "I need a word. Now," she said.

"Sure, Imogen!" said Ava, waving good-bye to her confused group of friends. "What's wrong?"

Imogen crossed her arms. "You can stop the 'I'm really nice' act," she whispered. "Where are my cousins?"

Ava's brow furrowed photogenically. "What do you mean? Aren't they in class? Have you lost one of them? There are a lot of them to keep track of."

"Three of them disappeared, and you know it. What did you do to them? Where are they?"

Ava gasped prettily. "This is terrible!" she said. "Have you called the police?"

"Who took them? Was it Gunther?"

Ava frowned beautifully. "Who's Gunther?" asked Ava. "I have no idea what you're talking about. I was at the charity committee meeting till seven. You can ask your friends."

Imogen decided to try a different tack. "How do you know where I live? I never told you."

Ava's eyes widened gorgeously. "Yes you did! You sent me a note about that loot your dad wanted to donate to the charity drive, to ask if I could come and pick it up. Remember?" She reached into her schoolbag and pulled out a letter—written on Imogen's monogrammed stationery, in Imogen's handwriting, with Imogen's favorite words in it: "serendipitous," "alack," and "Yours sincerely."

Imogen stared at the letter, as if it might make more sense the more she looked at it. She had no recollection of sending it whatsoever, and she usually remembered everything, even Wi-Fi passwords. *Did I write this note to Ava and then forget about it?* she thought. *Am I going mad? It has been pretty stressful lately, what with readjusting to life at home, and trying to rule Blandington Secondary School, and all that crime homework, and no one in the family committing any crimes, and the Kruks kidnapping my father. . . .* She suddenly felt quite overwhelmed. *What are the chances that Ava is a Kruk, really?*

It seemed horribly unlikely. She wanted to go home and get into bed and stay there until everything went back to normal.

"Are you okay?" Ava asked, touching Imogen's arm. "Is there anything I can do? I know a lovely therapist. I've never needed therapy, obviously, but she really helped my friend. Sometimes it's good to talk to someone—"

"No!" said Imogen, pulling her arm away. She had now completely forfeited any remaining queen bee standing she may have had. *Not that that's important,* she reminded herself. *What matters is finding out if Ava is a Kruk—and what she's done with my family.*

By the time Imogen got home, she felt dazed and frantic and as though she might start crying at any moment. She picked up Isabella, who was on the front path gnawing at some wires marked "Electricity Supply, Danger of Death," and opened the door. She wished that Nick and Nate would come bounding downstairs with Barney, or that Delia would make fun of her for staying for a full day of school. But the house was silent, apart from a low whirring noise that seemed to be coming from the kitchen.

Big Nana was chopping up a rutabaga, a Jerusalem artichoke, and a turnip—the three most miserable vegetables known to humankind—all of which looked bashed and battered and as though they needed someone to put them out of their misery. Big Nana, unfortunately, seemed to be causing them even more misery.

"There you are!" Big Nana shouted over the vacuum cleaner, which, for some reason, was running full blast in the corner of the room. "Ratatouille will be ready in twenty minutes."

"Shall I turn this off?" Imogen said.

"No!" said Big Nana, slapping Imogen's hand away from the vacuum cleaner. "The house might be bugged. We can't be too careful." She dropped the vegetables into a pot of tomato sauce.

"Did you *steal* those?" Imogen asked.

Big Nana sighed, closing her eyes. "No," she said. "I found them on the ground after the farmers market had gone. This is what this family has come to! We can't steal a thing, there's a huge hole in our house, and three of your cousins have disappeared like child actors who aren't Miley Cyrus after the age of twenty." She started stabbing at the ratatouille with a wooden spoon, flicking tomato sauce around the kitchen. The splashes of tomato on the white kitchen tiles looked like fresh blood—and that gave Imogen an idea.

"Look," she said. "Maybe it's time for action. Maybe we should strike against the Kruks now, before they do anything else. We can't just sit back and wait for Dad and Delia and the twins to come back home. We have to find them."

Big Nana put down her wooden spoon. "Okay, then," she said. "Let's see how much you've learned. What do you suggest we do?"

Imogen hadn't thought that far ahead. "I don't know," she said.

"Three words no Crim should ever utter," said Big Nana.

"We could go to Krukingham Palace," Imogen said, "and . . . set an alligator loose in there, or something?"

"Ha!" laughed Big Nana, though not in a fun way; more like in a you've-just-said-something-incredibly-stupid way. "'You come at the king, you best not miss.'"

That didn't sound like one of Big Nana's usual sayings. "Is that Shakespeare?" Imogen asked.

"No!" said Big Nana. "I thought you were top of the class in English."

"I don't think I am anymore," said Imogen, trying and failing to not care.

"That was from *The Wire*," said Big Nana. "I binge-watched a lot of TV when I was pretending to be dead. There isn't much else you can do when all your friends and family think they've been to your funeral. The point is, we shouldn't waste time thinking of petty ways to annoy the Kruks. When we strike, we need to deal a deathblow."

Big Nana was right, as usual. "All right, then," Imogen said. "In the meantime, I have some money left over from my birthday, if you want me to go to the store. I could buy some eggplant or zucchini or some kind of vegetable that's actually supposed to go in ratatouille."

"NEVER!" screamed Big Nana, brandishing her spoon like a weapon. "Even these pathetic, hard-to-digest, slightly brown vegetables will taste better than *bought* food." And to Imogen's horror, Big Nana started crying— really crying. Her tears dripped into the ratatouille pot. "Just as well!" she wailed. "We've run out of salt!"

Imogen had never been good at dealing with other people's emotions, so she turned off the vacuum cleaner and snuck out of the kitchen.

Without the vacuum running, the house was very quiet. Imogen walked through to the living room, where she found Isabella sitting alone on the couch, sucking on her pacifier and staring at her as if to say, "I've got my tiny, two-year-old eyes on you." Imogen felt a little unnerved. Where were the other Horrible Children? When you couldn't hear them, it usually meant they were making trouble—stealing a cat, or experimenting with glue, or inventing new uses for anthrax. But this time she had a feeling that they might be *in* trouble.

She searched the house, the sound of her footsteps

echoing in the empty rooms.

"Sam?" she called. "Henry? Freddie?"

"In the bathroom!" It was Freddie. "Give me a second?"

A second later (Freddie was a very accurate timekeeper these days), Freddie appeared on the landing in an inside-out dressing gown (old habits die hard). "I was just having the loveliest bath," he said. "I put a bit of lavender oil in the water, had a meditation podcast on, and I managed to relax! I haven't relaxed in thirteen years."

"Right," said Imogen. "Because that's when Delia was born."

"You're right! *That's* what was different!" said Freddie. "The cousins didn't interrupt me once! They didn't hammer on the door, or make fun of my rubber ducks, or throw a toaster in the bathwater—"

"And you don't think that's weird?" said Imogen.

Freddie's face fell. "A very good point. The house is eerily quiet. It's almost as if—"

"Exactly," said Imogen. "I'll look upstairs. You look downstairs."

Imogen searched everywhere for her cousins. She found her mother in the upstairs apartment, looking at a Harry Winston catalog and weeping at what might have been, and Uncle Clyde in his room, drawing up a plan to kidnap a princess from a European country that didn't exist, not even in the Eurovision Song Contest. But she couldn't find Henry or Sam anywhere.

"Freddie!" she shouted. "Have you found the boys?"

"Nope," said Freddie, appearing at the bottom of the stairs. "Unless you mean the Backstreet Boys?"

"Why? Are *they* down there somewhere?"

"No."

Imogen took a deep breath. *I can't with him today.* "What does this mean, Freddie?"

"It means that if we want to listen to really good nineties pop music, we'll have to go on Spotify."

"No!" shouted Imogen. "It means that the Kruks have struck again. Sam and Henry are missing."

Henry and Sam went to the skate park after school, as they often did. Sam liked skateboarding almost as much as he liked prank-calling Delia, pretending to be the ghost of a ferret she'd run over while joyriding a stolen car. Henry liked things that were made of wood, like skateboards and ramps, because they were easy to burn holes into.

Sam was showing off his kick flip, and Henry was kicking a small child whose name happened to be Philip, when a strange boy walked up to them.

He had piercing blue eyes—he looked at a BMX wheel,

and the tire exploded—and curly black hair. They knew he was strange right away because his skateboard had "strange" written across the top in big letters.

"Nice board," said Sam.

"Danke," said the boy, blinking his extremely blue eyes. "Why do you have such a squeaky voice?"

"Why are you speaking German?" asked Sam, who was still pretty sensitive about the squeaky voice situation.

"Ich bin nicht!" said the boy. "Which means 'I'm not.' In skater slang."

"Let's see what you can do, then," said Sam, sitting down on the ramp.

"Okay," said the boy. "That means 'okay' in skater slang. I should warn you, though. Some of the tricks I'm going to do are a little unusual. They might blow your Gehirn. Which means 'brain' in skater slang."

"Skater slang really does sound a lot like German," said Henry.

"All beautiful things do," said the boy. He kicked off and skated down the ramp—and then fell off his board and slammed face-first into the ground. "I meant to do that," said the boy. "That move is called 'a Nasenschnur.' All the Brooklyn skaters are doing it these days."

"Right," said Sam, who was beginning to think that the boy was even stranger than his skateboard suggested. "Can you do any flips?"

"Watch this!" said the boy. He kicked his board into the air, tripped over it, and then did a sort of somersault and landed on his back.

He didn't move for a few moments. He twitched a bit. "Oof!" he said eventually, wheezing. "That was called a full-body flip. It's quite an experimental move."

"Looked painful," said Henry.

"No pain, no skateboarding trophies, no million-pound sponsorship deals," said the boy.

"Want me to show you some of my tricks?" said Sam.

"Ja," said the boy. "But first I need to go to the toilet, which means 'bathroom' in skater slang. Do you know where the nearest one is?"

There was a bathroom just behind them, but the boy clearly hadn't seen it. Which was lucky, because Sam had a plan. . . .

"The nearest one is actually in the next town," said Sam. "It's a real pain. Literally, if you're desperate."

"You can get the bus from that stop there," said Henry, pointing to the bus stop just outside the park. "The 19."

"Thank you for your Freundschaftsbeziehung," said the boy. "Which means 'demonstrations of friendship' in skater slang."

"Skaters are weird," said Henry, eyeing the boy's skateboard. It looked so flammable . . . so easy to destroy . . . "Want me to look after your board for you?" he grunted.

"Yes, please!" said the boy, handing it over.

Sam and Henry grinned at each other. They'd gone days

without committing a successful crime. This almost seemed too easy.

Which, of course, it was.

As soon as the boy was out of sight, the boys high-fived each other, picked up the skateboard, and ran out of the park.

Henry beamed at Sam. "Big Nana is going to—" he said.

But we'll never know what Big Nana was going to do.

Because at that moment, two extremely strong hands grabbed Sam and Henry and threw them into a sack.

MEANWHILE

MY LIPS
ARE
SEALED

CHAPTER TEN

IMOGEN STAYED UP late that night, trawling the internet for information about a Kruk girl Ava's age. There was loads of information on all the other Kruks— far too much of it, in fact. She discovered Gunther Kruk's shoe size, and Elsa Kruk's favorite brand of blond hair dye, and some terrible poetry written by fifteen-year-old Dieter "Strange" Kruk, who she could tell was strange, because his name had "strange" in the middle of it. There was even a list of every Kruk's preferred dog breed—they seemed obsessed with dogs, particularly poodles and poodle mixes. But there was absolutely no record of a teenage girl Kruk.

So did that mean Ava wasn't a Kruk after all . . . ?

Imogen felt deeply confused, but she decided not to take any chances. She took out her criminal plans journal and scribbled down ideas for a plan to defeat Ava, until her eyelids began to droop and she found herself falling asleep and then jerking awake again, like a puppet with narcolepsy.

But when she finally went to bed, she couldn't get to sleep. She was used to a lot of background noise—Delia's snoring, Nick's night terrors, and Nate's all-the-time terrors (caused by Nick trying to kill him during his night terrors)—and tonight there was nothing, apart from the occasional howl from Barney, who missed his masters. *I know how he feels,* she thought as she stared at the ceiling, the headlights of a car occasionally flashing past the window. As she lay there, she became more and more certain that Ava Gud was somehow involved in her father's and cousins' disappearances. She had to be. Imogen *hadn't* given her that letter—she was sure of it. No one her age wrote letters. Which meant Ava had forged that, too—and it was a forgery of Kruk-level sophistication. Plus, Ava was far too rich and glamorous to be in Blandington without a good reason—or a very bad reason, like wanting to destroy the Crims.

How was Imogen going to face her tomorrow at school? How was she going to bear it as everyone else fussed around Ava, laughing at her jokes, telling her how brilliant she was?

How was Imogen going to get her family back?

The next day, Imogen walked into class to find Willa and Penelope sitting on either side of Ava, like lip gloss—wearing henchmen. Penelope gave Imogen a bit of a puppy-dog look, but Imogen quickly looked away. It was official—Ava was queen bee. With a sigh, Imogen reached up and pulled her ponytail out. Ava nodded at her with a superior, satisfied look. Imogen put the hair tie in her pocket, though—because she was determined that Ava's reign would be the shortest reign in history.

Still, for now, Imogen realized, Ava was winning at life. She had raised thousands of pounds on the charity drive. She was getting top marks in every class, which wasn't surprising since Imogen had stopped doing her school homework. And she'd taken Imogen's friends. Only one person remained unconvinced of Ava's greatness, and that was Imogen.

She's destroying my life, Imogen thought. *And now she's destroying my family.*

But one question kept niggling at the back of Imogen's mind: Why hadn't Ava targeted *her* yet? The whole throwing of the gold paperweight had seemed like a spur-of-the-moment thing—more to keep her out of the way than do any deadly harm. She could have poisoned her lunch, or kidnapped her after the charity meeting, or stabbed her to death with a compass. . . . *She probably wants to take everything from me first—my friends, my queen bee status, my family, my self-respect—before finally putting me out of my misery.* Then an even worse thought occurred to her. *Or maybe she doesn't care about me— Her* real *target is Big Nana.*

Hannah slid into the seat next to Imogen's—the seat that used to be Penelope's. "Penelope didn't want to join them," she whispered. "But then Ava invited them to stay in her parents' holiday home in Beverly Hills. Now they're pretty excited about it."

"They're easily pleased," muttered Imogen.

"I know," said Hannah. "Who wants to go to Beverly Hills, anyway? Just a load of movie stars and palm trees and swimming pools. And the weather is great *every day.* Boring."

She looked sideways at Imogen and grinned. Imogen smiled back gratefully. Hannah was still her friend.

"They don't really like her," Hannah said. "She's annoyingly perfect, all the time. They're just too scared of her not to do what she tells them. The other day Ava told Penelope to start laughing in the key of C, and Penelope's been walking around with a tuning fork ever since. And Ava said that if Willa didn't learn to look people in the eye, she'd pay the Rock to elbow her in the face."

Imogen tsked. "The Rock would never do that," she said. "Have you seen his Instagram feed? He seems like a really nice guy."

"*You* know that and *I* know that," Hannah said confidentially, "but Willa doesn't."

Indeed, when Imogen looked over at Willa, she saw that Willa was staring at everyone, looking terrified, barely daring to blink. Penelope and Willa were so weak—as weak as two extremely milky cups of coffee that barely tasted of coffee at all and were just slightly brown and warm and revolting. Again, Imogen suddenly missed Delia with a pang: She was a double espresso all day long.

But Imogen shook off her sentimental musings. Penelope, Willa, Delia . . . They'd all fallen victim to Ava in some way—she was sure of it.

And she was determined to get to the bottom of Ava's evil plan.

Hannah dashed off to netball practice at the end of class, so Imogen was alone, packing up her books, when Ava sauntered over to her. She sat on the edge of Imogen's desk, swinging her well-moisturized legs back and forth. "I've brought you a present," she said, holding out a bag of what looked like dried weeds. "It's herbal tea," she explained, noticing Imogen's blank look. "I find it really calms me down."

Imogen took the bag and forced herself to say, "Great. Thank you."

"How are you doing, anyway?" asked Ava. "Are you feeling . . . stable?"

"Never been better," said Imogen. She had to unsettle Ava somehow, to find out if she really was a Kruk. Drop a subtle accusation into the conversation, maybe. Luckily "subtle accusations" featured heavily in Big Nana's crime homework schedule.

"I've been worried about you," said Ava.

"Don't worry about me!" said Imogen. "Just been feeling a little bit . . . Kruk."

"A bit what?"

"A bit Kruk—it means 'under the weather.' It's a word my gran uses all the time. She's originally from the north, where they say things like 'Eeh, by heck' and eat a lot of pork rinds."

Ava patted Imogen's hand. "Maybe you should go home early if you're not well," she said.

She hadn't taken the bait. Worth another try . . .

"I just need a nice bath, probably," said Imogen. "And for someone to Kruk me dinner."

Ava smiled at her patronizingly again and handed her a business card. "I got that therapist's number from my friend for you, just in case. There's no shame in getting help, you know. Even Prince William says so." And with that she walked back to her desk, where Penelope and Willa were waiting for her.

Imogen stared after Ava. *I have to find out the truth,* she thought. *I have to prove you're a Kruk—and you're involved in this somehow.*

And then I have to get my family back.

After school, Imogen dropped by the cafeteria to steal some leftover chicken nuggets and corn—things were getting pretty desperate at Crim House, food-wise. Ava was there, chairing yet another charity committee meeting, standing in front of the fluorescent lights so that her hair lit up from behind like an incredibly annoying saint.

Imogen snuck into the kitchen without anyone noticing and filled her schoolbag with food. Then she decided to wait. This was her opportunity to follow Ava home—to find out who she was, once and for all.

Ava was the last to leave the charity meeting. Imogen followed her out of the building, hiding behind garbage cans along the way as Big Nana had always told her to: "No one looks behind a garbage can unless they are a rat, and rats never tell."

Ava turned down back alleys and ran up side streets, doubling back on herself and taking the longest possible route home. If she didn't know she was being followed, then she had a terrible sense of direction. She turned onto a main road—and then suddenly, Ava was gone. Imogen was impressed despite herself. Ava seemed to know all the criminal maneuvers, which just made it more likely that she was a Kruk. *It's a shame we're archenemies,* Imogen mused. *She'd really be able to help me with my crime homework.*

Imogen searched the street where Ava had disappeared, and ran round the block, but there was no trace of her. Imogen trudged home, feeling even more sorry for herself than usual. *I'll go and find Freddie,* she thought as she opened the front door. *He usually makes me feel better about things . . . except for when he's making me feel worse about them.* Either way, he was someone to talk to, in the absence of Delia. And her father. And most of her other cousins.

Freddie wasn't in the kitchen, or in the dungeon, or in the secret interrogation room. He wasn't in his bedroom, either, or in his poker room—but Big Nana was. Imogen found her lifting up the rug under the table, as though she expected to find something underneath.

"What are you looking for?" Imogen asked.

"Freddie," said Big Nana. "I know he's six foot four, but he's always been particularly good at hiding."

"Is *he* missing now?" said Imogen.

Big Nana nodded. "He went to the hardware store to try to steal some more netting for his booby traps and never came home. That was at eleven this morning."

Imogen shivered. "It won't be long until they come for us," she said.

"Let them try," said Big Nana. "I've got sharp teeth and a nasty case of rabies I never bothered getting treated."

But that wasn't much consolation.

Imogen felt so helpless. She hated thinking about what might be happening to her cousins and her poor father. Maybe it was time for desperate measures.

Maybe it was time to go to the police.

Big Nana held another family meeting that night—a strangely quiet one. The adult Crims were capable of making as much of a racket as the Horrible Children, obviously, but they seemed to have been stunned into silence. Well . . . almost silence. There was quite a lot of weeping and wailing, to be honest.

"My children!" wept Uncle Clyde.

"*My* children!" cried Aunt Bets.

"MY children!" wailed Josephine.

"Oh, shut up, Josephine," said Big Nana. "You've only got one child, and she's sitting right next to you."

Josephine looked at Imogen with obvious disappointment.

"Now," said Big Nana, waving her sharing stick in the air. "I've called you here because I have an important announcement: I am calling an end to the Crime

Directive. We can worry about the most wanted list when we've stopped being kidnapped."

"It's not like any of us were committing any crimes, anyway," muttered Uncle Clyde.

"It's humiliating," said Josephine. "I hardly dare show my face at the police station. You know the Masked Banana Bandit is still active?"

"No bananas anywhere," said Aunt Bets, nodding. "Just like during the war."

"You're not old enough to remember the Second World War," Imogen pointed out.

"I'm talking about the 1999 Blandington Fruit War, dummy," said Aunt Bets. "There was a real trend for smoothies that year. You had to be extremely cunning and violent to get your hands on a non-puréed strawberry."

"Back to the kidnappings," said Big Nana. "What did they all have in common?"

"THEY ALL INVOLVED OUR BELOVED FAMILY MEMBERS," said Uncle Knuckles, blowing his nose on a tablecloth. (He had such a big nose that he used them instead of hankies.)

"Apart from that," said Big Nana.

Imogen raised her hand.

"Yes, Imogen?" said Big Nana, passing her the sharing stick.

"It seems most of them disappeared while they were doing things that only other Crims knew they were going to do," said Imogen. "Nick, Nate, and Delia were headed to the arcade. . . . Freddie was headed to the hardware store. . . ."

"Exactly," said Big Nana, taking the sharing stick back and pointing it at each of the Crims in turn. "So how do the Kruks know what we're up to? We thought Gunther Kruk was the mole, but he's gone, and the Kruks are still targeting us. When was the last time one of us pulled off a crime?"

"I CAN'T THINK; IT'S BEEN SO LONG," said Uncle Knuckles.

"And now we're disappearing, a few at a time, like characters in a Scandinavian crime drama! Who, if you haven't noticed, usually end up murdered in very inventive ways! So has anyone got any ideas about what we can do to stop this madness and rescue our family? Anyone. Except you, Clyde."

Uncle Clyde, who had been waving his arm in the air, dropped it. "Not fair," he mumbled.

Imogen put up her hand.

"Yes, Imogen?" said Big Nana, passing her the stick. "You're always the voice of reason. Except when you're the voice of treason, which is even better."

"Okay, then," said Imogen. "This might sound crazy. But shouldn't we go to the . . . police?"

The Crims fell silent. Even Isabella stopped sucking on her pacifier.

"How dare you," muttered Josephine.

"I always knew she couldn't be trusted," said Aunt Bets.

"Look, I know it's not the ideal solution," said Imogen, standing up to get away from Aunt Bets, who was trying to stab her with the sharp end of her brooch, "but we're running out of options. We could go straight to PC Donnelly—he's family, so he's on our side. Usually. He got us off when Delia stole that ice cream truck."

"I think you'll find she *borrowed* it," said Uncle Clyde.

"And he gave me some good advice when I was figuring out The Heist. Like 'breakfast is the most important meal of the day' and 'horizontal stripes aren't flattering.' But also 'If you're wondering who set your family up, look for the person with the motive.' He might be able to help us."

The other Crims jeered and shouted and burst into such loud tears that Imogen stopped speaking and sat back down, putting her hands over her ears.

"SILENCE!" shouted Big Nana. And she turned her small, scary eyes on Imogen. "The only way I will ever enter Blandington Police Station is if my corpse is dragged in there by rats. And you know rats have a terrible sense

156

of direction, so that's never going to happen. We are CRIMS. Crims do not go to the police. The police are our mortal enemies. Except for Donnelly—he is a very nice boy; always remembered to wash behind his ears as a child—but still . . . He's on the other side. He's made his law-abiding bed, and he has to lie in it."

Uncle Knuckles nodded. "I HATE TO DISAGREE WITH YOU, IMOGEN, ESPECIALLY AS YOU HAVE SUCH LOVELY TEETH, BUT BIG NANA IS RIGHT. LIKE A CRYPTIC CROSSWORD PUZZLE, THIS IS SOMETHING WE'RE GOING TO HAVE TO FIG-URE OUT ON OUR OWN."

Aunt Bets grabbed the sharing stick from Uncle Knuckles and held it above her head like a spear. Glaring at Big Nana, she walked slowly toward her like a geriat-ric hunter stalking her prey. "When Big Nana was 'dead,' not one of us disappeared," she said. "Not even when you really, really wanted them to, like when Nick and Nate were going through that chainsaw phase. What's changed? Big Nana has come back. If you ask me, which NO ONE HAS because NO ONE LISTENS TO ME, Big Nana is behind this!" She was leaning over Big Nana now, hold-ing the sharing stick to her throat. "Yes, you!" she yelled. "You planned the whole thing—just like you faked your own death, you treacherous cow!"

Big Nana batted the sharing stick away and pushed

herself to her feet. "How *dare* you," she said, her hands in fists, her voice shaking. "Everyone knows that cows are the most trustworthy of all farm animals!"

"And you are the least trustworthy of all the Crims!" said Aunt Bets, grabbing one of her knitting needles and running back at Big Nana.

"Stop it!" shouted Imogen, managing to knock Aunt Bets out of the way just before she caused Big Nana a serious injury.

"You're in league with Big Nana!" shouted Aunt Bets, turning the knitting needle on Imogen.

"You're the one trying to stab us all the time!" shouted Uncle Clyde, turning on Aunt Bets. "*You're* the mole!"

"MY WIFE ISN'T THE MOLE!" shouted Uncle Knuckles. "CLYDE HASN'T SAID MUCH THIS EVENING. MAYBE *HE'S* THE MOLE! OR MAYBE HE'S JUST FEELING UNDER THE WEATHER. ARE YOU OKAY, CLYDE?"

"I'm fine," said Uncle Clyde, pointing at Josephine. "But she doesn't seem that sorry that Al's gone missing. I reckon it's her!"

"How dare you accuse me?" said Josephine. "I think it's Imogen. She's always been shifty, ever since she was a baby and had that so-called 'colic.'"

Imogen decided to ignore her ridiculous family. "Big

Nana!" she shouted above the din. "Do you really think anyone in this room is . . . *focused* enough to be the second mole?"

Big Nana's gaze lingered briefly on Isabella, who was babbling into a mobile phone.

"Oh, come on," said Imogen. "She's having an imaginary conversation in baby talk."

"Or is she speaking in code?"

Imogen raised her eyebrows. "Seriously?"

"Fine," said Big Nana. "You're right. Probably not."

"So maybe it's the house itself that's the problem," said Imogen. "Maybe it *is* bugged."

"I had the same thought," said Big Nana. "But we can't afford to keep the vacuum cleaner running all the time. Not when we actually *pay* for our electricity these days." She pursed her lips and shook her head, apparently overcome with grief. "There's only one thing for it: We'll have to move out of Crim House until things quiet down. Knuckles and Bets—you're in charge of stealing us a new house. Remember: We want at least six bedrooms, an eat-in kitchen, and period features."

"HOW WONDERFUL!" said Uncle Knuckles, dabbing at his eyes with his tablecloth, which was really quite dirty by this point. "IT'LL BE LIKE A SECOND HONEYMOON!"

Imogen turned to Big Nana and muttered, "Do you really think they're the best choice? Aunt Bets did *just* try to kill you—"

"Of course they are, my pot of local honey," said Big Nana. "Your aunt Bets is a sociopath. She's got a better chance than any of us of fighting off a kidnapper. No one will stick *her* in a sack and live to tell the tale!" She clapped her hands. "Now. All of you. Start packing. And don't forget: No one is to leave the house unaccompanied. No one is to *stay* in the house unaccompanied. If necessary, hire a piano accompanist to accompany you—there's a very good one in town who specializes in ragtime. Do you understand me?"

"Yes, Big Nana," everyone chanted.

Imogen went back up to her bedroom and started to pack her things. It felt like she was always packing and unpacking these days. She felt jumpier than usual. When her door creaked open, she spun around, picking up her desk lamp in case she needed to defend herself. But it was just Barney.

She ruffled his fur. "Did you see what happened to Freddie?" she asked him. But he didn't answer, which wasn't that surprising, considering he was a dog. She missed Delia with a pang. She could really have done with someone to confide in.

💣 💣 💣

Freddie had left for the hardware store at about four o'clock that afternoon. The sun had been setting in the sky, painting the beige houses an unusually attractive shade of peach. He had been feeling positive, like the exciting end of a battery. Sure, his cousins kept going missing. But at least something was finally happening to the Crims. Maybe a little bit of kidnapping was what his hopeless cousins needed; maybe they'd take the threat from the Kruks more seriously after this. Or maybe they'd die, painfully and slowly, at the hands of a small German child with unnaturally sharp nails. He shuddered. All he needed to do was set up one more booby trap—at the top of the house, where the 747 used to be. If he could just catch one Kruk, he knew he could get the information he needed. . . .

Freddie turned the corner into Blandington Secondary School Street—and heard a voice calling to him down a side road. He pulled out his penknife and approached carefully.

"Hey," said a figure in a hoodie. "It'th me. Pete."

"Oh!" said Freddie, putting his knife away. Unfortunate Pete was too unfortunate to be dangerous. He had lost every poker game he'd ever played and every tooth he'd ever had—thanks to Freddie, who'd made him punch himself in the face when he lost a game and failed to pay up. Plus, he had a habit of dropping money in the street—which didn't help his financial situation—and a brother called Fortunate Pete, which was just cruelty on his parents' part. Freddie almost felt sorry for him—but not quite. "You still owe me money," he said to him in his most threatening voice.

"I know, I know," said Pete, holding up his hands. "That'th

why I haven't bought any falthe teeth yet. You come firth. And I've come up with a way to pay you back! I thwear!"

"I'm listening," said Freddie.

"It involveth a bit of a con trick," said Pete. "Would you be up for playing along?"

Freddie looked at Pete. He didn't have much confidence in Pete's ability to pull off a con trick, no matter how small. But Pete did owe him money—a lot of it—and at this point, when it looked as though the Crims might be forced to start paying taxes any minute, he was eager to get it back. "All right," said Freddie. "What do you have in mind?"

Pete opened up his bulging rucksack. It was full of digital radios, smartphones, and tablets.

"Where did you get all this stuff?" asked Freddie, impressed.

"I made it!" said Pete. "It'th all fake—there'th thawdust inthide, where the electronicth should be. Thought I'd take it all back to the thtore. I made a fake retheipt— Look. That online Photothop courthe I did while I wath recovering from my . . . injurieeth . . . really paid off." He gave Freddie a reproachful look.

Freddie glanced away. Maybe making Pete punch himself in the face had been a bit cruel. He felt guilty enough that he agreed to Pete's ridiculous plan, even though he very much doubted that any electronics store owner would be foolish enough to be taken in by the fake goods.

But then he remembered: He was in Blandington, where a bandit in a distinctive mask could steal bananas over and over again without anyone stopping them; where the police officers played with My Little Ponies during team meetings; and where the electronics store owner was a little old lady called Doris, who thought that "wirelesses" were newfangled nonsense. (She'd inherited the store from her husband, who, ironically, had died in a terrible electricity-related accident, and she spent every night throwing darts at a portrait of Michael Faraday, the Victorian scientist who had discovered what electromagnetic conduction was. Still, she felt she had to keep the shop open for the sake of her husband. Poor Doris.)

"What do you want?" said Doris when Freddie and Pete walked into the store. She was very little indeed—the top of her head was only just visible above the counter.

"To return theeth faulty electronic goodth," said Pete, laying out his fake radios, tablets, and phones in front of her. "I bought theeth from you in good faith! And not one of them workth!"

"Not surprised," Doris said bitterly. "Full of wires and batteries. The devil's work!"

Freddie looked at Pete, who gave him a thumbs-up. This was a lot easier than he'd expected.

"Give uth our money back, then," said Pete, trying and failing to sound threatening.

"All right, all right," said Doris, counting out bills, apparently at random. She really was Blandington's worst businesswoman, which was saying something considering the town had a funeral parlor called Depressing Send-Offs R Us. "Just promise me you'll use this cash to buy something wholesome, like a pencil. Can't go

wrong with a pencil. How many people do you know died from dropping a pencil in the bath? None, that's how many."

Freddie and Pete practically skipped out of the shop, but they didn't, because they both liked to think of themselves as extremely masculine.

"That was amazing!" said Freddie. He'd forgotten how good it felt to deceive other people and trick them out of their hard-earned money.

And then a strange boy popped up from behind a garbage can on the other side of the road and gave Pete a thumbs-up. Freddie knew he was strange right away, because he had "strange" written across his forehead in marker.

"Who's that?" asked Freddie.

"Oh, one of my new poker palth," said Pete, laughing a high-pitched laugh. "He'th nowhere near ath talented ath you. But then, he'th not ath violent ath you, either."

"Hey," said Freddie. "I never laid a finger on you. I just persuaded you to lay a lot of fingers on yourself."

"I haven't forgotten," said Pete. "That'th why I'm tho keen to pay you back. Let'th go down thith alley tho I can give you the money away from prying eyeth."

He led Freddie down a dark, narrow path—and moments later, Freddie felt an impossibly strong person pick him up and shove him into a sack.

MEANWHILE

YOU SHALL NOT PASS

CHAPTER ELEVEN

IMOGEN WAS EATING her breakfast the next morning when her mother bustled into the kitchen, dressed in her Burberry raincoat.

Imogen paused, a spoonful of cereal halfway to her mouth. "You're not going out, are you?" she asked.

Josephine looked of her. "Of course I am, darling!" she said. "It's been a week since my color was touched up. I simply must go to the salon."

"Mom," said Imogen, "are you crazy? Haven't you noticed that our family has been disappearing? You shouldn't leave the house unless it's an absolute emergency!

And even then, Big Nana told us not to go anywhere alone!"

"But it is an absolute emergency! I spotted a gray hair in the mirror this morning! A *gray hair*! On *my head*! If I don't get my roots done, your father won't recognize me when he comes home!" Josephine pouted. "I suppose I could take Isabella with me."

"Isabella doesn't count. If you *do* get your roots done, you'll probably be missing by the time Dad gets home," Imogen pointed out.

"Stop being such a goody-goody," said Josephine. "You still leave the house to go to school."

"I *have* to go to school," said Imogen. "It's the law."

"I must be a terrible mother to have brought up such a law-abiding child," muttered Josephine.

"Anyway," said Imogen, choosing to ignore the insult. "I know how to look after myself."

"So do I," said Josephine. "Which of us spent months in jail without a stitch of Chanel to wear? *Moi!* You've no idea what it was like at night. . . . No aromatherapy pillows . . . no eye masks to keep the light out . . . no raccoon serum to keep my skin looking young . . ."

I have to stop her from leaving the house somehow, thought Imogen. She'd lost her cousins and her father—she couldn't bear to lose her mother, too.

She reached into her pocket and pulled out the stolen credit card that she'd found in Isabella's crib a few weeks' ago. Stolen credit cards were always turning up in Isabella's crib—or they *had* always turned up in the crib, until the crime drought. Now the only things Imogen found in there were used nappies and dolls with the heads chewed off. And you can't pay for a sandwich with those, unless you go to a very strange sandwich shop indeed. "Here," she said, holding the credit card out to her mother. "Why don't you have an online shopping day?" *That should keep her occupied. . . .*

"Imogen! It's beautiful!" said Josephine, snatching up the credit card and cradling it as if it were a newborn baby. She was still cooing "Who's a clever girl, then? I think I'll call you 'Amex'!" when Imogen left the house for school.

Imogen knew she shouldn't be going out alone, but the piano accompanist was busy walking Aunt Bets to her bridge club. What other choice did she have? She had to get to school. She had to keep an eye on Ava Gud . . . or, as she'd begun to think of her, Ava *Kruk*.

She turned the corner onto Blandington Secondary School Street—and there, walking to school ahead of her, was Ava, her glossy ponytail catching the light as it swung to and fro. *I wonder what conditioner she uses?* thought Imogen.

And then she shook herself. Her mother—unbelievably—did have a point. Anyone (like Ava Gud) who wanted to hurt her (which Ava Gud definitely did) would definitely try to reach her at school. She wasn't going to walk right into her trap. In fact, she was going to start fighting back. She hadn't forgotten what Big Nana had said: "You come at the king, you best not miss." But she couldn't just wait around for the Kruks to kidnap more of her relatives. She had to do something to warn them off. She turned and headed for home. She had a half-formed plan. . . . It might not work. But then again it might. There was only one way to find out.

Imogen went straight up to her apartment—she could hear her mother in the bedroom, singing a lullaby to the credit card—and carefully picked up the venomous tarantula she'd stolen from Blandington Zoo a few weeks ago (you never knew when they might come in handy). She put it in a plastic carrying case.

She caught the train to London Waterloo Station and walked along the river until she saw the Houses of Parliament gleaming in the autumn sunlight. Opposite Big Ben was a large, unassuming green roundabout. It looked pretty ordinary—it was ignored by Londoners rushing to work and tourists taking selfies of themselves in front of pointy buildings—but it wasn't ordinary at all. Because hidden in the middle of it was a solid, steel trapdoor. And beneath that trapdoor was the entrance to Krukingham Palace: the Kruks' headquarters.

Imogen stood on the pavement outside Big Ben and took a deep breath. There wasn't a crossing that lead to the roundabout—you had to really, really want to get to it; enough to hurl yourself across four lanes of traffic. But what had Freddie told her last time they were here? "The statistical likelihood of dying in a road traffic accident in London in any given year is one in twenty thousand. . . ." She'd survived the journey once before. She'd take those odds.

She ran out in front of the traffic like a rabbit that was ready to die happy because it had achieved everything it wanted to in life, and made it to the other side with all her limbs intact.

The roundabout looked different than it had a few months ago—the trees were barer and the grass was covered in fallen leaves—but the two bushes were still there. The smaller one, she knew, hid a security guard with a Napoleon complex. And the taller one covered the secret trapdoor.

Imogen stood still for a moment. The small bush didn't seem to have noticed her. Maybe she could sneak over to the trapdoor, throw the tarantula down the stairs into Krukingham Palace, and run back across the roundabout without being noticed.

She crept over to the tall bush as quietly as she could, silently cursing the fall leaves that crunched beneath her feet—but when she got there, she found that the heavy metal cover had been boarded over.

Imogen glanced down at the tarantula, still in its plastic case. *Maybe this is a lucky escape,* Imogen thought. Now that she was here, her plan seemed very half-formed indeed. Throwing a tarantula down an opened trapdoor and hoping it killed all the Kruks had about as much chance of success as Uncle Knuckles had of being cast as the lead in *Sleeping Average-Looking Person*, Blandington's annual Christmas ballet (less chance, actually—Knuckles turned surprisingly elegant pirouettes).

But then she heard a familiar, resentful-sounding voice behind her. "What do you want?" She turned—and there, all of a sudden, was the tiny bush, its twigs swaying aggressively in the breeze, the sparrows nesting in its branches eyeing her suspiciously. She stared into the leaves, trying to see the man hidden inside, but his disguise was just too good.

"Is the family home?" Imogen asked.

"Which family? The Kruks?" And then he slapped one of his branches over the place where his mouth must have been. "I'm not supposed to say their name out loud! Now I have to punish myself."

There was a bit of rustling and a snapping noise, and one of the bush's branches fell to the ground.

"Ow," said the bush.

"Does that actually hurt you?" said Imogen, curious now.

"Only symbolically," said the bush.

"Right," said Imogen. "So—are they home?"

The bush shook again, but didn't say anything.

"What was that? Are you still punishing yourself?"

"Sorry," said the bush. "I always forget I'm wearing this thing. That was me shaking my head."

"Oh."

"The family are away on an indefinite holiday. You can record a message for them if you'd like." There was more rustling—and then a digital recorder suddenly popped up in the middle of the sparrows' nest. The sparrows didn't seem that pleased about it, but Imogen was very impressed.

Imogen reached over, assumed the evil monologue position, and said in her most serious voice: "This is Imogen Crim. *And I'm going to take you down.*"

"Don't you want to say anything else?" asked the bush. "'Lots of love'? 'See you soon'? 'Hope you're enjoying the sunshine'?"

"Why? Are they somewhere sunny?"

"Darn! Did it again!" said the bush, snapping off another twig.

"I do have one more message for them," said Imogen. She picked up the tarantula carefully—and threw it, not very carefully, at the bush.

"Arrrrgghghghgh!" screamed the bush, running away, even though the tarantula was still in its plastic case. "A furry guinea pig!"

"It's a tarantula, actually. A venomous one."

"Arrrrghghhghg!" screamed the bush, even more loudly.

"That's right," said Imogen, nodding. "There's more where that came from." Which wasn't strictly true, but it sounded better than "That was the last venomous animal I had and I'm not sure when I'll be able to steal another one."

It was dark by the time Imogen got home. The house was dark too. The only light was coming from Big Nana's bedroom. As Imogen walked up the front path, dodging Freddie's booby traps, she saw her grandmother silhouetted in the window, practicing her maniacal laughter. Imogen felt a lump in her throat—she had just swallowed a cough drop—and sighed. The Crims hadn't had a reason to use their maniacal laughter for weeks.

And then it occurred to her—why were all the lights in the apartment off? Why wasn't her mother home?

There was a note on the kitchen table.

Made an online appointment for the salon, darling! Isabella's been practicing her kung fu all morning, so she'll make excellent protection! Back in a flash! It's nine a.m. now. Will be home for dinner. Maybe I'll cook. (Ha! As if!)

Imogen checked her watch. It was after nine p.m. *Way* past dinnertime. Her mother must have been taken—and Isabella too. Imogen waited for the panic—and the sadness and the anger—to hit her. But she felt nothing. She was so used to her family members going missing, she realized, that she had almost expected this.

Imogen went downstairs and turned on the dishwasher, and the vent fan, and the vacuum cleaner—to confuse any bugs—and the ice cream maker, to keep her spirits up. And then she knocked on Big Nana's bedroom door. It took a while for Big Nana to answer—that's what happens when you drown out all the noise in your house with electrical goods.

Eventually, Big Nana opened her door a crack. "Ah. You're home," she said, opening the door wider.

"But Mum and Isabella aren't," said Imogen. "I think they've been taken too. Which means there's just us, Uncle Clyde, Aunt Bets, and Uncle Knuckles left."

As soon as Josephine left Crim House, Isabella started scrybiting. Scrybiting was Isabella's signature combination of screaming, crying, and biting. Josephine had teamed Isabella with a beautiful pink leather handbag that perfectly matched her skin tone, but Isabella had chewed her way out of it before they reached the end of the road, and then started crawling, as fast as her short but surprisingly powerful legs would carry her, back to Crim House. It was almost as though she thought going to the salon was a bad idea. Josephine tutted. The child had a lot to learn. Going to a salon was never a bad idea. Unless it was a literary salon. Imogen had dragged her to one of those once. Just a lot of boring people with gray hair and moth-eaten cardigans reading books! Not a hair dryer in sight!

Josephine chased after Isabella, scooped her up, and marched back toward the main street. But just before she reached the salon, she noticed a sign, pointing down a dark alley. And written on the sign, in large red letters, were the words "Free Fancy Shoes."

Aha! *thought Josephine.* I like shoes! I like fancy things! And most of all, I like things that are free! *She turned to walk down the alley, ignoring Isabella, who was chewing Josephine's arm by this point—but then she stopped.* Hang on a minute, *Josephine said to herself.* "Fancy" isn't a name brand.

This is probably some sort of scam. *So she turned back and carried on toward the salon.*

But then she stopped again. Hang on another minute, *she thought again.* What if the sign says "Fancy" because the brands in question are *so* fancy that they can't be named for fear of starting a riot? Maybe this is like the circulars from Boring Shop, Exciting Prices that just say "Famous Brands"! *Josephine was even more thrilled with herself than usual for figuring this out (and she was always quite a high level of thrilled with herself). So she turned around again (she was quite dizzy by this point) and marched back into the alley.*

Isabella was scrybiting so loudly and violently that Josephine didn't notice the person coming up behind her. But she did notice, as anyone would, when someone behind shouted, "Ich habe dich!" and shoved her into a sack.

Isabella Crim
Crim House
3 Unusual Crescent
Blandington
BRD 4638

Dear Ms. Crim,

Thank you for reaching out to us about managing your considerable wealth. At Richbottom, Cooper & Stink, we believe your investment goals are as unique as you are. We also know that not everyone is cut out to understand the investment market—and they shouldn't be. We are happy to manage our clients' wealth with care and trust.

We know that with considerable assets like yours, trust is absolutely essential.

Toward that end, we must ask some questions about your situation. Specifically, it has come to our attention that you are a baby, or at least an unusually sophisticated toddler. And yet, you have amassed over three million pounds in assets.

Would you please agree to meet with us to address our concerns?

CHAPTER TWELVE

IMOGEN GOT UP with the larks the next day. The larks were really annoying—too chirpy considering how early it was—so Imogen got dressed and left the house to get away from them. She went to the only place she'd ever felt truly comfortable, no matter how many people there hated her or ignored her or were actively trying to kidnap her: school. She wasn't going to go to classes—she couldn't risk it; maybe this was the day Ava would decide to strike. She would go undercover and spy on Ava instead. If she followed her to the Kruks' base in Blandington, maybe she would find her family. . . .

Imogen thought back to the comment Big Nana had

written on her last crime essay, "Why Disguising Your-self as a Crosswalk Is Never a Good Idea": "When going undercover, find somewhere that no one else would want to hide. There's nothing worse than ducking behind a parked car and finding that someone's down there already." Imogen knew exactly where she *didn't* want to hide—the huge Dumpster just inside the entrance gate, which was full of the slimy remains of school lunches. So she held her breath and dived in. She drilled a peephole with the ama-teur dentistry kit Aunt Bets had given her for Imogen's last birthday, and waited.

By eight thirty, Imogen's back was in quite a lot of pain, and her feet were in a lot of orange peels and empty milk cartons. Just as she was cursing herself for getting in so early, a large, beige Cadillac pulled up at the entrance gate. (All the cars in Blandington were beige, apart from the Crims car, which was ARGHNO!, a color invented by a lexicographer who'd had the misfortune of seeing the Crims' car and invented a new word to describe its revolt-ing combination of red and gold and brown and green and silver and glitter and black and why?) A woman with curly blond hair stepped out of the Cadillac—hair so blond and curly and stiff-looking that Imogen imagined it might be able to resist bullets—followed by Ava.

Ava and the blond woman were having an argument. Imogen wasn't close enough to hear what they were saying, but she knew the international mime action for "I'm going to slit your throat" and the slightly less international sign for "I'm going to rip your bowels out when you get home. Good luck digesting your dinner."

The blond woman got back into the car and drove away, and Ava made the universal sign for "Please go away, I don't like you very much." The license plate on the car read NICELADY. But the blond woman didn't look very nice. Probably because she was a Kruk, too.

Imogen stayed in the Dumpster all day. She learned a lot about what flies like to eat for breakfast. She also learned a lot about why people kept cream in a refrigerator. She didn't learn a lot about Ava Gud.

After a few hours, Imogen worked up the courage to wheel the Dumpster toward a classroom window. She could see her fellow pupils in action. They were using Bunsen burners, which meant they were doing chemistry. Imogen loved chemistry. Last year, at Lilyworth, she'd managed to create a very effective new poison during lab. . . . She gazed into the flames, and suddenly felt very sleepy. Maybe if she just rested her head on this empty potato sack. . . .

BRIIIIINNNG! Imogen was woken with a start by the final bell. Just in time, she managed to climb out of the Dumpster, peel the chocolate wrappers from her shoes, and hide behind it. She was going to wait for Ava to appear. She would follow her home again—but this time, she wasn't going to let herself be outmaneuvered.

Keeping her distance—she didn't want Ava to turn around to find out where the revolting smell was coming from—Imogen tailed Ava through the streets. Ava took sharp turns down hidden alleys. Imogen followed her. Ava jumped over fences. Imogen vaulted over them after her. Ava ran down Blandington Secondary School Street, then skipped, then did a strange crab walk for a bit. Imogen didn't bother doing any of that—she still had her dignity. She kept Ava in sight, and her persistence paid off: This time, when Ava turned into the side street where Imogen had lost her the first time, Imogen saw her disappearing into a Chinese restaurant that no one ever went into because it had a hygiene rating of one out of ten proudly displayed in the window. Imogen waited for a few moments and pushed the door to the restaurant open—and realized it wasn't a restaurant at all. Behind the door was a narrow alley, a shortcut to Straight Crescent, a very ordinary Blandington street—and there, on the other side of the road, was Ava, walking up to a very nice, clean, normal-looking house with a white picket fence and a garden gno (like a garden gnome but more depressing).

Imogen hid in the next-door garden and watched Ava disappear inside the house. Moments later, a bakery truck pulled up outside the home. Imogen was immediately suspicious—hadn't Ava said her whole family was gluten intolerant?—but then Imogen realized the truck wasn't a bakery truck at all.

The vehicle's door opened, and two burly men climbed out and walked round to the back of the truck, doing that swagger-y walk that burly men do to prove just how burly they are. Imogen crouched down lower as they opened the double doors—and then she gasped. Not because their truck-opening skills were anything special—if anything, they seemed a bit hesitant about it. But then they unloaded three figures from the truck, and she understood why they hadn't wanted to get too close to them.

The three figures looked an awful lot like her uncle Knuckles, her aunt Bets, and her uncle Clyde. Which is because they *were* her uncle Knuckles, her aunt Bets, and her uncle Clyde. They must have been kidnapped while they were scoping out another house . . . but what was Uncle Clyde doing with them? Accompanying them, probably. He did have a portable keyboard, after all.

"Keep still!" one of the men said to Aunt Bets, in a gruff but terrified-sounding voice.

But Aunt Bets wasn't keeping still. She was dressed— or more accurately, restrained—in a straitjacket and a hockey mask. Her mad eyes stared out of the holes, looking madder than ever, and she was writhing around, muttering, "Bitey, bitey!"

Imogen looked again at the man who was holding her. One of his hands was covered in a bandage. . . .

"ARE YOU ALL RIGHT, BETS?" shouted Uncle Knuckles. "SORRY ABOUT MY WIFE," he said to the burly men. "SHE GETS A BIT OVEREXCITED WHEN SHE'S TIED UP. IT REALLY BRINGS OUT THE LION IN HER. SHE ATE HIM LAST SUMMER WHEN WE WERE ON SAFARI, AND HE POPS BACK UP AT THE MOST EMBARRASSING MOMENTS! I LIKE TO CALL HIM 'PHIL.'"

"Gives you terrible indigestion, lion meat," groused Bets. "Almost as bad as human flesh . . ." And she gnashed her teeth again.

Imogen watched from the next-door garden, feeling as powerless as an out-of-date cell phone. *I have to save them,* she thought. *But how?* She wished she had someone to help her. She cursed herself. What had Big Nana reminded her just yesterday morning? "Don't go anywhere alone, except to the bathroom, because no one needs to see that."

The burly men—looking quite terrified now—led her uncles and aunt down the side of the house to the back door. Imogen waited until they were safely inside and then crept up to the building and peered through the windows.

Ava was in there, hands on her hips, watching Imogen's relatives being led to the basement. And she wasn't alone. Standing next to her were a group of children, dressed in bow ties and party dresses, and an icily blond man with a thin face.

She recognized them all from somewhere. . . .

From a party she'd been to—a terrible party, involving chocolate fountains and the threat of tigers and a surprising number of otters.

Gustav Kruk's sixty-fifth birthday.

The cold-looking man was Stefan Kruk, who had stolen the *Mona Lisa* and replaced it with a Very Good Fake—she recognized him from her internet research.

I knew it! I KNEW IT! Imogen forced down the urge to do a little dance of victory.

I knew no one could be as intelligent and likable and beautiful as Ava without also being completely evil, thought Imogen. It was weird that she hadn't been able to find anything on the internet about Ava's existence, or in the book she'd recently borrowed from the library, *A Family Tree That Really Should Have Been Cut Down and Made into Firewood: The Kruks Through the Generations* . . . but she was most definitely a Kruk.

Imogen reveled in her triumph for a moment. She loved being right, almost as much as she loved other people being wrong. But then she realized this meant the Kruks definitely had her family. And that was not a good thing. To say the Kruks were more powerful than the Crims would be like saying machine guns are more powerful than underpants. There was no comparison. And the Kruks had kidnapped her *entire family*. Apart from Big Nana.

Imogen felt sick. What chance did she and Big Nana really stand of saving the Crims if the Kruks had them? What chance did they stand of saving themselves? This could spell the end of the Crims.

Imogen walked home, dazed. It felt like her heart was trying to beat its way out of her body. She didn't blame it. Her body was probably about to be kidnapped by Kruks.

I did have a good reason for doubting the Kruks were behind this, she told herself, trying to assuage her guilt. *When I was looking for the person who had set my family up for The Heist, PC Donnelly told me to look for someone with a motive. And the Kruks have no motive for targeting us.* Was Elsa really crazy enough to try to take down an entire family just because she felt like it? The Kruks controlled half the world (they left the cold bits—like Russia, Antarctica, Alaska, and Glasgow—to the mafia). The Crims controlled . . . parts of Blandington. (They left the bits where talking was frowned upon—like the library and the church—to the mafia. Not that the mafia was remotely interested in them.) What was in it for the Kruks? They'd never been punished for the lunch box heist; they hadn't actually been involved in it in the first place. Maybe the Kruks knew that Imogen had been investigating them? But how?

Imogen broke into a run. She had to get home and find Big Nana, to tell her what she'd learned. If Big Nana was still there . . .

Please don't let Big Nana be gone too. Please. I'll do any-thing. . . .

She pushed open the front door.

The house was suspiciously silent.

"Hello?" she called.

And then she heard a sort of wailing—the sort of wailing you'd expect from a whale trapped in Wales (there isn't much entertainment for marine mammals in Cardiff).

"Big Nana?" called Imogen.

"Waaaaaaaaah!" wailed the whale, or whatever it was. The sound was coming from the kitchen.

Big Nana was at the dinner table, sobbing, surrounded by balled-up tissues.

"What's wrong?" asked Imogen. "I mean, apart from the obvious."

"Knuckles and Bets and Clyde have been taken!" Big Nana cried snottily.

"I know," said Imogen.

And then she had a thought. A thought so terrifying that time seemed to stop: Whoever had taken her relatives had known where they would be. There *had* to be a mole in Crim House. And she and Big Nana were the only Crims who hadn't been kidnapped yet.

Which meant that one of them had to be the mole.

She looked up at Big Nana, who must have seen the fear in her eyes.

"Please don't tell me you think I'm the mole," Big Nana said wearily.

Imogen didn't say anything.

"It's fine," said Big Nana, still crying. "I thought you could be the mole, too, for about five minutes. But then I came to my senses. You're a Crim through and through, Imogen—you always have been. I know you couldn't work against the family. Unless you are an imposter like Gunther Kruk was."

"Which I'm not."

"So prove it: What nickname did you give me when you were a little girl?"

"Big Banana," said Imogen.

Big Nana nodded, satisfied.

"Now *you* have to prove you aren't the mole," Imogen pointed out. "What was the first real crime I ever committed?"

"You stole Freddie's bike when you were seven."

Imogen nodded and laughed a little with relief.

But Big Nana wasn't laughing. "It's definitely the

house. It must be bugged," said Big Nana. And she started crying again. "I can't believe I let this happen. Bets and Clyde and Knuckles—all gone!" She put her head in her hands and gave into her sobs.

Imogen noticed a note underneath Big Nana's elbow. A long note, written in cursive handwriting. "Wait—what's that?" she asked.

"They left a ransom note," said Big Nana, her head still in her hands.

"They wrote their own ransom note?"

"No! I'm just too distressed to be grammatically correct!" Big Nana lifted her head and passed the ransom note to Imogen. "I found this in the mailbox."

This note, like all the others, was made from letters cut out of magazines. But this time the letters were tiny, and there were lots of them—the note was very long and very creepy. Imogen read:

My dear Gerda Crim,

It has been a long time, has it not? You've done very well for yourself. Built a very interesting house. Produced a fair few heirs to your crime empire. Pulled off a few half-decent heists--kudos on the Pentonville Prison job, by the way. We wish we'd thought of that. But your glory days are over. Your house is in tatters. You haven't committed a real crime for weeks now. And your entire family has been kidnapped! Apart from that annoying, ponytail-wearing, philosophy-quoting granddaughter of yours.

So here's our demand: Bring us a million pounds in unmarked bills in a Gucci suitcase (the red one that's half price on Net-a-Porter at the moment will do). Make us another round of those brownies you baked last week (bet you didn't even notice they were missing, did you?). And we will release your family.

But here's the catch.

You have to bring us the brownies and the money in person. And you'll never go home again. We've made up a lovely bedroom for you in Krukingham Palace. Well, I say "bedroom"--it's more of a dungeon, really.

Are you willing to sacrifice yourself for your family?

If you don't, you'll never see them again. It's been a while since the tigers had a decent meal. And the weasels are pretty hungry, too.

Yours,

Elsa

Imogen could see why Big Nana was so upset.

"Why are they so determined to bring you down?" Imogen asked.

"They're probably threatened by my incredible criminal talent," said Big Nana, blowing her nose.

Imogen wasn't sure that Big Nana's criminal talent had been shining all that brightly since her return to Blandington, but she didn't want to kick Big Nana when she was down.

"What does it matter, anyway?" cried Big Nana. "They've won!"

"Look," she said, "Don't give up. I know where Aunt Bets and Uncle Knuckles and Uncle Clyde are."

Big Nana looked up, her eyes swollen from crying. "You do?"

Imogen nodded. "In a house on Straight Crescent. They've been kidnapped by the Guds. Who are actually the Kruks."

"Well, of course they are," said Big Nana.

"Okay," said Imogen. "So let's rescue them! We just need a plan!"

"It's too late for a plan," said Big Nana, dropping her head into her hands for a third time. "You and I are the only Crims left. The Kruks outnumber us ten to one—and you should see their arsenal of weapons. This is what I feared. I just hoped we'd be stronger when it happened. . . ."

Imogen was beginning to feel pretty guilty for not taking her crime homework more seriously. "We can't give up!" she said. "I have an idea! I think Ava is the weakest link. We could kidnap her—and then we can get information out of her. Or maybe we could ransom her and do some sort of prisoner exchange? We could make a deal with the Kruks, so they'll leave Blandington for good. . . ."

"I doubt it," said Big Nana, shaking her head. "This is the Kruks we're talking about. You know how our family motto is 'Nothing is more important than family. Except dinosaurs'?"

Imogen, unfortunately, did know this.

"The Kruks have a motto too. . . ."

"I know," Imogen said. "It's on their family crest. Also, incidentally, the combination to their Loot Room: *'Wir werden Sie zu töten und nehmen Sie Ihr Geld'*—'We will kill you and take your money.'"

Big Nana sighed impatiently. "That's the public family motto, Imogen. It's all PR."

"That's terrible PR," Imogen said. "They should fire their publicist."

Big Nana waved her hand, bored. "As I was saying, within the family, they say something else: 'Lots of things are more important than family. Including, but not restricted to, money, pride, and really good roast chicken.' Elsa would throw her sister under a bus if she looked at her the wrong way. In fact, she has done that. Twice. She only has one sister left, who usually walks around with her eyes closed, just to be safe."

Imogen had never seen Big Nana so defeated. But *she* wasn't defeated. Not yet. "We have to try," said Imogen. "We *can* kidnap Ava. And who knows what will happen after that?"

"I have a pretty good idea," said Big Nana. "And it involves at least one coffin."

Imogen felt close to tears—tears of frustration and helplessness. "So what's the alternative? Hand yourself over and hope the Kruks keep to their word, for the first time in their lives, and give the others back? Or abandon the rest of our family to their fate without even *trying* to save them?"

Big Nana sighed. "I suppose it's worth a try, Imogen, my barbecued pork rib. I'll help you make a plan."

Imogen looked up at her grandmother—and saw real fear in her eyes. Which made her wonder: What had the Kruks done to Big Nana to make her so scared? Sure, the note was pretty scary—no one liked to be fed to weasels— but Imogen couldn't shake the feeling there was something Big Nana wasn't telling her. Was Delia right that Big Nana knew something she was holding back? Like why the Kruks were going to such lengths on a personal vendetta against Big Nana?

💣 💣 💣

Aunt Bets and Uncle Knuckles had found the one—the perfect house. It had running water, central heating, was close to transport links, less than a ten-minute walk to Blandington Secondary School, and only had three broken windows. Sure, it had graffiti on the walls, but it read "Henry Crim woz ere," so it made them feel right at home. They persuaded Uncle Clyde to come for a viewing.

Uncle Knuckles elbowed one of the broken windows, sweeping away the glass so that Aunt Bets could slip inside and open the front door for him and Uncle Clyde.

"Very nice!" said Uncle Clyde, striding into the living room. "Dibs on the bedroom nearest the bathroom."

"NO WAY," Uncle Knuckles boomed, his voice shattering yet another window. "YOU KNOW WHAT MY BLADDER'S LIKE."

And then he stopped. Because someone was already in the living room: a strange hobo with a squashy hat and a sack on a stick, with startlingly blue eyes.

"Guten Tag," he said intensely in a German accent. He stepped aside, revealing a pile of large, sturdy-looking sacks.

They knew he was strange because he was an old-timey German hobo squatting in an abandoned house with a pile of sacks. And because he immediately began shouting at them.

"You're too late!" he said. "This is MEIN Haus. I live here. I've already used the toilet."

"We were here first!" yelled Aunt Bets. "We have dibs!"

191

"But then you left, to fetch your little friend over there," said the hobo, nodding to Uncle Clyde. "And I moved in. You schlafe, you lose."

"You'll use that toilet again over my dead body," said Aunt Bets. "Or actually, yours. Knuckles—flush him down the lavatory."

"HE'S TOO BIG TO GO DOWN IN ONE PIECE, DEAR," said Uncle Knuckles.

"Then pass me my ax."

"I DIDN'T BRING IT WITH US, MY DARLING!" shouted Uncle Knuckles. "ALL I HAVE IS SOME SUGAR-FREE CHEWING GUM, SOME DIARRHEA MEDICATION, AND A LEAFLET ON HOW TO MEDITATE. WE COULD GIVE HIM SOME PAPER CUTS? OR CONSTIPATION?"

"Ahahaha!" the hobo laughed Germanly. "Constipation! It will take more than that to make me leave!"

"I don't think so!" yelled Uncle Clyde, running toward the hobo with his penknife. But the hobo clearly did think so. He disarmed Clyde with a swift karate move and bundled him into one of the sacks.

Aunt Bets cracked her knuckles—and then she cracked her Knuckles, whacking him over the head with her handbag for being so hopeless—and then she attacked.

She threw herself at the hobo with the force of a thousand

tigers, which, if you were wondering, is quite a lot of force. But the hobo was too quick for her. He feinted to the side and dodged her punches, and she tumbled into a wall and knocked herself out.

"MY WIFE!" cried Uncle Knuckles, which was true. "MY POOR DEFENSELESS WIFE!" he wailed, which definitely was not.

A second hobo emerged from the kitchen. For some reason, this one was carrying a hockey mask and a straitjacket—and what looked like a Teflon sack.

Uncle Knuckles fell to the ground. It was a long way down, so he hurt himself quite badly. "DON'T HURT HER!" he cried. He was actually sobbing. Huge great tears were splashing from his eyes and onto the floor.

"Let's get them out of here before they flood the place, ja?" said the first hobo.

"NO!" shouted Uncle Knuckles. "TAKE IT! YOU CAN HAVE THE HOUSE! JUST SPARE MY WIFE! AND SET MY BROTHER FREE! WE'LL GO AND LIVE—"

But we'll never know where Uncle Knuckles planned to go and live. Because that's when someone came up behind him, chloroformed him, and put him into a sack.

CHAPTER THIRTEEN

IMOGEN WOKE UP the next morning with something cold and smooth stuck to her cheek. She sat up and peeled it off—and realized it was a photograph of Ava Gud she'd printed out from Hannah's Instagram feed. She had been planning to pin it to the middle of her plan, beneath the heading "How to Kidnap Ava Gud and Get My Family Back Without Being Turned into Exotic Pet Food." She sat up and looked at the notice board—there were mug shots of the Crims and illegible notes on index cards and lots of pieces of string connecting the different stages of the plan together. She was pretty impressed with what she had managed to come up with at three in the morning, although she was struggling to read her own sleep-deprived handwriting. She couldn't quite work out what she had planned to do to Stefan Kruk with a cage full of canaries.

She checked her watch—it was just past midday. Not too late, then. She picked up the photo of Ava and pinned it to the middle of the plan. She stood back and looked at it.

"Oh Imogen, my little overflowing recycling bin, it's perfect!"

"Aah!" yelped Imogen. She hadn't heard Big Nana come in.

"Now, now," said Big Nana, wagging her finger. "Never be surprised by a relative, unless it's your fiftieth birthday and they're throwing you a party." She turned back to the plan. "But I'll let you off this time. You *were* paying attention to your crime homework! Let's see: 'Step one: Put on believable disguises, using real human-hair wigs, because the Kruks can spot a synthetic wig at a hundred paces.' Couldn't have put it better myself. 'Step two: Play Wagner to pacify the guards.' Inspired. 'Step three: Take a dog with you, because the Kruks really like dogs.' Yes, yes, and yes again." Big Nana leaned over and gave her shoulders a squeeze. "I *knew* you could do it," she said. "I knew you were the one who would follow in my footsteps. It's hard sometimes, because my footsteps are very large and strange, and I often take quite roundabout routes—but you did it. Thank you."

Imogen felt the warm glow you only get from praise or sitting too long in a room full of radioactive waste. "Thank *you*," she said. "Thank you for teaching me everything I know. Apart from the math stuff—I learned all that at Lilyworth."

"Numbers," said Big Nana, pulling a face. "Yuck."

A few minutes later, Big Nana was dressed in her finest fake Chanel dress, adjusting her curly blond wig (made from the hair of ex–beauty-pageant contestants). Imogen was out front with Barney, putting the finishing touches to the NICELADY license plate she'd made—Big Nana's welding homework had come in handy much sooner than she'd thought it would. She gave it one last polish and then screwed it over the real license plate on a black sedan she'd rented using one of Isabella's stolen credit cards. She looked up and did a double take when she saw Big Nana, who looked remarkably like the well-groomed but bad-tempered Kruk she'd seen at school with Ava.

"Have you got the sack?" Imogen asked.

"Of course," said Big Nana, pulling it out of her handbag like a criminal Mary Poppins. "I went for the extra-strong ones—the ones with the ad where they put the grizzly bear inside."

"That poor bear," said Imogen. "I'd be grizzly too if I was shoved into a sack."

Barney barked, as if to say, *Me too.*

They climbed into the car, and Barney bounded in after them. He couldn't help bounding—he was that sort of dog.

"Lie down in the back," Imogen said to him. "Your job is to watch out and alert us to danger. Okay?"

Barney barked happily.

"What am I doing?" Imogen asked herself, shaking her head. Which was a good question—Barney wouldn't have known danger if it came up and introduced itself really politely, wearing a "Hi. My Name is Danger" name tag. She threw a blanket over his head, and he lay down, thumping his tail on the back seat. "Right," she said. "Let's go, Big Nana. Next stop: Blandington Secondary School."

Big Nana checked her mirror and signaled before pulling out of the driveway. "Is this really how ordinary people drive?" she asked.

"Yes," said Imogen.

"But how do they get away from the police cars?"

"You're much less likely to get chased by police cars when you're not breaking the speed limit," Imogen pointed out. "It's actually quite relaxing." She leaned over to the dashboard and turned the radio dial to Naff Classics. A string quartet was playing *Pachelbel's Canon.*

"What is this noise?" demanded Big Nana.

"It's classical music, Big Nana," said Imogen. "To help us focus."

"This is no fun," said Big Nana, reaching over to turn the radio off. "We're about to win our family back and stick it to the world's most powerful crime family. You know what this calls for?"

Imogen had a horrible feeling that she did. "Please, no . . . ," she muttered.

Big Nana held up her phone and shouted "Kitty Penguin!" into it. "Delia got me into her," she explained to Imogen. "She's very talented, considering she can't sing in tune."

Kitty Penguin started blaring out from the tinny cell phone speakers, "singing" (screeching) one of her "tunes" (unbearable sequences of unpleasant noises).

Neither of them said anything for a minute. *Where's Delia now?* Imogen wondered. *She would have loved to be part of this. And the rest of my family?* Imogen hated to think of what they were going through—but she shook herself. *They're all fine. They're just hanging out in a cozy dungeon somewhere, waiting for us to come and get them, which we are doing, right now.*

Big Nana closed her eyes—which was a bit worrying, driving-wise—and started singing along to "Get Fierce," Kitty Penguin's latest number one.

"'I don't get fierce. I stay fierce,'" sang Big Nana. "'I've got sharp nails, and I could pierce/ Balloons with them if I wanted to, but I don't.'"

"Such beautiful lyrics," said Imogen.

"They really are," said Big Nana, who didn't get irony. "Come on! Join in!"

Reluctantly, Imogen cleared her throat, and started howling along with the music.

"We'll kill you if we like.
Or we might just steal your bike.
Or change our names to Mike.
We do what we want, cuz we're fierce!"

Big Nana turned and smiled at her, the wind blowing her fake hair away from her face. "See? Don't you feel better?"

And Imogen realized that she did. She had come up with a brilliant plan, and she was setting out with Big Nana to pull it off.

They were finally fighting back.

There was a huge line of traffic outside the school. Big Nana honked her horn.

"What are all these people *doing* here?" she asked.

"Picking their kids up."

"People really do that?" Big Nana shook her head, baffled.

It was getting hot in the car, and neither of them had had breakfast—they'd eaten the last of the chicken nuggets the night before. Big Nana was getting increasingly irritated, particularly with the slower kids. "Why are they looking both ways before they cross the road?" she asked.

"So that they don't get hit by a car."

Big Nana tutted. "Getting hit by a car builds character."

They pulled up next to an ice cream truck—a familiar one. Imogen's cousins had hijacked it the day she'd come home from Lilyworth and given her a very uncomfortable ride back to Crim House. She felt a pang of nostalgia as she remembered Delia swerving into oncoming traffic, and Henry trying to graffiti his initials on her knuckles, and Isabella beating her up with her tiny fists. . . .

Big Nana's stomach growled. It was the least polite of all of her internal organs. She dug some coins out from the side of the car's seat and handed them to Imogen. "Jump out and get us an ice cream."

"Really?" said Imogen. "Now?"

"A little ice cream never hurt a kidnapping," she said. "A lot of ice cream, on the other hand, can play havoc with your interrogation technique."

Imogen shrugged. She was done doubting Big Nana:

She was, it turned out, always right. She opened the car door, climbed out, and strolled up to the truck's window.

"Yep?" said the bored-looking man in the ice cream truck.

"Two ice creams, please. With flakes," said Imogen.

The ice cream man looked in his freezer. "I'm out," he said. "Let me go and check in the back."

Imogen glanced back at the traffic. There were still several cars ahead of Big Nana. She still had time.

But that's when the ice cream truck's door opened and a hand reached out, grabbed Imogen, pulled her inside, and shoved her into a sack.

The first thing Imogen thought was: *Ooh, nice burlap. This is like a* professional *sack.*

The second thing she thought was: *Help!*

Imogen was shaken out onto a dusty floor, covered with curled wood shavings and a dark stain that might have been blood or might have been hot chocolate.

The room she was in felt familiar for some reason. The whole place smelled of freshly sawn wood. The lights were dim, but she could make out benches and saws and drills and huge planers, and there were planks of wood stacked up against each of the walls. *I'm in the school woodshop,* she realized. She'd only been in here once, to try to bribe the Design Technology teacher into donating to the charity drive by letting him know that she knew his first name: Hilary.

She heard a familiar laugh. Maniacal yet tinkling; irritating yet likable . . .

Could it be?

Yes, unfortunately, it could.

"Hello, Imogen," said Ava. She was holding a knife—a really expensive-looking, diamond-studded, pink one. Dangerous, yet the sort of thing a teenage girl might ask for for Christmas. She turned to the large, unfriendly looking men who had shaken Imogen out onto the floor and said, "You can leave us now. We have a lot of catching up to do. Don't we?"

Why is Ava so much better at everything than I am?? Imogen fumed as the massive men left the room. *I planned to kidnap her, and she kidnapped me!! This is unacceptable! I will not let her win!*

Imogen stumbled to her feet. "You're a Kruk," she spat at Ava.

"Yes, I am," said Ava, twirling her knife.

Imogen straightened her back. *Never let them know you're scared.* "You've been after me this whole time."

"Right again," said Ava.

"You came to Blandington Secondary School so you could kill me."

"Aww," Ava said patronizingly. "You *have* been doing

your homework! Except it's not really *me* who wants you dead. This is all my mom's idea." She shook her head. "*Parents*—am I right?"

Her mom must be the blond woman who was driving the NICELADY car, thought Imogen. She hadn't recognized her from the pictures of the Kruks she'd found, either—but then the blond hair was probably a disguise. Was Ava's mother Ida, the musical Kruk who specialized in throttling her victims with ukulele strings? Or Mona, the amateur dentist with a taste for hand drills? Or the craziest, deadliest Kruk of all—Elsa?

Ava pointed the knife at Imogen's throat and said, "Do me a favor, would you? Climb up on that workbench over there."

Imogen looked at the workbench. It was attached to a huge circular saw, and there was a plank of wood lying on top of it. A plank as long as Imogen's body. "I'd rather not, if you don't mind," she said in her sweetest voice.

"Oh, but I do mind," said Ava. "I have to kill you before dinner, or I'll be grounded. And I can't be grounded because it's the charity auction next week, and you dropped out of it, so it's on me to organize the *whole thing*, so really, this is all your fault." She stepped toward Imogen. The knife looked nastily sharp.

Come on Imogen. Think. But the only thing in Imogen's head was "Get Fierce," the lyrics spinning round and round in a terrible, screechy loop. *I don't get fierce. I stay fierce. . . . Great,* she thought as she clambered up onto the workbench. *The soundtrack to my death is going to be the world's worst pop star rhyming "fierce" with "ears."*

"There," said Ava, tying Imogen's arms and legs to the workbench. "That wasn't so hard, was it?" She leaned over to press the saw's on button—but then she paused.

"Ready?"

Imogen didn't say anything. Of course she wasn't ready. She had to come up with a plan. But apart from Kitty Penguin, her mind was horribly empty, like the kitchen fridge had been that morning.

And then she remembered something—something that would hopefully make her imminent death slightly less imminent. . . . *Please let it work,* she thought to herself.

"I'm ready," she said.

Ava raised her eyebrows. "Okay. You asked for it!" she said, and flicked the switch.

The saw started to spin, blade flashing, and cut through the plank, slowly moving toward Imogen. The wood seemed to scream, and who could blame it? It was being cut in half by a teenage maniac.

The saw was slowly approaching Imogen's feet, spitting sawdust into her face. But Imogen wasn't worried. Okay, she was a bit worried—anyone would be, with a screaming saw approaching their feet. But she knew it would never reach them because the saw had a safety cutoff. When she'd surprised Mr. Hilary Jenkins in the woodshop all those weeks ago, he'd been in the middle of chopping the worst student projects up into little pieces so he could throw them on a fire and forget that they had ever existed. He'd jumped when Imogen walked into the room, and his hand had slipped . . . But instead of cutting his fingers off, the saw had juddered to a sudden halt. "If the saw gets too close to your hand, it stops automatically," he'd explained. "Which you'd know if you took woodshop. Why don't you, by the way? Hammering is very cathartic."

And then she'd blackmailed him into handing over a month's wages, and he'd seemed quite happy about her not taking woodshop after that.

But Imogen's feeling of relief only lasted for approximately twenty seconds. Because that's how long it took for Ava to open a box of dynamite.

Humming in tune with the screaming saw, which was still working its way toward Imogen, Ava moved around the workbench, arranging dynamite around Imogen's body symmetrically; the same way she'd arranged the brownies on plate in the charity committee meeting. But then Imogen spotted something in Ava's pocket. A book of matches! If she could just somehow reach them . . . If only her hands weren't tied to the bench . . .

And then Ava brushed right past the bench—and as

she did so, Imogen managed to reach out with her fingers and snatch the book of matches just in time. She pushed them up her sleeve before Ava could notice, and her heart thumped with relief. *I've saved myself,* she thought. *I'm not going to die. Just yet.*

Ava adjusted the angle of one of the sticks of dynamite and stood back to admire her work. And then she cleared her throat.

Oh no, Imogen thought. *She's not going to do an evil monologue, is she?*

In fact, that's exactly what Ava was going to do.

"Who would have thought it would end like this?" started Ava.

It was all Imogen could do not to roll her eyes. "Talk about a cliché introduction . . ."

Ava glared at Imogen and then carried on monologuing. "It's a shame, really. I'm killing you without an audience. Without anyone knowing what I can do with a little bit of determination, some dynamite, and a large collection of high-quality woodworking tools. But what does that matter? What matters is that you'll end up dead. Because the Kruks are far superior to your pathetic little family, and always will be! Mwahahahahahahaha!"

Imogen had to admit Ava's maniacal laugh was, as the kids at school said, all extra. But whatever—she was not going to sit here silently and let Ava have the last word. She cleared her throat and launched into her *own* evil monologue.

"I always knew you were a Kruk," Imogen muttered. "I followed you home and saw you there—with your overdressed little cousins and your uncle Stefan."

Ava gasped.

"Yes, that's right," said Imogen. "You say you're so superior—and yet you forgot to close the blinds when you were bringing prisoners into the house. Rookie mistake, Ava. Rookie mistake."

Ava gave a nasty little laugh. "I heard a lot about you before I got to Blandington," she said. "I heard you were smarter than the other Crims, and popular, and good at physics. But you're pathetic. It took me about five minutes to take your spot as queen bee. Plus, I got an A on that string theory test and you only got a B+."

"That's because the questions were worded confusingly! And I'd been up all night knitting a bulletproof vest!"

"Yeah? Well, you should have made a *saw*proof vest."

"Should I, Ava? *Should* I?"

The saw was at Imogen's leg—and then, all of a sudden, it cut off, shuddering to halt.

Imogen cackled. *Nice dramatic timing.* She felt pretty

smug for a person who was maybe about to be blown to death by eighty evenly spaced sticks of dynamite.

Ava let out a cry of frustration. "NOOOOO!" she wailed. "STUPID SAW! HOW AM I GOING TO KILL YOU NOW?"

"Well . . . you do have the dynamite."

"Oh yeah. Good point," said Ava, reaching into her pocket to get the matches. "NOOOO!" she groaned again when she found it empty. "I FORGOT THE MATCHES! Why is this SO HARD?" She flopped down onto the floor.

"You also have that knife," Imogen observed.

"But I don't really *want* to hack you to death," whined Ava. "It'll get really messy, and this T-shirt is new."

"It's a good color on you," said Imogen.

"Thanks!" Ava said brightly. "I got it on sale." And then she pouted again. "My mom told me I had to brutally murder you. But I think it's stupid."

"She used the word 'brutally'?" Imogen said.

Ava nodded. "She used some other words, too—'sadistically,' 'inventively,' 'slowly'—but I thought 'brutally' kind of covered it. Why can't our family just TALK to your family? Why do they have to go all scorched-earth? They're so *embarrassing*!"

"Tell me about it," said Imogen. "Imagine your family,

with all the malevolence and fondness for sharp objects, but with none of the talent. That's the Crims."

Ava hopped up onto the workbench next to Imogen. "Don't be so hard on yourselves," she said. "You *do* have talent. I didn't really mean what I said just now."

"Oh, don't worry, I get it," said Imogen. "Big Nana always makes us exaggerate in our evil monologues. We have to practice them in front of the mirror."

"Oh my God! Same!" said Ava.

Imogen smiled at Ava. *She actually seems to like me,* Imogen thought. *Perhaps I can manipulate her into freeing me and my family—and then throw her down a well or something.* But then she realized, she didn't actually want to throw Ava down a well. She liked her, too. If they had met in different, less murder-y circumstances, they might actually have become friends.

Ava looked at Imogen curiously. "I've never met someone who grew up in a family like mine."

"Nor have I," said Imogen. "Everyone else is all 'My dad is always away for business, it's so annoying,' and I'm like 'My grandmother faked her own death, and my mother preferred the guy disguised as my father to my actual father because he was better at stealing diamonds.'"

"Really?" said Ava, fascinated. "My mom killed my dad because he stole her a sapphire necklace for their

anniversary instead of an emerald necklace, and it didn't quite match her dress."

"I'm so sorry," said Imogen.

"Don't be," Ava said dismissively. "He always called me Ivan because he wished I was a boy, and he threw darts at me at breakfast time to toughen up my skin. I still can't see a bowl of cereal without flinching."

Imogen and Ava smiled at each other shyly.

"We have to pretend we're still enemies," said Ava.

"Does that mean we're not?"

"We're not. So I probably won't kill you."

"I'd appreciate that." Imogen smiled. It would be impossible to describe the relief that flooded through her at that moment. If you've ever been spared from a violent death at the very last minute, you'll know how she felt. "I don't suppose you'd untie me, would you?" she asked.

Ava looked at her. "Okay," she said. "But don't try anything funny."

"I won't," said Imogen. "I'm not very funny."

Ava used her knife to cut Imogen's hands and ankles free. Imogen rubbed her wrists and sat up, clearing a space for herself among all the dynamite. "Do you know what's going to happen to the rest of my family?"

Ava shook her head. "The Kruks are a totally top-down organization. They just tell me what I need to complete my mission. Only my mom really knows what's going on."

"Your mom?"

"Elsa. She's crazy. My brothers actually tried to run away to Siberia to get away from her, but there was some passport thing, so . . ."

Imogen felt as though a cold weight had dropped into her stomach. Ava was Elsa's daughter. Which meant the blond woman in the NICELADY car was almost certainly Elsa. "I have a question," she said. "Why is Elsa so interested in our family anyway? She doesn't just want to control Blandington, does she? It's a bit . . . boring."

"I KNOW!" said Ava. "I have to put on a mask and steal bananas from the supermarket just to keep myself awake."

"*You're* the Masked Banana Bandit!" cried Imogen. "You're the most wanted criminal in town!"

Ava laughed, shaking her head. "That is *tragic*. You guys really need to step it up."

"Tell me about it," said Imogen. "Listen—I don't suppose you could do me a favor?" She realized she was pushing her luck at this point, but she had to ask. "Could you just—you know—set my family free? It's not like they're any kind of threat to you. . . ."

"I'm sorry," said Ava. "Mom would kill me. Did you hear about that whole grizzly bear–shark thing? She's developing a new animal-based murder technique, involving a giant squid and a bald eagle, and I really don't want her to test it out on me. It's going to be hard enough to explain why you're not dead—"

"Thanks anyway," Imogen said quickly, before Ava could change her mind about the Imogen-not-being-dead thing.

Ava smiled apologetically. "I could go down into the dungeon and take them some cheese and crackers?" she offered.

"That would be great," said Imogen. "Otherwise, they'll start eating one another, and you really don't want to have to clean up after that."

"Ew. No, I don't. Cannibalism is *so* suburban." She pushed herself off the workbench and helped Imogen down, too. "Shall we get out of here?"

Imogen grinned. "Yes, please," she said. "Just one more question: How come there's no record of you anywhere? I Googled you and looked on Instagram and Facebook and in all the official Kruk biographies, and the unofficial biographies, and the Kruk Reddit—"

Ava pulled a face. "They're *brutal* on there."

"—but there's nothing about you anywhere."

Ava rolled her eyes. "That's because Mom and the other senior Kruks are grooming me to be leader someday. They want me out of the spotlight till then. So I don't even get to perform in my end-of-term ballet shows, which is so unfair."

"No way!" said Imogen. "Big Nana wants me to be the leader of the Crims, too!"

"Shut up!" said Ava, and high-fived her.

"It's a shame we'll be mortal enemies one day."

"Yeah, well. We have a while before that happens."

"Tell you what," Imogen said as they walked toward the woodshop door. "I've had an idea to explain the whole me-being-alive thing."

Ava crossed her arms. "I'm listening."

"We set off some of the dynamite and tell everyone that the Masked Banana Bandit was trying to blow up the school. You can say that you tracked me down to murder me, but found me wrestling with the Masked Banana Bandit—and then the school newspaper turned up and took loads of photos of us together, so you'd have been the prime suspect if I'd gone missing. So you helped me overpower the Masked Banana Bandit instead."

"I like it." Ava nodded slowly. "Plus, the school newspaper really is going to love this story."

"Are you kidding? It'll be the most exciting thing that has ever happened in Blandington."

"Since I turned up," said Ava, flicking her ponytail.

"And we'll *both* be the most popular girls in school when everyone hears about what heroes we are."

"Just one problem," said Ava. "We have dynamite, but we don't have any matches."

"I do," said Imogen, producing them from her sleeve.

Ava shook her head. "You are *good*," she said. "Let's do this."

CHAPTER FOURTEEN

BY THE TIME Imogen got home from blowing up part of the school, Big Nana was nowhere to be seen—not by Imogen, not even by a wood pigeon with particularly good eyesight who was hanging around in the tree outside.

"Hello?" Imogen called, walking through the eerily empty hall.

Nothing.

Please don't let them have taken Big Nana too. . . .

"Hello? Big Nana?" she called, opening the kitchen door.

Nothing there either.

"Barney?" she called. But he didn't come running.

Imogen went outside—the black sedan was parked outside, so Big Nana must have come home after the failed kidnapping. So where was she? And where was Barney? He wasn't in the back of the car where they'd left him. Had he been taken too?

And then Imogen remembered: Crim House was full of secret passages.

She ran back inside and pressed on the picture of Great-Uncle Umbrage, and the door to the tunnel swung open. Imogen ran down it and explored every turn, but she couldn't find Big Nana anywhere.

She must be in another passage, thought Imogen. *If I were Big Nana, which thankfully I'm not because she has much worse dental hygiene than me, where would I dig a secret tunnel?*

I'd want the tunnel to be as close to my bed as possible, in case the Kruks turned up in the middle of the night.

Imogen ran up to Big Nana's room. She hadn't been in there for years, but it hadn't changed at all. The walls were still papered with a pattern that looked like a harmless, chintzy floral print from a distance but from close up, turned out to be a twisting pattern of deadly nightshade and barbed wire; there were little porcelain figurines on the mantelpiece—a pickpocket, a serial killer, and a small child throttling a lamb. The only thing that was different were the framed photographs; Big Nana had added to them over the years as the children had grown up. There were Nick and Nate, stealing first prize in the Blandington Talent Contest from the tap-dancing poodle that had won; there was Isabella, riding her first stolen tricycle; and there was Delia, all dressed up for the Blandington Spring Fling, her reluctant date—one of the members of No Direction, a really, really awful local band—handcuffed to her wrist. Imogen felt a pang. *At least I know where they are and that they're alive. All I have to do is find Big Nana and get them all back. . . .*

Imogen knocked on walls and levered up loose floorboards, searching for the passage. She emptied Big Nana's closet, tossing aside caftans and seventies trousers and one extremely horrible, pink, ruffled dress—and there, at the back, she found a patch of wall that was a slightly different color from the wall around it.

Imogen pressed on the wall, and a hidden door sprang open. She noted with disappointment that it didn't lead to a secret passage; it opened a small, secret enclosure. Inside was the large toy hippo that Imogen had found in the Kruks' Loot Room—the toy hippo that Big Nana had loved as a child. And next to it was a children's picture book that Imogen hadn't seen since she was very, very young: *Ten Little Mice in the Woods*. Big Nana used to read this to her when she was babysitting!

The cover showed ten terrified-looking mice cowering in an ominous, bird-shaped shadow. She opened the book and started reading. The story started innocently enough: *Once upon a moonlit night* . . . But then an owl turned up and started stealing the mice with its sharp, owl-y talons, taking them back to its horrible, twiggy nest. And then, on the final page . . . the owl ate all the mice.

What kind of picture book is this? Imogen thought. She had forgotten how disturbing the story was.

Imogen turned the page, expecting some kind of happy ending—wouldn't a Red Riding Hood character turn up and cut the owl open and release the mice? Wouldn't it all turn out to be a dream? But that was it. No more pages.

So that's why I have recurring nightmares about creatures with massive beaks, Imogen realized.

But something else about the book made her feel uncomfortable—something other than the creepy plot and horribly realistic colored-pencil illustrations. She felt as though she'd read the story recently. Or had seen some kind of adaptation— Had it been turned into a musical? Or a terrifying Netflix series? Not that she could think of. *Probably just* déjà vu . . .

And why did Big Nana hide the book in the secret compartment at the back of her closet, like it was one of her most treasured possessions?

Imogen flipped back to the front of the book and noticed an inscription on the title page that she'd missed the first time around. An inscription in Big Nana's handwriting.

To Elsa, my psychotic little kumquat!
Love and kisses from your favorite aunt
xxxx

"Kumquat"?

"Your favorite *aunt*"?

Elsa?

The hippo?

What?

Where?

Who?

Why?

And then it hit Imogen like a ton of imaginary but upsetting bricks.

BIG NANA IS A KRUK.

It seemed impossible. She couldn't believe she was even *thinking* it. But the more she thought about it, the more she realized that it was the only plausible explanation.

That was why the hippo had been in the Kruk's Loot Room.

That was why Big Nana had such piercing blue eyes.

That was why—

Imogen glanced up and screamed. Because Big Nana was standing in the closet doorway, watching her.

Imogen shoved the hippo and picture book back into the secret compartment and stood up, terrified.

"Sorry, my broken, little stained-glass window," said

Big Nana, smiling. "I didn't mean to startle you. I'm just so relieved to see you!" And then she noticed that Imogen didn't seem that pleased to see her. "Are you all right?" she asked.

Imogen started backing away, her skin prickling. She hit the back of the closet. So she started backing away in the other direction.

"What's wrong?" said Big Nana, taking a step toward her.

"Stay back!" shouted Imogen, cursing herself for not having a weapon on her. Ava would never have made a mistake like that. "You *know* what's wrong! You *lied* to me! AGAIN!"

"What?"

"*You're* the mole! You've been leaking our secrets to the Kruks!"

Big Nana looked shocked. "How can you *say* that to me?" she asked. "What's got into you? Have you been eating pick-and-mix again? I've told you, too many gummy cola bottles make you paranoid. Gobstoppers give you delusions of grandeur—much more fun—"

"You're a *Kruk*!" shouted Imogen.

Big Nana looked stunned.

And then she looked ashamed.

And then she looked angry.

And then she looked upset.

She was really very good at conveying her emotions through her facial expressions.

Imogen was slightly less good at conveying hers, so this is what they were: fear, horror, and revulsion.

Big Nana looked at the ground. And then she looked up at Imogen, sadness and guilt in her Kruk-like eyes. "You're right," she said at last. "I should have known you would figure it out eventually." She took a deep breath and started to pace the room.

She's gearing up for an evil monologue, Imogen realized. She was dreading what she might hear but riveted at the same time. She would finally find out the truth.

"My legal name is Gerda Kruk," monologued Big Nana. "I am Luka Kruk's twin. When I was in my early twenties, the question of who would succeed Niklas Kruk came up. I wanted and deserved to lead the family. But because Luka was the male, Niklas made him his heir. Even though he was a terrible leader! Our father was a great man, and a brilliant shoplifter—also a talented part-time wizard—but he was no feminist."

Imogen couldn't believe what she was hearing. *Big Nana is Luka Kruk's twin?* She still stood with her back to the wall, rigid with fear.

Big Nana stopped walking and put one hand on the mantelpiece, as if to steady herself. "Luka changed the whole structure of the family," she continued. "He wanted me to start over at the bottom and 'earn' my position at the top. Can you imagine? *Me!* I'd already invented the Beatles and caused the Cuban missile crisis and forged the Sphinx . . . That took a lot of skill and a lot of mud, I can tell you." Big Nana shook her head. "I was furious, as you can imagine. So that night I walked out of Krukingham Palace and never returned.

"That same evening—before I walked out on the family forever—I'd started reading Elsa a bedtime story. Lovely book it was—*Ten Little Mice in the Woods.* I used to read it to you when you were a baby too. But before I could finish it, Luka called me out of the room to talk to him. Just like him—such a selfish man. And I was so upset by his whole start-from-the-bottom nonsense that I decided to leave, right there and then. And I completely forgot to finish Elsa's story." She sighed. "I've kept the book ever since, as a reminder of the life I left behind. And I'm beginning to think Elsa hasn't forgotten it, either. . . ."

Imogen felt a chill. Big Nana—the woman she had known all her life—had once read bedtime stories to Elsa Kruk, the craziest, most dangerous, blondest criminal of her generation. How could Imogen ever trust Big Nana again?

"I'm not the mole," Big Nana continued. (She certainly had more monologuing stamina than Imogen.) "Leaving the Kruks was the best thing I ever did. As soon

222

as I started living in the real world, I realized how wrong it was to be violent and terrifying all the time, and so cruel to bees. And a couple of weeks after I left, at a Bank Robbers Anonymous meeting, I met Herbert Crim. Your grandfather. We started a new crime family—one that cares about one another as much as it cares about making it onto a Top Ten Deadliest Police Chases list. One that doesn't cause so much harm. Well, apart from Aunt Bets. But what can you do? I can't control who marries into the family. . . ." She looked Imogen in the eye. "Believe me, my squashed fruit fly. I grew up in Krukingham Palace. I know the Kruks. And I know that I'm right to be scared of them. Elsa is crazy. Not the way crazy golf is crazy. Not even the way crazy paving is crazy, though what were people thinking in the seventies? Front paths shouldn't be so stressful to look at." She shook her head. "No. Elsa's crazy like Jack the Ripper was crazy, but more so, because at least he had the decency to die in the nineteenth century. I don't know what she's going to do to us, but I know that it is going to be unbelievably painful and unpleasant. People are going to make true crime dramas out of this."

But Imogen had had enough. "Stop," she said. *Who are you?* she thought. She was finding it hard to look at Big Nana, so she closed her eyes for a moment. "I need to be alone," she said. "I need to absorb all of this."

Big Nana nodded, head bowed. "You are the least

absorbent of all my grandchildren. The others are like sponges—silly, soggy sponges."

But Imogen wasn't listening. She had thought she knew what it felt like to be betrayed. But she hadn't. Not until now. "I'm going home," she said.

Somehow she managed to stagger upstairs to her apartment.

She collapsed on the couch.

She couldn't seem to move.

She couldn't even seem to blink. But then her eyes got very dry, so she did.

Big Nana. A Kruk?

What did this mean for her?

What did this mean for the rest of her family?

What was she going to *do*?

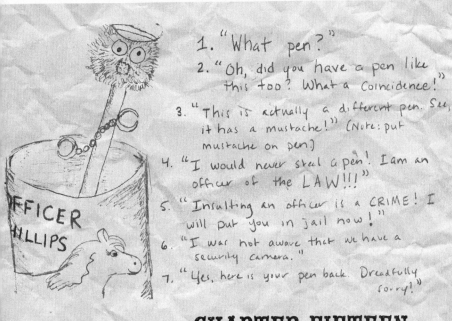

1. "What pen?"
2. "Oh, did you have a pen like this too? What a coincidence!"
3. "This is actually a different pen. See, it has a mustache!" (Note: put mustache on pen)
4. "I would never steal a pen! I am an officer of the LAW!!!"
5. "Insulting an officer is a CRIME! I will put you in jail now!"
6. "I was not aware that we have a security camera."
7. "Yes, here is your pen back. Dreadfully sorry!"

CHAPTER FIFTEEN

IMOGEN WAS IN the middle of a dream. A terrifying one—like a nightmare, but worse. A night-stallion, if you will.

She was dreaming that she was a Kruk, which meant she had lovely blue eyes and was wearing a very nice Stella McCartney shirt, but which also meant she was completely psychopathic and was about to kill Big Nana. She was rooting around in a drawer filled with venomous snakes and child-sized handguns, looking for something . . . and then she found it: a syringe, filled with poison . . .

And then suddenly, a huge monster was standing over

her—a monster with overly curly fur, a monster that was drooling . . .

Imogen woke up with a start. The monster wasn't a monster. It was Barney. He was panting, and drooling, and staring right into her eyes.

Imogen pushed Barney away, groaning. He really was the most pathetic attack dog in the history of pathetic attack dogs, which is long and filled with adorable puppies that chased butterflies while their owners were murdered, often with machetes. Almost every single Crim had been kidnapped, and Barney hadn't done a thing to intervene. When Imogen had been hauled into the ice cream truck outside school, Barney had just laid there and watched them take her. And he was doing the same thing now—sitting there, panting, staring at her.

"Go away!" she shouted. "I don't have any dog food. Go and catch a rat or something if you're hungry." But Barney stayed right where he was.

Imogen sat up in bed and rubbed the sleep out of her eyes. She was truly alone in her fight to get her family back now. And she was ready for the most desperate of desperate measures: She was ready to go to the police. She knew Big Nana would hate her for it. But Big Nana was a Kruk—so did it matter what she thought anymore?

She stood up and looked down at Barney, who was still just sitting there, staring at her.

Hang on, thought Imogen. *Did I just see something flash in Barney's eyes?*

"Barney," she said, patting her knees. "Here, boy."

Barney padded over to her, wagging his tail, still staring straight at her.

She grabbed his collar and pulled him onto her lap. He really was extraordinarily heavy for a dog. . . .

And then she remembered . . . Barney had come home with Al. *Fake* Al.

Who was actually Gunther Kruk.

She felt around Barney's neck. Nothing. There was nothing on his stomach, either. But underneath his ear . . .

A switch.

She flicked the switch. There was a whirring noise, and Barney just sort of—turned off.

Imogen stared at the dog, stunned.

Barney was *a robot.*

What the . . . ?

Imogen wasn't sure what to do. Why would the Kruks send a robot to Crim House? *Because robots can record things and transmit data. . . .* Imogen felt sick. *Barney is the mole.*

And she had let him sleep *in her bedroom.* Ugh! She couldn't even trust animals anymore!

And then she heard the front door crash open—and then footsteps, running up the stairs. Too many and too heavy and too dangerous sounding to be Big Nana.

She heard maniacal laughter. *Evil* laughter. *German* laughter.

And then she heard someone shout: *"Wir werden Sie zu töten, und nehmen Sie Ihr Geld!!!"*

It was the Kruk family motto: "We will kill you and take your money!"

Imogen sat extremely still, with her hands shaking. She hardly dared to breathe. *It's actually happening,* she realized, *just like Big Nana said it would. The Kruks have come to get us. The dog-mole must have deactivated the electronic security system. . . . But where is Big Nana now? Have they found her already?*

Feeling sicker than ever, Imogen ran down the back stairs to the Loot Room—Big Nana's designated emergency meeting place.

Please let Big Nana be here. She punched the code into the door.

And for once, her wish came true.

There, waiting for her, was her grandmother, dressed all in black, strands of red hair escaping from beneath her balaclava. Imogen felt a rush of relief.

"Thank badness you're okay," said Big Nana, giving Imogen a rather painful hug. "It's time. We have to go to the bunker."

"The bunker?" said Imogen.

"You know," Big Nana said impatiently. "The bunker."

Imogen didn't know. She'd never heard of the Crims having a bunker.

"Every family has a bunker to escape to when their rivals break down their front door and threaten to kill them all," said Big Nana.

"I'm not sure they do," said Imogen.

Big Nana shrugged. "Maybe it's just a Crim thing. And a Kruk thing. Anyway. There's a secret passage right behind that collection of coronation mugs for King Edward VIII, who was never crowned, rendering the mugs totally pointless. Let's go!"

Imogen followed Big Nana down a dark, dank tunnel. The floor of the corridor was damp and muddy, and the whole thing smelled worryingly of gas. They crawled blindly, and in silence, until Imogen's knees started to cramp up.

"I hate to sound like Delia on a long car journey," Imogen said, "but are we nearly there yet?"

"And I hate to sound like myself on a long car journey," said Big Nana, "but shut up and be grateful I haven't left you behind to be murdered by a woman who carries a nuclear warhead in her handbag."

They crawled on, not speaking. The tunnel seemed to get narrower and narrower the farther they went. And then, just as Imogen noticed a nasty, insistent, ratty-sounding squeaking coming from above her, the tunnel spat them out into a cold, dark room, as though they tasted revolting.

"Bunker, sweet bunker!" said Big Nana, turning on the light, which buzzed and flashed a few times and then stayed on, casting a greenish wash over the windowless room.

Bunkers are, by definition, pretty depressing places, but Imogen couldn't imagine a more depressing bunker than this. The walls were made of cinder block, and a label on the ceiling read "Asbestos Tiles. Do Not Touch Unless You Want to Die a Slow, Painful Death." There was no furniture, unless you counted a broken, fly-covered toilet, which Imogen didn't. The only food was a few cans of spaghetti and meatballs, labeled "Best Before: 2001." Scattered across the floor were some *Reader's Digest*s, dated from 1992. Imogen spotted more than one fanny pack.

Big Nana lowered herself onto a moldy-looking beanbag on the floor. "This isn't so bad!" she said, which was exactly the opposite of what Imogen was thinking. "We can stay here for a few years at least. I've got some sesame seeds stuck in my teeth from breakfast. If I plant them in the mud, maybe they'll grow. . . ."

"No," said Imogen. "Absolutely, definitely not. What did you teach me? When the Kruks attack, we have to take action. Our whole family has been kidnapped. We know who's behind it. And now they have taken over our house, too. We only have one option left."

"That's right: stay here until the coast is clear, and catch up on early nineties fashion tips. What do you think of bodysuits?"

"No." Imogen took a deep breath—this wasn't going to go down well. "We have to go to . . . THE POLICE."

"THE POLICE?"

"THE POLICE."

Big Nana was horrified. "I can't! Never! Not unless the rats carry my corpse in!"

Imogen was getting frustrated. "It's better than your plan. You seriously think we should just sit here, hoping that the Kruks get bored of having our family around and let them go?"

"It's a possibility—have you ever been in a room with Knuckles for more than ten minutes? Very damaging to the eardrums."

"They won't let them go!" said Imogen, who was starting to feel furious as well as frustrated. "Why would they? Elsa is crazy. You've told me that yourself enough times. And they've put masses of effort into staging the kidnappings. It's almost as if—" And then it hit her—what *Ten Little Mice in the Woods* had reminded her of. It wasn't a musical adaptation, or a Netflix series. It was *her life.* "It's almost as if she's trying to recreate the way the mice disappeared in *Ten Little Mice in the Woods.*"

Big Nana stared at Imogen, nodding, horrified. "Elsa

is certainly crazy enough to do that. . . ."

"*Please*, Big Nana," begged Imogen. "Elsa's going to kill them all in one of about four hundred very painful, experimental ways! We *have* to go to the police."

But Big Nana shook her head.

"Come on," said Imogen, softening. "We'll refuse to talk to anyone except PC Donnelly—he hardly counts as a policeman. He's got Crim blood."

"People will see us *walking into a police station of our own accord*! I have my street cred to think of!"

"You're way too old to have street cred. And anyway, we can wear disguises."

Big Nana sighed. "Fine," she said. "Just like every time we play backgammon, you win," she said. She heaved herself onto her feet and unzipped a suitcase that was lying in the corner of the bunker, under several 1970s copies of *Rogue* magazine—*the* style bible for criminal couture. Clouds of dust rose into the air as she did so, and she had a coughing fit so extreme that her face turned purple. Imogen had to go and hit her on the back until she recovered. "Thank you," she said. "Now . . ." She opened the suitcase and pulled out two disguises—a Victorian maid's costume and a chimney sweep's outfit, complete with brush. "These belonged to your great-great-grandfather Jimeny Crim," she said. "Times have changed, so these aren't exactly the

232

latest fashions, but they'll do the job."

Imogen squeezed into the maid's dress and tied the lace bonnet onto her head. She looked like a character from a period drama—a really bad one that wouldn't even win a technical award for lighting design. She turned around to see Big Nana pulling the chimney sweep's cap on. Her grandmother looked surprisingly like a nine-year-old Victorian boy, just with more wrinkles and slightly nicer teeth.

"Let's go," said Big Nana, pulling aside one of the cinder blocks to reveal another secret passage. "This one leads straight to the police station parking lot." She dropped to her knees and muttered, "I'm getting too old for this nonsense."

The passage brought them out into an unused shed behind a row of parked cars. Imogen dusted herself off and was about to march into the police station when Big Nana called her back.

"I can't just walk in there, Imogen," she said, stepping from foot to foot, as though she needed a wee (maybe she did—the bunker's broken toilet was too disgusting to sit on). "I'm going to find a crime to commit. Just a little one. That way they'll bring me in in handcuffs, and I'll be able to hold my head up high."

"Fine," said Imogen. "But hurry up!"

Big Nana whipped a skeleton key out of her pocket and jimmied open the door of one of the many beige Volvos parked nearby.

"Stealing a car is not a little crime!" hissed Imogen.

"I'm not stealing it," Big Nana said, slipping into the driver's seat. "I'm moving it. To the disabled parking space. Because as you may have noticed, I'm not disabled at all! Psych!"

"Please don't ever say 'psych' again," Imogen said as her grandmother swerved into the disabled spot and stepped out of the car, looking very pleased with herself.

"Now we just need to wait for them to arrest me," said Big Nana, leaning on the hood, as if she were posing for a very niche fashion shoot.

But no one seemed to want to arrest them.

Imogen could see the back of a police officer's head through the station window. She was pretty sure it was PC Donnelly. He was concentrating very hard on his computer screen and didn't seem at all interested in what was going on in the parking lot. Which wasn't surprising, because the only interesting things that happen in parking lots take place after dark and are extremely unpleasant.

"Back in a minute," Imogen said. "I'll just go and let Donnelly know that you'd like to be arrested."

She pushed open the glass door to the police station. PC Donnelly didn't look up—he had his headphones on and was watching a movie. A movie about horses, Imogen realized as she approached the desk. A movie about tiny horses, running around a field in slow motion, shaking their tiny manes and smiling tiny smiles.

She knew a police officer who was very keen on little horses. And it wasn't PC Donnelly . . .

Before she could creep back out of the station, the police officer turned around.

PC Phillips. Imogen cursed herself for not being more careful.

PC Phillips didn't look any more pleased to see Imogen than she was to see him. He minimized his screen and said: "Don't know what that video was. Just popped up on my screen while I was reading a very official police article about handcuffs and pepper spray and muscles."

"Is PC Donnelly here?" Imogen asked.

"Nope," said PC Phillips, clipping and unclipping his handcuffs. "He hasn't been here for a week. No idea why. He hasn't called in sick or anything."

Imogen hit her forehead with her hand, because sometimes you feel so stupid that you actually do that sort of thing. *Of course!* PC Donnelly was a Crim. Why hadn't it occurred to her to check in on him? He must have been kidnapped too!

"Hey," said PC Phillips, who was now looking out of the window at the parking lot. "Is that your grandmother?

And is that my car? And is it in the disabled parking space? And did she put it there?"

"Yes . . . ," said Imogen.

"To which question?"

"All of them."

PC Phillips snatched up his handcuffs and marched outside, looking unpleasantly pleased with himself. Imogen hurried after him.

"'Ello, 'ello, 'ello," he said to Big Nana, rocking on his heels.

"Good-bye, good-bye, good-bye," said Big Nana, and she ran back to the secret tunnel entrance—but PC Phillips was too fast for her.

"I'm arresting you in the name of the law, which, as everybody knows, is Sandra," he said, snapping the handcuffs onto her wrists.

"I'll speak only to PC Donnelly!" Big Nana cried as PC Phillips pushed her toward the police station.

"Then you'll be silent for a very long time," said PC Phillips, grinning madly, like an overexcited cat. "PC Donnelly has gone missing."

And then Big Nana swore, which made PC Phillips very happy, because it meant he could charge her with verbally assaulting a police officer; he loved charging people with crimes almost as much as he loved miniature ponies.

He marched Big Nana down the long corridors, past

the cell the Crims had been released from a few weeks' previously. "Wait," said Imogen. "We need to tell you something! We need to report a crime! A really serious one!"

"Then you're in luck," said PC Phillips. "Because I'm taking you to see the new chief constable."

Big Nana stopped walking. "New chief constable?" she said.

"Yes," said PC Phillips, pushing her in the back so she stumbled forward, stopping outside a big, black door. "He's got a great mustache. And a good name. Literally: Norman Gud."

Imogen looked at Big Nana.

Big Nana looked at Imogen.

Imogen was feeling rather guilty for insisting they go to the police. She had a sinking feeling that, like *Ten Little Mice in the Woods*, this was not going to end well.

Chief Constable Gud's office looked like an ordinary chief constable's office—lots of photographs of him shaking hands with famous people, a box of doughnuts, several speed handcuffing trophies—except that the famous people he was shaking hands with were all terrorists, or dictators, or members of U2.

Chief Constable Gud himself looked a lot like an ordinary chief constable—shiny buttons on his uniform, very good posture, a really marvelous mustache—but his hair was so blond, it was white, and his eyes were piercing and blue, and his name tag said "Stefan Kruk," which was a bit of a giveaway.

"So," said Stefan Kruk. "We meet again."

"Actually we meet for the first time," said Imogen, who was a stickler for accuracy in stressful situations.

"Whatever," Stefan said dismissively. "You Crims are all the same. Pathetic. Stupid. Bad at chess."

Imogen opened her mouth to protest—she had been president of Lilyworth Chess Club and was famed for her use of the Sicilian defense—but Big Nana gave her a "shut up" look, so she shut her mouth again, and pretended she'd just been doing an impression of a turbot.

"You have fallen right into my trap," Stefan continued, leaning back in his chair.

"Actually, we *walked* into it," corrected Imogen.

Stefan looked at Big Nana. "Is she always this much of a pedant?" he asked.

Big Nana nodded, rolling her eyes, as if to say, *What can you do?*

Stefan steepled his fingers and leaned across his desk. "If you ever want to see your family members alive again, you will come with me. OR ELSA!"

"Else," Imogen said quietly.

"No. *Elsa*," said Stefan. "That was an intentional pun. What, you don't like puns?"

"Of course I do," said Imogen. "I dote uh-pun them."

"That was terrible," said Stefan.

"Not my best," Imogen admitted. "But I am under quite a lot of stress at the moment."

"Using puns against us," muttered Big Nana, shaking her head. "The Kruks are even more diabolical than I remembered."

Stefan clapped his hands and shouted, "Up!" Big Nana and Imogen scrambled to their feet.

"Out!" he shouted, and they walked silently out of his office, past PC Phillips, toward the parking lot.

"In!" he shouted, and Big Nana and Imogen slid into the back seat of a waiting police car.

"Drive!" Stefan yelled as he climbed into the front seat. "Oh, wait. You can't do that. That's my job."

We have to get out of here, Imogen thought—and a plan began to form in her mind. . . .

Stefan started up the engine and pulled away, humming a sinister tune as he drove through Blandington.

"That's the Kruk's premurder anthem," hissed Big Nana. "They sing it to relax themselves before a really big killing spree, often involving goats. We need to get out of here."

"I don't get it!" Imogen whispered back. "Why do they want to kill us? What's in it for them? It can't be to get Blandington. . . ."

"Let's not worry about that now, my prize turnip. We need a plan."

"I have one," said Imogen. "I think. Play along."

"I haven't brought my flute," said Big Nana.

Imogen looked at her.

"Sorry," mouthed Big Nana, and she squeezed Imogen's hand. "I trust you, whatever your plan is. Let's do it."

Imogen closed her eyes, took a deep breath, and started twitching and yelping; eyes rolling and mouth agape.

"She's having a seizure!" screamed Big Nana. "Stop the car! My granddaughter has diabetes, and she hasn't had anything to eat today! She's going into a coma!"

"Ah well," said Stefan, eyes firmly on the road. "I was going to kill her anyway. It'll save me the effort."

"Pathetic!" said Big Nana. "You're not man enough to kill her yourself."

"Of course I am," said Stefan, taking his eyes off the road. "I am extremely man. I have extra man chromosomes and everything." As if determined to prove it, he pulled the car over, climbed out, and walked around to the back seat. . . .

Imogen waited, eyes closed.

She had to get the timing just right.

Click. The door opened. And so did Imogen's eyes. She head butted Stefan, knocking him back into the street, and ran as fast as her gold-medal-in-the-hundred-meter-race legs would carry her, which was really quite fast.

"I don't think so!" Stefan shouted, catching up.

If she could just push a little bit farther . . .

But she couldn't. Stefan grabbed her by the hair and shoved her to the ground.

Imogen tried to get up, but Stefan's grip was too strong. She lay there, defeated.

But then she heard Big Nana scream from the car behind her: "Keep going! I'm counting on you! All the Crims are!"

Stefan looked up. He was obviously debating who was the bigger prize—Imogen or Big Nana. Imogen took her chance. She swiveled herself around and kicked Stefan as hard as she could in a place that men really don't like to be kicked, and then she pelted away as fast as she could.

Never buy avocados again! Plant a tree and always have free avocados!

HOW TO MAKE RATATOUILLE OUT OF ANYTHING

FREE PATTERN! Adorable quilted weapon cozy...

20 TREASURED MONUMENTS RIPE FOR STEALING!

CHAPTER SIXTEEN

IMOGEN RAN THROUGH the streets of Blandington, not daring to look back. At first she heard Stefan's footsteps chasing after her, but at some point he must have given up and turned back to Big Nana, because by the time she arrived at Crim House, she was alone.

Imogen wasn't really sure why she'd come back here. And she wasn't really sure what to do next. She stood on the street corner, panting, trying to get her breath back, watching the house for signs of movement.

Were the Kruks still inside?

It didn't look like it. . . .

Using Big Nana's Extremely Silent and Sneaky

Walking technique, she crept up the back path, stepping around Freddie's booby traps, and opened the door.

The house was silent. It was also extremely messy. More messy than usual, which is saying something, because you usually had to step over several tortoises and a couple crossbows to go to the bathroom.

The place had been ransacked. Every cupboard was open; stolen takeout containers and jewelry and balaclavas were scattered across the floor. Pictures had been ripped from their frames, and every single book had been torn from the bookshelves. Imogen spotted Delia's signed Kitty Penguin poster lying on the living room floor and carefully picked it up. *Delia will be home soon,* she told herself. *Although I could use her help right now. . . .*

Imogen picked her way downstairs to the Loot Cellar. The door was hanging from its hinges. It had been blown open, by the looks of things. Imogen stepped inside, fear spreading up her spine.

What have they taken? Imogen had spent a lot of time looking around the Loot Room—too much time, you might say. Time she could have spent doing something useful, like learning Mandarin or figuring out how to stop her relatives being kidnapped. She worked her way around the Loot Room from front to back, but as far as she could tell, everything was still here—Uncle Knuckles's tap shoes; the original Broadway cast of *Cats*; even Uncle

Clyde's million-pound lunch box.

Imogen was puzzled, and not by the sudoku collection Sam had stolen from the local old people's home. Sure, the Crims' collection contained a lot of rubbish. But there were some valuable things down here, too. The lunch box, for instance.

If the Kruks weren't interested in the Crims' valuable belongings, then they must have been looking for something specific.

But what?

Could it possibly be . . . ?

Imogen ran to Big Nana's room. Her grandmother's things were everywhere—the framed photographs had been pulled from the walls and trodden into the carpet; the pillows had been slashed open and lay on the floor, as if a duck massacre had recently taken place there; and Big Nana's clothes were all over the bed. The only thing missing from the room was Big Nana.

Imogen pushed aside the mattress, which had been thrown against the closet, which had been ransacked—but the secret door at the back was shut. She pressed on it, and it sprang open once again.

The space behind the closet was untouched. The toy hippo and the picture book were still inside.

Imogen picked up the book and flipped through it. What was it that Big Nana had said? *That she never went back to finish reading the story.* . . . Imogen turned to the very front of the book and read the inscription. *To Elsa.*

Everyone said that Elsa was crazy. And word just got out that Big Nana was still alive. How crazy *was* Elsa, exactly? Crazy enough to destroy an entire family because she didn't know the ending to a picture book?

"Barney!" Imogen called.

She heard a bark, and sure enough, Barney came bounding toward her, wagging his creepily realistic tail. The Kruks must have left him behind to guard Crim House.

She held up the book.

"Is this what you want?" she asked.

The dog made an assortment of beeping sounds and lunged toward the book. Imogen yanked it away just in time. Barney growled a metallic sort of growl that made Imogen shudder, and then he lunged at her again. He missed and chewed through Big Nana's iron bedpost instead, as though it was no more substantial than a stick of licorice.

"Not so fast," Imogen said. "I'll come on my own, in my own time. And if you don't want me to destroy this book, you won't touch a single hair on the head of a single Crim. Unless it's one of Josephine's gray hairs—she's always asking people to pull them out for her, so she'd probably be quite grateful. Got it?"

She didn't wait for a reply. She reached for the switch under Barney's ear and flicked it off. The dog gave a strange, metallic sighing noise and crumpled to the floor.

She pulled on her coat, put the picture book in her pocket, and, staggering under the weight of the robot dog thrown over her shoulder, she left Crim House and headed down the hill. *Time to pay a visit to the Guds . . .*

CHAPTER SEVENTEEN

IMOGEN STOOD OUTSIDE the Guds' white picket fence, eyeing the garden gno, watching for signs of life (or death) at the windows. She saw a curtain in one of the upstairs rooms twitch. Mind you, if she were a curtain belonging to a Kruk, she would twitch too; the poor thing was probably traumatized by whatever horrors it had witnessed.

She had no idea what was going to happen next, but she had a feeling—a strong, unpleasant, terrifying feeling—that she wasn't going to like it.

Imogen powered up the robot dog again. It stood up and shook itself off, and then Barney was back, barking and licking Imogen's face. She looked into Barney's eyes. "I'm here," she said, hoping she sounded braver than she felt. "And I want to see my family."

The door to the house creaked open, and a stiff-looking butler appeared on the doorstep—the same stiff-looking butler she'd met at Krukingham Palace, who had been so keen on coloring books and poisoning people with cyanide.

"Welcome," he said, but he didn't sound as though he meant it.

Imogen stepped into the house. The inside was just as boring as the outside—the floor was covered in the same beige carpets favored by everyone in Blandington (apart from the Crims) and the walls were papered in a revolting floral pattern that managed to be simultaneously dull and exhausting to look at. Gold-framed, soft-focus family portraits were dotted around: a school photograph of Ava; Ava with Elsa, laughing on a beach somewhere; Elsa with a strange-looking boy, who Imogen knew was strange because he was wearing a T-shirt with "strange" written on the front . . .

"Follow me," said the butler, and led Imogen down a hall, and down some stairs, and down some more stairs, and then down an escalator, and then down an elevator, until Imogen started to worry he was taking her right to the center of Earth to be melted to death by molten rock. But he wasn't, luckily.

The elevator opened on a gold-plated entrance hall. *Of course,* Imogen thought as she followed the butler out of the lift. *The Kruks' Blandington headquarters isn't just an ordinary, boring house. The ordinary, boring house is a cover for a very extraordinary, exciting underground palace.* And from the looks of things, the Kruks had really gone to town this time. Literally—they had stolen landmarks from all over London to decorate their Blandington pad. The statue of Eros from the middle of Piccadilly Circus was taking up most of the entrance hall, and Imogen noticed the London Eye—a huge Ferris wheel that usually sat next to the river Thames—in what looked like a children's playroom.

"This way," said the butler, stepping into the hall—and slipping over straightaway. Gold floors are pretty slippery, it turns out. The butler swore under his breath and gripped on to the handrail on one of the walls. This was clearly a regular problem.

Imogen followed suit—the butler was wearing a very distinctive suit—and the two of them slipped and slid their way down the entrance hall, crashing into Eros more than once, gripping on to the handrail like people who have never been ice-skating before and never want to go again.

Eventually, after falling over a few more times, they arrived at a big, black door with a sign that read: "Basement Torture Room. Protective Clothing Advised." *This is a bad sign,* Imogen thought. She'd never seen a nastier sign, not even the one in Krukingham Palace that read "Sensory Deprivation Chamber."

The butler unlocked the door with a massive key, and the door swung open. Imogen stepped onto the tiles that lined the outside of the room, and suppressed a scream—because inside the room, which was really more of an indoor swimming pool, was her family. Imogen was glad to see them, but what made her scream was that they were suspended above the swimming pool in a small, square wire cage, looking a bit squashed and unhappy. The adult Crims were standing on the floor of the cage, but there wasn't enough room for the Horrible Children down there, too, so her cousins had climbed up the walls of their prison and were clinging on, looking terrified. Delia spotted Imogen, and her eyes widened. Imogen shook her head just slightly: *Don't say anything. Not yet. . . .*

Big Nana was right at the front of the cage, the side closest to Imogen. She caught Imogen's eye and jerked her head toward the pool. Imogen glanced down and noticed that the water seemed unusually dark and writhe-y. She looked at it more closely—and then wished she hadn't. Because swimming around in the pool, thrashing their small but powerful tails and gnashing their small but powerful teeth, were too many piranhas.

Now I get why Big Nana made me do laps in the piranha pond, thought Imogen. *But there are only about eight piranhas in our pond. It looks as though there might be eight thousand in there. . . .*

"Imogen, darling!" Josephine blowing her a kiss from the back of the cage. "I *knew* you'd come! You could have dressed up a bit for the occasion, though. I always think silk is the best fabric to wear when staging a dramatic rescue."

"Is it really you?" said PC Donnelly, who was squashed up next to Uncle Clyde, looking particularly miserable. "I've never been so pleased to see a Crim in my life! No offense," he said to Aunt Bets, who was baring her teeth at him.

"Hurry up and get us out of here!" said Delia. "The finale of *The Z Factor* is tonight!" *The Z Factor* was Delia's favorite show—a load of people who had failed to make a career in show business competed for the title of world's worst entertainer. Not being forced to watch it had been the one good thing about Delia going missing.

Imogen felt a little surge of joy at seeing her family back together again, despite the piranha-filled circumstances. But there was one person she was particularly anxious to see. . . . "Is Dad there?" she asked.

A hand and a spectacle-wearing head appeared beneath Nick and Nate. "Hello," said Al. "It's been a while. Thirty-four days and nineteen minutes, to be exact."

"I love it when you're exact!" said Imogen.

251

Then a blond, curly haired woman stepped into the room from the gold entrance hall—the same blond, curly haired woman Imogen had seen at school with Ava—and the joy surged right back out of her.

Elsa Kruk.

Imogen had been hoping against hope that Elsa wouldn't appear until she had freed her family. But here she was. Things had just gotten even more dangerous.

And next to Elsa, panting, still looking ridiculously cheerful, trotted Barney.

"Barney!" said Nick and Nate.

"Don't bother," Imogen told them. "He's the mole. The second one. And he's got a circuit board instead of a heart."

The Crims all gasped.

"I knew I was right to hate that dog," muttered Aunt Bets.

"YOU HATE EVERYTHING, THOUGH, YOU DELIGHTFUL SOCIOPATH," pointed out Uncle Knuckles.

Barney stayed by the doorway while Elsa walked around the edge of the room to the tiled area closest to the cage and rested her hand on a lever on the wall—a lever that seemed to be attached to the cage. . . .

And then two Kruk boys, who Imogen realized must be Ava's brothers, followed their mother into the room, with the air of children who have been dragged to their mother's office when they'd much rather be outside playing football. Except that they were wearing tuxedos, because they were Kruks.

"It's *you*!" said all the kidnapped Crims at once, pointing at the boys because the taller of the two was the one who had shoved them all into sacks. And the shorter of the two boys was the strange boy who had tricked them all. They could tell it was him at once, because he had "strange" written across his cummerbund in Swarovski crystals (the Kruks must have been cutting back, diamond-wise).

Imogen recognized them both—they had been two of the children who had sung at Luka Kruk's birthday party, which she and her cousins had crashed for complicated reasons—but they had clearly started experimenting with hair dye.

And then an even more familiar figure followed the boys into the room and hovered behind them, near the door, as though she'd rather not be there—a figure with a great ponytail and a perfect grade point average.

Ava Kruk.

Imogen hadn't seen her since Ava had tried to kill her and they'd made a temporary peace. She looked different— like she hadn't slept much recently. And for the first time since Imogen had met her, she looked a little nervous.

Imogen tried to catch Ava's eye, but she was staring at

the floor, like there was something really interesting about it, which there was (the tiles were made of solid unicorn bone).

Elsa looked annoyed and bored. "Let's get this over with, shall we?" said Elsa. She removed her hand from the lever, took up her evil monologue pose—one arm on her hip, one in the air—and cleared her throat.

"Four score and ten years ago it has been since you betrayed me, Big Nana." She stared right at Big Nana, who was watching her, apparently quite unimpressed, from her position at the front of the cage.

"I don't think that's quite right," piped up Al from the middle of the cage. He was just as pedantic as Imogen and much worse at knowing when to shut up. "A score is twenty years, so that would be ninety years ago—"

"SILENCE!" screamed Elsa. "But point taken." She cleared her throat again. "One score and ten years ago, you, Big Nana, betrayed me. ME! Elsa Kruk! And I have never forgiven you. And I never will."

"If you could just tell me what I did, maybe we could clear this whole thing up," said Big Nana. "We've all been absurdly curious."

"You *know* what you did!" shrieked Elsa like a very bad actress delivering a hammy, amateur performance of Lady Macbeth. "You never finished reading me my story!" She pouted like a six-year-old, but she was thirty-six, so it looked all wrong—like a baby in a suit, except a lot less adorable than that sounds.

I knew it, thought Imogen. She couldn't resist giving herself a mini–high five. A clap, essentially. But no one noticed, which was okay.

"I never got to finish that book!" wailed Elsa. "And it was my *favorite* book! And I've never been able to find another copy—not on eBay, not even on AbeBooks. I have trawled the internet for years! I have trawled the seas, too, for good measure! All I have to show for it is a very advanced knowledge of cyberslang and a lot of halibut. I've even looked in libraries. LIBRARIES! Do you know what libraries smell like?"

"Books and rubber stamps and ink and self-adhesive tape," Imogen muttered wistfully.

Ava looked over from the doorway and gave her a warning "shut up" look.

"WRONG!" shouted Elsa, stamping her food. "They smell of DUST AND OBEDIENCE!"

None of the Crims said anything. There isn't really anything you can say in answer to the phrase "dust and obedience" except "Wouldn't that have been a lovely name for a Victorian novel if someone had thought of it at the time?"

"And now," said Elsa, her evil monologue building to its crescendo, "NOW I WILL HAVE MY REVENGE!"

She looked at Imogen. "You. Get in the cage."

"It looks quite full already," said Imogen.

"I SAID GET IN!" screamed Elsa, leaning toward her, her eyes squeezed shut in fury.

The butler rushed over and grabbed a ladder that was leaning against the wall near the lever, and then rested it against the cage. He climbed up, pressed a button, and the top of the cage popped open. He climbed down and bowed to Imogen. "After you," he said.

Imogen didn't really have much of a choice. She walked around the edge of the room and started to climb the ladder. *Please don't let the Kruks see my hands shaking. . . .* She climbed into the opening at the top of the cage, and Uncle Knuckles, who looked quite relaxed about the whole imminent-death situation, reached up a hand to help her down. She clung on to the side of the cage, right above Big Nana and between Nick and Nate, which was her least favorite place to be, apart from in a pool full of piranhas, which was where she was about to be.

The butler climbed back up the ladder and shut the cage's door. Imogen had no idea how they were going to get out of this one. . . .

She looked down and saw that Uncle Knuckles was now sitting on the floor, poking his feet down into the pool.

"What are you doing?" she hissed.

"IT FEELS GREAT," he "whispered" back. "THE PIRANHAS ARE NIBBLING OFF MY BUNIONS!"

"*You fools!* You thought you could mess with me?" shrieked Elsa, reaching for the lever. "Haven't you heard what they say about me? 'Don't mess with Elsa.' I even have a line of bumper stickers!"

And she started pulling the lever down, to lower the cage into the pool.

Imogen saw Ava squeeze her eyes shut. *Won't you try to stop her?* she thought hopefully. But it was clear that Ava was too afraid of her mother to do that.

And then . . .

"WAIT!" shouted Imogen. She let go of the edge of the cage with one hand, reached into her pocket, and pulled out the copy of *Ten Little Mice in the Woods*.

Elsa let go of the lever. She looked as though she couldn't believe what she was seeing, which, when you consider she was looking at a girl holding a children's picture book, in the middle of a cage full of eccentric criminals, moments away from plunging into a pool full of piranhas, maybe wasn't all that surprising.

Elsa turned to Big Nana. "Are you saying you've had the book *all this time*?"

"I didn't say anything," said Big Nana, "but now that you mention it, yes, I have."

Imogen was confused. "I thought you knew she had

it," she said to Elsa. "I told Barney—the robot dog—"

Elsa turned to the butler, who looked as though he'd been hoping to sneak out of the room, and shouted, "WHY DOES NO ONE AROUND HERE TELL ME ANYTHING?"

"Because most of the people who tell you things end up dead, ma'am," said the butler, with a stiffer bow than usual.

Elsa chose to ignore this remark—luckily for the butler. She turned back to Big Nana and said, "If you still *have* the book, well, that changes everything."

"I always felt terrible that I didn't get to finish reading it to you," said Big Nana. "That's why I kept it. That, and the fact that it's a real collectible. It turns out there was a little misprint at the end. . . ."

"Why don't you finish reading the story now, Big Nana?" said Imogen, looking down at her grandmother. "Wouldn't that fix everything?"

There was a long, tense silence—as long and as tense as a tightrope between two very tall buildings, and just as dangerous—and then, at last, Elsa nodded.

"All right," she said. "I'll hear the end of the story. And then I'll decide whether I still feel like killing you." She turned to the butler, snapped her fingers, and said, "Bring me the story-time chair!"

The butler walked out of the room backward, and

slipped over on the solid-gold floor. And then he picked himself up and went off in search of the chair.

"I'm not promising anything," Elsa said when the butler came back in, carrying the story-time chair (a very old child's chair with an "*E* is for 'Execution'" cushion on it). "I might still kill you all. I'm in a very murderous sort of mood today."

Imogen managed to catch Ava's eye at last. She looked at her as if to say, *Help us!*

Ava gave her the tiniest nod—a nod so small it might not have been a nod at all—and then she stepped forward. "Mom," she said. "Isn't this whole thing kind of weird and mean? Like, how much did this whole piranha tank room even cost? Shouldn't you be saving for my college education?"

"Yeah, Mom," said one of the Kruk boys. "I've been wearing the same tuxedo for, like, three years now. I can barely do my bow tie up, it's so tight! And it's hard playing football in a cummerbund. You say there's no money to buy me a pair of sneakers, but you have plenty of money for piranha tanks—"

"BE QUIET!" shouted Elsa.

They were quiet.

Ava rolled her eyes at Imogen and mouthed, "Parents."

Imogen held the book up in the air again. "I'm going to give this to Big Nana now. Okay?" she said.

"Okay," said Elsa, and settled herself in the story-time chair. "I am sitting comfortably. Big Nana, you may begin."

Big Nana held her hand up, and Imogen passed her the book.

"Right," said Big Nana, opening the book to the first page.

```
"Once upon a moonlit night,
Ten little mice got an awful fright—"
```

"I can't hear you properly!" Elsa shouted again. "Big Nana, you may leave the cage. Stefan! Point your gun at her! And if she tries anything funny, *shoot* your gun at her!" The butler, looking a little put out by all the rushing backward and forward, lowered the ladder back onto the cage, ran up to open the hatch at the top, and climbed back to the ground again. Big Nana, surprisingly nimble, made her way down and waited close to the water's edge while the butler relocked the cage and pulled the ladder away before any of the other Crims could get any ideas. To be honest, they were all too scared to have ideas.

"Stand here!" demanded Elsa, pointing to a spot directly in front of the story-time chair.

Moving slowly, which is how you move when a mass murderer is pointing a gun at you, Big Nana took up her position. She opened the book again. "Ready?" she said.

"Yes," said Elsa, folding her hands in her lap.

Big Nana started to read again.

```
"They were walking through the woods one day,
When one little mouse was taken away.
He was adding up numbers, 'One, two, three,'
When a nasty owl swooped down from a tree—"
```

"NO!" shrieked Elsa, waving her hands madly. "STOP! I want THE VOICES!"

Big Nana sighed. "All right, Elsa, my terrible case of halitosis. I'll start again."

So Big Nana started all over again, this time with THE VOICES.

Imogen listened, rapt, to the story of the ten little mice who lived in the wood, who were just minding their own business, doing things that mice like to do—eating cheese, squeaking, reciting poetry about cats—when for no apparent reason, they started disappearing. The first mouse was captured by the nasty owl while it was doing math problems; the second was taken while it played in the forest amusement park (a glade full of particularly exciting twigs); the third was lured in by the owl's impressive skateboarding tricks. . . . The whole thing was strangely familiar. And Big Nana's performance was masterful. Each mouse had a different, distinctive voice—one had an Irish accent, another an Australian one, a third sounded French—and the owl sounded uncannily like Elsa Kruk herself. Not that Elsa seemed to notice. It was so brilliant that Imogen could understand why Elsa was so angry that Big Nana never finished reading the story. Although nothing could excuse the piranha tank.

Big Nana continued reading:

"The mouse looked up from its cheese, but then
The mouse became victim number ten."

Elsa was on the edge of her seat, her eyes shining with delight (and a little bit of craziness, but mostly delight)— she looked happy. *This is working,* thought Imogen. *We might just get out of this alive. . . .*

Big Nana turned the page to read the very end of the story.

Everyone held their breaths.

But just as she was about to start reading, Ava stomped over to her and grabbed the book out of her hands.

CHAPTER EIGHTEEN

AVA WALKED OVER to the piranha pool and dangled the book over the water. The fish writhed and snapped their tiny jaws.

What was Ava *doing*?

Imogen groaned. This was their one chance of getting out with all their limbs intact. Big Nana *had* to finish reading the story. Imogen had thought Ava was on her side. Had she been wrong?

Elsa fell to her knees. "Don't do it!" she cried. "Please! Don't be cruel to your poor, defenseless mother!"

"Poor? Defenseless? HA!" laughed Ava. "You have a

hand grenade in your pocket right now! And it's made of solid diamond!"

"I have standards," Elsa muttered sulkily.

Ava flicked through the book. "This book is *terrible!*" she said.

"Please!" Elsa said again. "Don't rip the pages!"

Ava shook her head and held the book above the piranha-infested pool again. "*This* is what's so important to you? Important enough for you to uproot your daughter from a wonderful private school in London and drag her to THE MOST BORING TOWN ON EARTH?!"

"Actually," said Freddie, from the back of the cage, "it's not the most boring town on Earth. That particular honor belongs to a town in Iceland where everyone is called Jon and most people die in their thirties of acute interest deficiency."

Ava ignored him. She was focused on her mother, who was cowering at her feet, which means pretending to be a cow out of sheer desperation. "Moo!" said Elsa. "Please! Have mercy!"

"I *told* you moving here was a stupid idea," said Ava, who did not have mercy. "I *told* you the piranha tank was ridiculous. But you said that everything you were doing was necessary—that our family was in danger. And now it turns out you just wanted to find out the end of a picture book that involves TALKING MICE and is illustrated in

COLORED PENCIL??"

Uncle Clyde and Henry and the twins all cheered.

"I'm tired of doing whatever you tell me to do, Mum!" cried Ava. "Don't I deserve to be happy too? I wanted to go to the anime convention in Japan with Uncle Dedrik, BUT NOOOOO! Now I'll never get to meet a grown woman dressed up as a massive rabbit, or sit on a talking toilet."

"You could visit Jack Wooster," said Uncle Clyde. "He has some talking toilets."

"I WANT THE TOILETS TO TALK IN JAPA-NESE!" screamed Ava.

"It's not too late!" said Elsa, weeping openly now. "I have loads of air miles! I can book you a flight to Tokyo! Business class, if they still have seats available!"

But it *was* too late.

Because Ava tossed the book into the pool.

Imogen watched as it spun through the air, pages fanning out, as if in slow motion, and plunged into the water—where it was instantly eaten by the piranhas, that obviously hadn't had a decent meal for days.

"NOOOOOO! WHYYYYYYY?" screamed Elsa, prostrating herself on the ground and banging her fists into the solid unicorn-bone tiles.

"Because you're THE WORST LEADER EVER! Worse than Great-Great-Aunt Sibylle, and she sank the

Titanic while she was trying to steal it!"

"HOW DARE YOU COMPARE ME TO SIB-YLLE?" screamed Elsa. "We do not talk about her! Your great-great-grandmother TOLD her not to disguise herself as an iceberg!"

"Whatever, Mum," said Ava. "I'm not scared of you. You're pathetic."

"Yeah!" shouted Henry. "Down with the system! Down with parents!"

"Good for you, Ava!" called Uncle Clyde.

"Clyde, you fool," said Josephine, weeping. "This is not good for *us*. We're about to be *killed*!"

"Good point," said Aunt Bets, whipping out a sharpened colostomy bag, which did indeed have a good point on it. She held it up to Imogen. "Kill that Ava girl for me, will you, before she gets us murdered? If you lean out really far, you might be able to reach."

Elsa, by this point, was rolling around on the floor, sobbing. "Now I'll never know the end of the story!" she wailed.

"ALL THE MICE DIE!" yelled all of the Crims at once.

"Actually," said Big Nana, "interesting fact: That ending was the misprint. The owl wasn't supposed to eat the mice—he was supposed to rock them gently to sleep. The copy editor obviously had a macabre sense of humor!"

Elsa stood up, shaking with rage, her hands in fists, and her face a purple ball of fury. "I HATE SPOILERS!" shouted Elsa. "EVEN MORE THAN I HATE CRIMS! AND YOU ARE CRIMS! AND YOU JUST SPOILED *TWO ENDINGS* OF MY FAVORITE BOOK! YOU WILL WATCH YOUR FAMILY DIE! AND THEN *YOU* WILL DIE!"

And, before anyone could stop her, she reached over and pulled the lever.

"NO!" screamed Big Nana, rushing over to Elsa and wrestling her for control of the lever.

"YES!" yelled Elsa, pushing Big Nana so that she staggered backward, almost slipping into the piranha pool.

Stefan Kruk marched up to her and put his gun into her back. "You are lucky I was reloading just then," he said. "Next time you try anything like that, you die."

There was a whirring and a clicking, and the cage began to shake. Elsa had obviously blown her budget on the unicorn-bone floor and the solid-gold entrance hall and gone for the budget cage option, Imogen reflected, as the rickety structure began rattling and slowly dropping toward the pool.

"OOH, LOVELY. I HAVEN'T HAD A BATH FOR DAYS," chuckled Knuckles.

"Stop it!" Ava ran over to the lever and tried to wrestle control from her mother so she could push it back up.

"You can't do this to people!"

Imogen looked over at Stefan, who seemed to be having an internal crisis about whether to threaten Ava with his gun or keep it on Big Nana.

Elsa was too strong for Ava, too. Imogen had read in *Art, Murder, Money, and Mythical Creatures: At Home with the Kruks* that Elsa practiced weightlifting with particularly heavy blackbirds. It was evidently paying off.

Imogen stared at the cage, willing it back up with her eyes. Which didn't work, because she wasn't magical. *It's really happening,* she realized. *Big Nana was preparing me for this exact scenario in my first crime homework essay. Well, plus some claustrophobia and minus the acid.*

And yet she just sat there, too rattled to do anything (literally—the cage was making quite a racket as it descended toward the water).

Come on, she told herself. *What was the plan I came up with in that essay? Big Nana gave me 90 percent, so it must have been a good one. I just need to remember the steps. . . .*

Imogen tried to clear her mind. But all she could think of was the piranhas and how hungry they were. . . .

Concentrate, she thought. But she was finding it hard, because the Crims had started pushing and shoving one another in an attempt to get away from the bottom of the cage.

"Oi, Aunt Josephine!" Henry shouted as Josephine

climbed over him. "You just trod on my head!"

"Have some respect for your elders! Especially when about to die!" shrieked Aunt Bets, planting a punch on Henry's nose.

Think, Imogen. Imogen closed her eyes—and at last her plan began to come back to her.

First, distract the master criminal.

Well, she thought as Elsa laughed at the fighting Crims, *that seems to be taken care of.*

Then work out a cunning plan to free your family.

A plan. A cunning one . . . What did Big Nana always say about plans? Start with what's right under your nose.

The thing that was right under Imogen's nose at that moment was her father's head, which was cowering from Aunt Bets's sharpened colostomy bag, which she was jabbing blindly in every direction. But right in front of her were the bars of the cage. And now that she looked at them, the spaces between the bars were fairly wide. If she could just find a way to cut through one or two of them, they'd be able to climb out. . . .

She patted her pockets, on the off chance that she was carrying something useful like a crowbar or a stick of dynamite—but there was nothing apart from Barney's ridiculous dog bone.

That's it! she thought. She reached into her pocket and held the bone out to Barney, who was still standing by the door, panting electronically. "Here, boy!" she called, holding out the bone, feeling a bit ridiculous, because she was, after all, talking to a robot. "Come and get it!" And she threw it onto the floor of the cage.

True to form, Barney ran up to the edge of the tiles and leaped across the water to reach the cage—and then, in his determination to get to the bone, he started to *gnaw through the bars with his robot teeth.*

Yes! It worked! Imogen gave a quick victorious fist pump.

Now they just had to get to dry land. . . .

Big Nana came to the rescue. While the Kruks were screaming and shouting—mostly rude things about Barney in German—she raised the lever to stop the cage from descending, then ran over to the ladder and lowered it toward the hole in the cage.

Imogen climbed out of the hole Barney had gnawed in the bars and made her away across the ladder as quickly as she could, followed by the twins, followed by Delia, and Freddie, and her aunts and uncles, her mother, and lastly, her father.

"Get back in there!" screamed Elsa, suddenly looking up from her bickering family to realize what was going on.

But the Crims were sick of doing what she told them to.

Imogen glanced over to Stefan, who had raised his gun toward the Crims—and then she saw Ava give him a very

270

slight shake of the head, and he lowered it again. She really *was* powerful. And she was on their side. Sort of.

Big Nana beamed at Imogen. "You did it!" she said, giving her a slightly sweaty hug. "Thank you!"

"Thank *you*," said Imogen. "The ladder's what saved us, really. And I just did what I learned in my crime homework—"

But their mutual appreciation–fest was cut short. The Kruks had started to fight again, rather violently, among themselves.

"See?" Ava shouted at Elsa. "I told you this was a stupid idea!"

"How *dare* you talk to me like that, you glossy-haired pony, except less useful than a pony, because at least ponies take you on scenic countryside rides and DON'T ANSWER BACK!"

"Oi!" said one of the little tuxedo-wearing Crims. "Don't talk to Ava like that!" He pulled something from his cummerbund that looked suspiciously like a garrote.

While Elsa was wrestling her garrote-wielding son, Imogen waved her arms to get the other Crims' attention. "Follow me!" she hissed.

She led them into the solid-gold hallway, and they slipped and slid all the way to the reinforced-steel door.

But it was locked.

And as soon as Imogen touched it, an alarm sounded.

"INTRUDERS DETECTED. HOUSE ON LOCK-DOWN" boomed an automated message.

And then came the awful sound of footsteps running in their direction.

The stiff-looking butler was sprinting toward them, followed by quite a flexible-looking butler, followed by several butlers of medium-looking flexibility. "Stop them!" shouted the first butler, which wasn't really necessary since the Crims were cornered by the door and weren't moving at all.

"If only Sam had his rats," Imogen whispered.

"I found some new ones," Sam said, pulling one out of his pocket. "The Kruks spent all their money on making the house look good and forgot to hire a cleaner."

Sam set the rats on the floor and whispered: *"Get them!"*

The rats, which had been treated extremely badly by the butlers—who had been trained in butlering school to stamp on rodents when they saw them—launched themselves at the men's legs with their nasty, gnawing teeth.

"Now, run!" shouted Imogen, and the Crims skidded back down the solid-gold hallway, turning into the first corridor they saw, which was carpeted, much to everyone's relief.

"Quick! In here!" hissed Nick (or Nate—Nick had

lost his hat, so it was once again impossible to tell the difference between them). He opened a door, and the Crims squeezed inside (it was an extremely small room), just as the butlers came running around the corner.

"Which way did they go?" asked the stiff-looking butler.

"Down here, I think," said the flexible butler, and their footsteps padded off down the corridor.

"Hey, guys," said a familiar-sounding voice from underneath Aunt Bets. "Would you mind not sitting on my head? I've got a lot of solid-steel steak knives to polish and not a lot of time to polish them in."

"Don Vadrolga!" cried Imogen, not just because she liked saying the names of fading Hollywood actors during times of stress, but because Don Vadrolga was there, sitting on the floor, looking a little squashed, since Aunt Bets was sitting on his legs. "We can get you out of here!" said Imogen. "Hopefully. Either that or we'll get you killed along with us. . . ."

"Oh, don't worry about me," Don Vadrolga said wearily. "I'm used to the Kruks now. They feed me . . . and they only beat me up when they're really bored . . . and the butlers lend me their coloring books when I'm feeling stressed, so I'm pretty zen about life these days. Plus, the paparazzi can't get in here, and no one makes *Friday Night Chills* jokes, so I have it pretty good."

Imogen had a sudden, overwhelming desire to sing "Feelin' Alive." Luckily, she was good at resisting overwhelming desires.

"Oi. Don Vadrolga," said Aunt Bets, turning on him, her pointy-teeth bared. "Is there another way out of this house? You have five seconds to answer before I blow you up with my portable explosive device." She pulled it out of her handbag to show him. "It doubles as a powder compact."

"Since you asked so nicely, yes," said Don Vadrolga. "Turn right out of here, and go up the first spiral staircase— the one that isn't made of Grammy Awards. At the top you'll find Elsa's bedroom. Don't worry about the bats. At the very back of the room, you'll see something that kinda looks like a laundry hamper, but it's actually an escape chute. It'll take you out right in the middle of Blandington Park."

"Thank you," said Big Nana. "You are very kind for a man with such a big dimple on his chin."

The Crims ran out of the room and up the spiral staircase that wasn't made of Grammy Awards (it was made of the bones of everyone who Elsa had ever overheard calling her "crazy," but luckily, the Crims didn't know that). Sam took out his skeleton key and jimmied open the door to Elsa's room.

And everyone gasped.

Because Elsa's bedroom was the creepiest bedroom any of them had ever seen, and they lived with Uncle Clyde. You'd never have guessed it belonged to a professional psychopath with too many butlers and a penchant for inflicting pain on innocent people. The room looked as though a child lived there. A six-year-old child. The walls were pastel pink and covered with childish drawings showing lynchings and bear smugglings and poisonings, each of them signed "By Elsa Kruk" in a crayon scrawl. Dotted around the room were the remains of what had once been teddy bears, but were now horrifying Frankenstein's monster–type nightmares—a doll with the head of a penguin and the legs of an octopus; a teddy bear with no limbs, dressed as a prison warden; and a tiny doll that looked exactly like Big Nana, with pins sticking out of it . . .

"So *that's* why my sciatica has been so bad recently," murmured Big Nana.

And then there were the bats. They were black, and they were asleep, and they were everywhere—hanging from the wardrobe door, and the ceiling, and the clown-shaped ceiling light. And unfortunately, the laundry hamper/escape chute.

Uncle Clyde pulled at his unnecessarily red hair, frowning. He was coming up with one of his plans, Imogen realized. "Nick and Nate, if you walk on your hands toward the laundry hamper; and Freddie, if you sing 'Tingle, Tingle, Little Scar' to calm the bats down; and Imogen, if you sort of cartwheel through the air without touching the ground—"

"Shut it, Clyde," said Big Nana, and she picked her way across the floor, which was covered in broken toys and bat droppings and actual bats, to the laundry hamper. She opened it carefully, trying not to wake the bats.

Imogen held her breath. . . .

But there wasn't an escape chute in the laundry hamper. There were a lot of dirty T-shirts and a note, made of letters cut out of a magazine:

FOOLED YOU AGAIN! IDIOTS!

Uncle Clyde used one of Big Nana's favorite swear words. And unfortunately, it seemed that bats don't like swear words. Because suddenly they weren't asleep at all.

They flew at the Crims, squeaking and batting their leathery wings, and getting tangled up in one another.

"There's a bat in my hair!" shrieked Josephine.

"Ther'b a bat id my mouth!" spluttered Sam.

"Be quiet, everyone!" hissed Imogen, running back to the door. "Let's get out of here, before—"

What was Imogen going to say? "Before Elsa gets here," probably. But it was too late for that. Because just as she was about to run out of the room, Elsa appeared in the doorway in front of her.

"Looking for me, were you?" she said in her insane, singsong voice. "Quiet, my pretties," she said to the bats, who instantly settled down and fell back to sleep.

Imogen couldn't help but be impressed, even though she tried quite hard not to be.

"I have you cornered now," said Elsa. "And it's time for DINNER!"

"I'M NOT HUNGRY, THANKS," said Uncle Knuckles. "I GET A BIT GASSY WHEN I'M NERVOUS."

"You're not going to *eat*," said Elsa. "You're going to be *eaten*! Why do you think Don Vadrolga was in such a hurry to polish those steak knives? I think I'll start with fillet of Imogen, followed by rump of Josephine. . . ."

And then the door burst open again, and a lot of Kruks tumbled into the room—too many to count, which is a really bad number of Kruks.

And they were angry. And they were all holding explosive-looking weapons—machine guns, flamethrowers, mortars. Even the smallest, tuxedo-wearing Kruk had a nasty-looking grenade.

Imogen felt sick. They had been so close to getting away. But now they were definitely, definitely going to die. At least it would be quick, from the looks of the weapons.

But then she looked at the Kruks themselves—and she

realized that they weren't actually pointing their weapons at the Crims.

They were pointing them at Elsa.

"Enough is enough, Elsa," said Stefan Kruk in his extremely German voice. "We love crime. We love feeding people to wild animals. But only if they really deserve it. And the Crims—they do not deserve it. Ava is right. We have let you order us around for far too long. And your orders are terrible. Even when you order food from the Chinese restaurant, you get it wrong. We have had enough."

They raised their weapons. And Elsa, for once, did the sensible thing: She turned and ran out of the room as fast as she could. The Kruks chased her down the spiral staircase, and the Crims leaned over the hallway banister to see what would happen.

But then someone whispered "Hey! Imogen!" from farther down the hallway: Ava! She beckoned the Crims toward her. "Look what I've got!" she hissed, holding out a sack of dynamite. "I've brought a match this time! Want me to bust you out of here?"

"Yes, please," said Imogen.

Ava laid the dynamite symmetrically around the reinforced-steel door.

She lit the fuses.

The Crims stood back and put their fingers in their ears.

And then . . .

KABOOM!

The steel door blew apart into a thousand twisted pieces.

The Crims were free!

"Thank you!" Imogen called to Ava, as she ran through the door.

"You're welcome!" Ava called back.

They ran out into the passageway and took the elevator to the escalator to the stairs, to the other flight of stairs. They were pretty out of breath by the time they stepped, coughing and spluttering, into the boring Blandington street.

"GROUP HUG!" insisted Uncle Knuckles. He reached around all the Crims with his extremely long arms and pulled them into a suffocating embrace. He let them go moments before accidentally committing mass murder through the medium of extreme affection.

Imogen found herself next to her father, who was blinking and polishing his glasses, looking a little lost, as though he didn't really know what was going on.

Imogen gave him an extra, nondangerous hug. "I missed you," she said. "Once I'd realized you'd been usurped by a Kruk, I mean. Sorry about that."

"'Usurped' is a very good word," said Al, smiling at Imogen proudly.

"I know! I never thought I'd have a reason to say it out loud!"

"Every cloud has a silver lining made out of dictionaries," said Al Crim. And he hugged her again. "I *knew* you'd find me."

"Hey," said a voice behind them. It was Ava, looking a little bit gunpowder-y and disheveled. "Just wanted to check you all got out okay."

"We did," Imogen said, smiling at Ava—and feeling strangely shy. It occurred to her that she actually *liked* Ava, and she was pretty sure she was never going to see her again. "I can't thank you enough," said Imogen. "We'd be dead if it weren't for you."

"No worries," said Ava, waving her hand like it was nothing. "I would say buy me an ice cream sometime—or one of those frozen yogurts your friends are so into—but I don't suppose we'll see each other anytime soon. Which is actually . . . a shame."

"It *is* a shame," said Imogen. "Would it be okay if I . . . hugged you?"

Ava looked around. "Quickly, before any of my family see."

And for the first and probably the last time in history, a

Crim hugged a Kruk, and not just in an I'm-about-to-get-you-into-a-headlock-and-kill-you sort of way.

"Now get out of here!" said Ava, and she disappeared back inside the house, where a serious Kruk family argument was clearly still taking place. (Imogen could hear gunshots and smashing glass and someone shouting "Not the sharks!")

Imogen clapped her hands because the Crims had started to fight among themselves too—Sam had stolen some piranhas and was trying to shove them down the twins' pants. "Right, everyone," she said. "Let's run for it!"

And together, screaming and yelping and throwing deadly fish at one another, the Crims ran off into the sunset. Not that you could see the sunset, because the air pollution got in the way.

That's what you get when you live in Blandington.

CHAPTER NINETEEN

A MONTH LATER, the Crims were thriving
again—if by "thriving" you mean "hurting one another
with hammers on a regular basis and occasionally stealing
one anothers' underpants." Now that the Kruks weren't
sabotaging every crime they tried to commit, and the
Masked Banana Bandit had mysteriously stopped stealing
bananas, they were back on top of the most wanted list.
Isabella had committed her first armed robbery (she used
her arms to steal milk cartons from the other kids at the
nursery); Henry had burned down the skate park; and Sam
had set fire to Henry's matches and lighters and amateur

tattooing equipment in revenge for him burning down the skate park. Al Crim had made Josephine the happiest woman in the world by buying her an extremely expensive diamond brooch and pretending he'd stolen it. Which, when you think about it, is sort of like fraud. Everything, in other words, was back to normal.

Delia committed Imogen's favorite crime of all: She stole the bouncy castle from Isabella's third birthday party and used it to replace the Boeing 747 on top of the house. "MUCH MORE FESTIVE," said Uncle Knuckles, who loved bouncing around in his new bedroom. He had to confiscate Aunt Bets's needles, though—and her sharpened colostomy bag, her pointy false teeth, and her sword collection—because she kept puncturing the walls, and he was getting sick of patching and reinflating the castle every morning.

"Ha!" Uncle Clyde had said in delight, when he went to the supermarket and found it fully stocked with bananas. "Now that we're back in top form, no one can compete with us! We've scared that stupid bandit out of Blandington. I wonder who he was. . . ."

Typical Uncle Clyde, Imogen thought, *assuming that a successful criminal must be a man, when all the best Crims and Kruks are women.* But she never gave away the Masked Banana Bandit's true identity.

Imogen was back at Blandington Secondary School, where, without Ava to compete with, she had easily retaken her position as queen bee. Her friends seemed to be extremely relieved that Ava had left.

"She was horrible," admitted Penelope.

"And quite scary," said Willa.

"And not nearly as fun as you," said Hannah.

"I haven't been much fun either since I came back," Imogen said. "I'm sorry I was so awful. I had some . . . problems at home."

Her friends forgave her—of course they did. After all, now that Crim House had a bouncy castle, it was the most fun to have sleepovers in. And Imogen resolved to be kinder to them in the future. Kindness, she was beginning to realize, was a very effective means of control.

The only trouble was, school was a little bit boring with no one to challenge her . . . so she persuaded Delia to join her as co-chair of the charity drive.

"I don't want anyone to actually think I, like, *care* about anything, though," Delia said. They were holding their first co-chair meeting late one evening in the living room of Crim House.

"What's wrong with caring?" Imogen said. "Kitty Penguin is always campaigning to save seabirds. . . ."

"Hmm," said Delia, which Imogen took to mean, "Very good point, Imogen. I am convinced by your excellent argument."

Imogen opened up her charity drive notebook. "We need to think of an autumn fund-raiser."

"*You* need to think of an autumn fund-raiser," Delia said, looking out the window to the front yard, where Henry was teaching Isabella to eat fire.

"We could always have a bake sale," Imogen said.

"Ugh, no," said Delia. "*Pathetic.* If kids are going to pay to do something, it has to be something they *want* to do but aren't *allowed* to—like get tattoos."

Imogen tapped her pen on her chin thoughtfully. "That actually isn't a terrible idea," she said. "We could get some temporary tattoos—"

"*Temporary* tattoos?" Delia asked, staring at Imogen as though she'd lost her mind, which she hadn't, although she'd come pretty close to it in the past few weeks. "What's the point of *that*? I've already got a real one."

She pulled up her shirt to reveal a curly black *C* on her lower back.

"Wow," said Imogen. "I'm impressed with your family loyalty."

Delia frowned. "What are you talking about?"

"The *C*. It's for 'Crim,' right?"

"No!" said Delia, tucking her shirt back into her skirt. "It's for 'cucumbers.' I hate them. And reminding yourself of the things you hate keeps you sharp. Am I right?"

Imogen did not think she was right.

"Anyway," continued Delia, "I'll go and talk to the guy who runs the tattoo parlor in town. He was saying the other day that everyone in Blandington gets the same tattoo—'Mum' on their upper arms. I bet he'd love a bit more variety."

Imogen decided it was time to change the subject. "I'm really glad you're working on this with me," she said. "You're so full of . . . ideas."

"Yeah, well," said Delia, looking at the floor. "I had quite a lot of time to think while I was in that dungeon."

"It was weird without you," Imogen said. "And I'm sorry I didn't listen to you sooner. About the whole Kruks thing."

"*Seriously*," Delia said, grinning at her. "I know you're not as smart as me, but that was *really* stupid."

Imogen couldn't let that slide. "*I'm* the one who figured out how to get you all free," she pointed out.

"Only after the rest of us basically wrote 'IT'S THE KRUKS' on the living room wall."

"Henry actually did write that. Above the mantelpiece, in indelible marker. Except he spelled 'it's' with a *Z*. But most of his graffiti makes no sense at all, so can you blame me for ignoring it?"

Imogen's phone beeped before Delia could reply: an Instagram alert. Ava had posted more pictures of Japan, mostly of her dressed in anime costumes—as a demon, as a massive rabbit, and as a schoolgirl with an offensive weapon, which wasn't much of a stretch for Ava. Imogen showed them to Delia.

Delia shuddered. "I don't know why you follow her. I never want to see her or her creepy family ever again."

Imogen ignored Delia and quickly liked Ava's photos— if she didn't, there was always the risk that Ava would think that she was passively-aggressively not liking them on purpose and send an assassin to her house. It had already happened once. Fortunately, Imogen was able to prove that her phone's battery was dead, and she simply hadn't seen the photo of Ava dressed as an angry (yet somehow cute) potato. *I wonder if I'll ever see Ava again in real life,* she wondered. She sort of missed her. . . .

And that's when there was a knock at the door.

"I'll get it!" called Big Nana from upstairs.

Imogen and Delia walked into the hallway behind her to see who it was.

Big Nana opened the front door—but there was no one there.

"My friend Invisible Mike must be up to his old tricks again," said Big Nana—and then she looked down, and gasped.

Sitting on the doorstep was a large poodle with a bow tied around its neck.

The dog gave a little bark and jumped up to lick Big Nana's face. And then it trotted into the living room, sat back on its hind legs, opened its mouth wide, and projected a hologram onto the wall.

It was another robot dog . . . which could only mean one thing . . .

The hologram showed someone sitting in a high-tech office chair—someone with a glossy ponytail. The chair swiveled around, and there, smiling at them, stroking a sinister-looking white cat, was Ava Kruk.

"Hi!" said Ava, waving to them. "Or as we say in Japan, *konnichiwa!*" She held the white cat up toward them. "This is Mittens. I stole him from the cat café. He's a Siamese attack cat. Isn't he adorable?"

Mittens was not adorable. Mittens was terrifying.

Delia shook her head. "I'm getting out of here," she said, and ran upstairs to her room.

Ava pouted. "I don't know why Delia's never liked me. All I've ever been is kind to her. Except when I helped kidnap her, obviously. . . ."

"How are things with your family?" Big Nana asked

tentatively. "The last time we saw you, things were looking a bit . . . tense."

"Oh, that was nothing, really," said Ava, shrugging. "Just a little tiff. The boys always get the machetes and sharks out when we have an argument."

"So Elsa is still alive?" Big Nana asked carefully. It seemed unlikely.

"Oh yes," said Ava. "She decided to get out of town for a while until things cool down a bit. She says she's gone on a spiritual quest, whatever that means. She's tracked down the author of *Ten Little Mice in the Woods*, and she's persuading her to write a sequel."

"How lovely," said Imogen, who had a horrible feeling that "persuading" meant "tying her to a chair and threatening her with a machine gun."

"So Elsa's not in charge of the family anymore?" Big Nana asked.

"No," said Ava, sitting up in her chair. "Actually, that's what I wanted to talk to you about. Uncle Dedrik's taken over, and the family's totally changing. We're becoming a bit less Bond villain—though obviously we all still wear expensive Italian clothes, and drive nice cars, and swivel around in chairs with fluffy white cats on our laps." She stroked Mittens, who hissed at her and bared his teeth. "We're on a diversity drive—we commit equal-opportunity crimes against everyone, no matter their race, gender, sexuality, or age. And we want to make the Kruk family itself more inclusive, too." She smiled at Imogen and Big Nana. "I'm glad Delia's gone—because you two are the ones I *really* wanted to talk to. I saw a lot of potential in you, Imogen. And you too, Big Nana. So I have a proposition for you: Would you like to join the Kruks? Rejoin, really, in your case," she said, nodding to Big Nana.

Imogen felt a jolt of excitement. Or was it fear? She caught Big Nana's eye. It was fair to say they hadn't been expecting this.

"What do you think?" Ava said. "You guys would be rich. And you'd have real power. And you'd get to travel the world. Did you know there's a community of people in Peru who have never experienced a *single armed robbery*? We can help change that! Plus, I'm going to run the Kruks one day, and I'll need good people by my side. By which I mean, walking three paces behind me."

A few weeks ago, Imogen would never have dreamed of joining the Kruks. But she liked Ava. And she liked being the best at things. And there was no doubt that the Kruks were the very best at crime. . . .

"By 'good people' I mean you guys," Ava said. "Just in case that wasn't clear."

"That's very flattering," said Big Nana. "Almost as flattering as that lovely Italian dress you're wearing, Ava."

"You like it? It's Armani."

"I can tell," said Big Nana. "But . . . what about the other Crims?"

Ava gave a sad little smile. "I was afraid you'd ask that," she said. "Not actually afraid, obviously—I'm not afraid of anything, except this really scary movie I watched the other day, which involved a beautiful woman and a needle and an eyeball. Japanese horror is *weird*! The thing is, we really don't have any use for the other Crims."

"Nobody does," Big Nana said sadly.

"I'm sure we could find a way to keep them busy, though," said Ava. "Don Vadrolga can't do all the silver polishing on his own. And I wondered whether Josephine would like to head up the Kruk Repertory Theater Company? Plus, there are always people who need murdering—that should keep Aunt Bets busy."

Part of Imogen longed to say yes to Ava's offer—but the rest of her, the best bit of her, knew that she could never abandon her family. She caught Big Nana's eye—and both of them shook their heads.

"It's a really tempting offer," Imogen said.

"But no thank you," said Big Nana. "If the last few months have taught me anything, other than the fact that children's books can be very dangerous in the wrong hands, it's that I'm a Crim now. Not a Kruk."

"Me too," said Imogen.

"Even if that means you have to stay in *Blandington* for the rest of your life?" Ava asked.

"Even that," said Imogen, though she felt a sudden rush of horror at the thought of it.

Ava shrugged. "Fine," she said, ruffling Mittens behind his ears. "As long as you understand that you're either with us or against us. Like, I can't imagine I'll ever want to go back to Blandington." She shuddered. "There's only so long you can stay in a town that only sells cheese pizza. But I can't promise you'll be safe if you don't join us."

"I'm not worried," said Big Nana.

I am, thought Imogen. *But a bit of fear is good motivation.* She was going to take her crime homework much more seriously from now on—and she was going to make sure the rest of the Crims took it seriously too.

"Okay, then!" said Ava. "See you! Wouldn't want to be you! If you know what I mean . . ." She gave a little wave—and the hologram flashed off.

Imogen grabbed the robot poodle, which had started to chase its tail, and flicked off the button under its ear before it could start spying on them. "Well," she said to Big Nana. "*That* just happened."

"Yes," said Big Nana. "It did."

Imogen felt a slow dread creep up from her stomach. Had they made the right decision? Was it really worth it, turning down a life of success and money to stay with the rest of the family, who were mostly extremely irritating, especially when they were awake?

Big Nana turned to Imogen and squeezed her hand. "You don't need to worry, my buttered crumpet," she said. "We fought off the Kruks' attack. And if we can do something like that, which involved too many piranhas and a surprising number of very high-quality sacks, we can do anything—when we work together."

Imogen felt a bit better. "You're right," she said.

"Of course I am," said Big Nana. "Come here." She opened her arms for a hug. She smelled comfortingly of lemon drizzle cake and gunpowder.

Imogen suddenly felt really tired, which wasn't surprising considering the number of extremely high-stakes decisions she'd had to make in the past few weeks. "'Night, Big Nana," she said.

She smiled to herself as she walked upstairs. She was home, safe—for now—in Crim House, and there was nowhere she would rather be.

Despite everything . . . she was proud to be a Crim.

Acknowledgments

Thanks, as always, to my brilliant writing friends Sarah Courtauld and Zanna Davidson. Writing wouldn't be nearly as much fun without them.

And very many thanks to the wonderful editors at Working Partners and HarperCollins, particularly Stephanie Lane Elliot, Conrad Mason, Samantha Noonan, and Erica Sussman.

Thanks, also, to my wife, Victoria, for making the porridge in the morning when I'm writing.

And thank you to porridge for being so delicious.

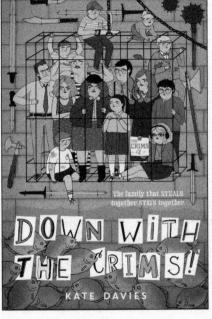

31901064424502